Brothers

and

Wives

Praise for *My Sister's Ex*

One of *Essence* magazine's Best Reads of 2009

"Cydney Rax has a way [of] adding a twist to her plots; she makes you think about things that for some are unimaginable and unforgivable."
—The Pink Reviewers

"With a feel-good quality . . . this book is a must-read and will have you begging for more."
—Cheryl Hayes, APOOO Book Club

Praise for *My Best Friend and My Man*

"There are some parts where Cydney has you laughing out loud and others where you want to reach in and throttle the characters. Cydney has another hit on her hands!"
—Desiree Day, author of *Crazy Love* and
One G-String Short of Crazy

"Smart, sexy, and wickedly funny . . . Once again, Cydney Rax displays her keen ability to weave a story of romance and mayhem with characters that you'll both love . . . and love to hate."
—Nancey Flowers, *Essence* magazine bestselling author of
No Strings Attached

"Cydney Rax is phenomenal with her pen game. This blueprint on how to win in the game of love is sure to be a bestseller."
—Joy King, author of *Hooker to Housewife* and *Superstar*

"Truly a satisfying read that pulled me in from page one . . .
I couldn't put it down."
—Cheryl Robinson, author of *Sweet Georgia Brown*

"Whatever's in the water in Houston, Cydney Rax should drink eight glasses a day."
—Patrik Henry Bass, senior editor, *Essence* magazine

Praise for *My Husband's Girlfriend*

"Provocative."
—*Ebony* magazine

Brothers
and
Wives

a novel

Cydney Rax

THREE RIVERS PRESS
NEW YORK

Copyright © 2010 by Cydney Rax

Published in the United States by Three Rivers Press, an imprint of the
Crown Publishing Group, a division of Random House, Inc., New York.
www.crownpublishing.com

Three Rivers Press and the Tugboat design are registered
trademarks of Random House, Inc.

Library of Congress Cataloging-in-Publication Data

Rax, Cydney.
    Brothers and wives : a novel / by Cydney Rax.—1st trade
paperback ed.
        1. African Americans—Fiction.   2. Triangles (Interpersonal
relations)—Fiction.   3. Domestic fiction.   I. Title.
    PS3618.A98B76 2010
    813'.6—dc22   2010004536

ISBN 978-0-307-46009-7

Printed in the United States of America

Design by Maria Elias

10   9   8   7   6   5   4   3   2   1

First Edition

This one is dedicated to all my loyal readers.

Sometimes reader interest can birth books. After *My Husband's Girlfriend* (MHG) was released, I received a variety of responses from readers. Some folks thought the topic was implausible—and they didn't hesitate to tell me just that. Actually, I understood what they were feeling. This wild and crazy story line is strictly fiction, right? But then the e-mails started pouring into my Inbox. One older male reader confessed that he and his wife were going through the same problems as the characters Neil and Anya. He sadly told me that his own wife actually suffered from FSAD (female sexual arousal disorder). They weren't having sex. Period. "What should I do?" he asked me. I responded with a nice e-mail, and afterward I felt like, *Whoa! I'm not an advice columnist.*

A few other readers sent e-mails stating they, too, could relate to the MHG drama. One guy had encountered his own "Dani" in real life, and so on. And quite a few wanted to know, "Cydney, when are you going to make this into a movie?" Ha! If only it were that easy . . . I'd be somewhere right now . . . (okay, let me focus).

One librarian in Grand Rapids, Michigan, said MHG

was one of the best urban fiction novels she's ever read. I was shocked and thrilled. Authors love receiving this kind of e-mail. Trust me.

But the e-mails I received from a slew of others are the reason I wrote *Brothers and Wives*—the stand-alone sequel to MHG. Simply put, some folks demanded, "When's the sequel coming out?" At first I told everyone, "Nope, no. No sequel." But a couple of years after MHG, the characters began talking to me again. Creativity started flowing. And here in your hands is the result of fan interest. Plus it was great to get involved again with Neil, Dani, and Anya and find out what's going on in their lives these days.

I love the book. I hope you do, too. From the bottom of my heart, thank you, for every ounce of your support.

Cydney Rax

Brothers
and
Wives

PART 1

RULES OF ENGAGEMENT

DANI

More Than Just a Pretty Face

It's the last weekend in July. I've just pulled my pickup into the parking lot of the Bear Creek Pioneers Park on the west side of Houston. I open the door of my Toyota Tundra and carefully lift my nearly three-year-old son, Brax, from his car seat. "Come on, baby, watch your step," I tell him and watch him closely so he won't stumble on parts of the picnic grounds that dip unevenly. We walk toward the aroma of hickory-smoked meat. From a short distance, I can see a flurry of activity in front of a covered pavilion that's draped by a large banner with the words Meadows Family Reunion.

Once I arrive at our picnic area, I set my red cooler, a family-size bag of pita chips, and several containers of hummus on a green rectangular metal table. I rearrange my orange and red bikini top so that my nipples aren't totally showing and give my white Bermuda shorts the once-over. I nervously inhale and take in the scene around me and do a quick count. It looks like seventy-something people are here already. Some folks are holding little mini fans in their hands trying to stay cool; they are wasting their time—it's so hot outside I feel like I'm swimming in a pot of boiling water.

"Mommy, I'm thirsty."

"Okay," I tell Brax and reach for a bag of cups that's on the table and pull one out. I fill it with cold water from a huge orange beverage container and watch him take a long swallow.

The sound of laughing children captures our attention, and we both practically run toward a play area where dozens of his cousins are swinging, climbing monkey bars, and going for rides down the sliding board. Brax plays on the swing until a teenage cousin asks for my permission to include him in a group of kids who are going for a quick visit to the wildlife habitat. I say okay and make them promise to try and bring my son back within a half hour.

I walk back toward the pavilion, where I'm drawn to thumping, mesmerizing music that's blaring from a few speakers. Several feet away, about a dozen couples are partying on a concrete floor in an open area right by the picnic tables. Riley Dobson, Neil Meadows's next-door neighbor, grins and waves at me from the dance floor. I wave back. Thank God for a friendly face. In the past, when I was going through hard times, she temporarily let me live with her, and I've always appreciated her generous heart.

Feeling spirited and confident, I squeeze past folks till I reach the dance floor. It's been a while since I've been around some of Neil's relatives. I want to relax and not feel uncomfortable. I'm sure there're still some relatives who are upset over the fact that Neil, a married father, got me pregnant with Brax a few years ago.

Even though I lack a dance partner, I twist my ass to the new Ray J song, snapping my fingers and singing quietly. Right in front of me is the deejay booth, which holds a long, transportable table that stands on a slightly raised platform. A couple of laptops and mixers are spread across the surface. Two guys are standing behind the table; one is an average-looking guy sporting nerd glasses. But the man working the turntable makes me ask myself, *Who the hell is this?*

He's wearing an army-green wife beater and dark cotton shorts. His thick, round arms remind me of Vin Diesel with biceps so large that Brax could probably do pull-ups on them. Yep, dude looks completely edible to me.

The handsome man rocks his head to the beat, and his lips are moving like he's chatting with his partner. But the second he glances into the crowd and rests his pretty eyes on me, his conversation stops.

His partner nods like everything's cool and he'll keep the music going. The man removes his headphones, steps down from the deejay table, and walks slowly over to me. Grinning, he leans in with his mouth near my ear and offers me a pleasant "What's up?"

"Hey," I answer as I continue dancing.

"You look familiar."

"Hmm, you look kind of familiar yourself. You spin on the weekends?"

"Naw, nawww, baby girl. I just got back into the H last night. I've been posted up in Motown and only been back in Houston since yesterday. I'm Scottie Meadows."

At first I think, *Hmm, probably a younger cousin who went away to college.* Yet Scottie doesn't look like he'd be stuck somewhere in a residence hall with his head buried between textbooks. The black bandanna tied around his head and twisted to the side gives him a dangerous air.

"And I'm Danielle Frazier, but my friends call me Dani."

"Hi, Dani," he says, winking at me.

I tilt my neck to peer at him with greater interest. Scottie reaches out like he's about to shake my hand, but then he grabs my fingertips, intertwines them in his, and gently pulls me closer, as if he can't help himself. I roll my eyes and emphatically shake my head like, *Don't even try it.* I'm not opposed to being held and frisked by an incredibly good-looking man, but this dude won't be getting Dani's cookies this fast and easy, I don't care how dangerously handsome he is. I decide that if I *do* let him have me, he's going to have to wait for and *earn* this scrumptious piece of deliciousness.

After he releases me, I slow my dancing down a notch. Scottie continues talking over the drone of the music. "You look really, really nice today."

"You're too kind. Thanks." I smile, wanting to say, "So do you," but I don't.

"Who invited you?"

"Neil."

He looks shocked as hell, then replies, "Oh yeah? That's my older brother."

And SHAZAM, like a superhero with magical powers, Neil bursts onto the scene out of nowhere and interrupts us.

"Don't even think about it. Don't ask, *Scottie.* Don't!"

"What you talking about, Neil? We're just holding a conversation, minding our own business, and you walking up in here like you the big boss man." Scottie throws up his hands in exasperation and leers at his brother. His six-foot-four body towers over Neil by a few inches.

"Baby bro, I'm nobody's boss," Neil continues. "I'm just saying Dani is off-limits."

"What the hell?" I mumble, annoyed at Neil for having the audacity to try and control who speaks to me. I stop dancing, unable to take my eyes off Scottie and Neil.

"Say what?" Scottie jumps in. "Shouldn't you be saying your wife, *Anya,* is off-limits? You getting me messed up, *brotha.*"

"You're already messed up," Neil snaps. "And Dani doesn't need to get caught up in all that."

Neil's not talking to me, yet I freeze. His harsh voice is a long blade shoved and twisted against my neck. Rage twinkles in Neil's piercing eyes. This man isn't playing. But neither am I. *Nobody* cock-blocks Danielle Frazier.

"What the fuck?" I screech.

I don't care if Scottie is Neil's relative or if he's a stranger that wandered into their family reunion begging for a hot dog—Neil had no freaking right to put the brakes on someone trying to talk to me. It makes me so mad, especially since he is the one who invited me to this function in the first damned place.

"Dani, you don't understand," Neil says. "My brother isn't someone you should be getting to know."

"Wait a minute, Neil," Scottie speaks up. "This is a family reunion. Dani here is probably going to be talking to everyone, not just me. Am I right, or am I wrong?"

I smirk at Neil. I love that a man I barely know is sticking up for me.

"Scottie, you know you're full of . . ."

Then this tall, big-eyed girl with braids springing out of her head like long-stemmed flowers excitedly hops toward us and cuts in on our heated conversation. She looks like she's in her early twenties and is wearing purple boy shorts and an orange tank with a plunging neckline. When she walks, her boobs bounce like basketballs and nearly flop out of her skimpy top. She tilts her head and stares at me with a mixture of hurt and disgust. She then swiftly parks herself right in front of Scottie. *Who* is *she?* I move next to Scottie to get a good view. The girl smiles, then looks like she's about to burst open and a river of tears is going to spill out. He glares at her like now is not the time to be in his face.

"Aw, Scottie, why you gonna act like that, huh? You know you're not right." She raises her voice, competing with the music. *Why is she doing that?* I want to discreetly tiptoe out of here while I have a chance, yet I can't. I *won't.* Scottie and I have just started a conversation. If I can get Neil off my case, I won't be leaving until his brother and I finish talking.

Neil pleads, "LaNecia, please stop all that yelling. Go on and help serve lunch."

"I don't give a flying fuck about barbecue and chicken wings right now. These greedy-ass Negroes can serve themselves. Do I look like I work at Hooters?"

Yep, I think to myself and stare her up and down.

The Ray J song is coming to an end. There's a pause before the next song starts.

LaNecia continues whining and jumps up and down like a self-centered kid. "I want to talk to Scottie. I need to talk to him."

"LaNecia, please calm down, cousin."

Ahhh. It suddenly hits me. *That name sounds familiar. I've heard about LaNecia, one of Neil's imbalanced kinfolks.*

Neil squeezes in between LaNecia and Scottie, and Scottie takes the opportunity to move a few steps back from the line of fire.

"Shut up, nerd!" she shrieks. She presses her thick lips together, then opens her mouth and blows hard. A thick, nasty glob of saliva lands squarely on Neil's striped polo. He makes a face and raises his hand in the air, but his fist hangs suspended—as if he realizes he can't throw a punch at his young relative.

I cover my mouth with my hands and discreetly laugh my butt off. Whew, his family is nuts. Thank God my dreams of being married to Neil never came true.

Neil exhales loudly, grabs a hankie from his back pocket, and quickly wipes off the spit. It looks so yucky. Neil clasps LaNecia by the shoulders and violently shakes her. Her long braids fly every which way and smack her in the eyes, nose, and lips. That's when I feel a tap my shoulder. Startled, I spin around. Scottie gestures at me to follow him. I gladly walk away from the drama.

LaNecia is yelling so loud I don't have to see her to know what's happening. "I swear to God, y'all men ain't shit. You always make up the rules, but the world wasn't made just for you, was it, you annoying bastard."

Scottie extends his hand to me. I reach out and accept. His palm is surprisingly warm and comforting. He guides me to a less crowded area of the picnic grounds. As we're walking, he suddenly starts cracking up. I join him, and we shake our heads in amazement. I clutch my belly with my free hand because I'm laughing so hard it hurts.

Scottie points to a wooden bench, releases my hand, and takes a seat. So I plop down beside him, kick off my flip-flops, and start swinging my feet back and forth.

"Damn, now where were we?" he says as his laughter subsides. He dabs his eyes with his thumb.

"Awww, don't cry," I say teasingly and grin. Jeez, this man's green-gray eyes make me want to stare at him all day. "Like I was trying to tell you before we were interrupted, I'm Dani, the proud parent of one. My little boy, Brax, is somewhere around here running wild with his cousins. And, uh, I guess I should mention Neil and I know each other from way back."

"I could tell something was up with you two, but he's married, so . . ." Scottie says, his voice drifting off. He continues to stare at me. "You got a man?"

"Um, not really. I hang out, but no one serious."

"You shitting me, Mariah Carey?"

"What you call me?" I grin and blush over the fact that he compared me to the attractive singer, even though I'm hardly as old as that narcissistic chick. His intense staring makes me feel beautiful, desirable, and the center of his attention.

Scottie reaches out and boldly brushes his fingers through my curls. He plays with my hair, twisting my locks around in a wide circle.

"You're so fucking pretty that, just like Mariah, I know you make any other woman feel ugly. And," he continues, his eyes running me up and down, "your body is scorching hot, mama. You oughta have ten men's babies, not just one."

"Yeah, that's what I keep hearing, but reality is a trip." His compliments make me feel like a princess. And even though we've just met, I decide to guide him past the typical outer-beauty crap and let him know me on a deeper level. "To be honest, Scottie, I–I'm at a point in my life where I want to find the right guy, fall in love, get settled, all that. I wouldn't want ten men even if I could have 'em."

"I hear ya. That's what's up."

"And you?" I ask, offering him an encouraging smile. "You got someone?"

"Me? Naw, I'm not married." He gives a pained look,

stares into space, then mumbles, "No kids." Then he says louder and looks dead in my eyes. "No commitment."

"Ah, how old are you, if I may ask?"

"You can ask whatever you like," he sings in a silly voice. "You can ask whatever you like. Yeah!" He bursts out laughing, and I do, too. "I'm twenty-five, babyyy."

"Twenty-five, huh?" I gawk at him, impressed. I love his cockiness. Some younger guys still act like they're afraid of the pussy, but not Scottie.

"Well, I'm in my late twenties. But a woman never tells her true age."

"In my eyes you'll never be past your twenties. You've got the type of looks that'll keep you young forever."

"So," I say, glowing, "are you sure you don't have a woman stashed away somewhere?"

"Positive."

"Then why was LaNecia yelling at you?"

"Too damn long of a story . . . I'll tell you about it one damn day."

"Oh," I respond, surprised. "Does that mean you plan to talk to me *after* today?"

"You damn fucking right I want to talk to you. I want to talk to you every day after today. Gimme your digits."

I chuckle but don't make a move to respond.

"What's wrong? Am I making you nervous?"

"Nooo, Scottie." I twist around in my seat until we're facing each other. His eyes are so sincere, yet I detect sadness underneath the surface, like he has a story to tell, but he may not be willing to add it to his Facebook wall just yet.

"Scottie, I just want to do things different this time," I tell him in a calm, measured voice. "I mean, in the past I've made, what, a thousand mistakes in relationships, and I–I am not in the market to get hurt again. Hurt *hurts,* ya know?"

"I know, darling."

"You put all your hope on a guy, wishing things'll work out. . . . One day you're declaring your utmost love to each other. . . . By next week you're telling the man to go to hell. He's hollering so loud that neighbors can hear, calling you a cunt. Oops," I say and laugh self-consciously. "I'm telling way too much."

"No, do tell. I'm listening."

"Bottom line is, I gotta make different choices. That make sense?"

"So you want my digits?"

I beam and give in. "Sure. If I feel like I want to talk . . ."

"Believe me, you *are* going to want to talk to me."

"Like I said, if I *feel* like I want to talk to you, Scottie, I will definitely give you a call."

I surrender my PDA and let him punch his contact info into my address book. He offers me his phone, and I input my number. Looking satisfied, he says, "Don't forget, we made a pact. From now on we promised to talk to each other every day for the rest of our lives."

"I didn't say that."

"You don't have to say it, just do it. Okay, Dani?" He looks so adorably sincere, like a loving, oversize puppy. I nod and wonder what I'm getting myself into.

He tells me, "If you haven't heard by now, people consider me a fuckup, but ask me if I care."

"Nope, I haven't heard a single thing about you."

"Then let me be the one to tell you, mama."

He takes time to fill me in on how some of the family either treats him like they expect him to fail or are waiting to hear the latest bad news about him.

"It ain't like they perfect. Everybody got flaws. But for some reason, some of them are always pointing fingers at the kid, trying to make me feel like I'm not going to amount to anything. But I'll prove 'em wrong. They my family and I love 'em, but fuck 'em."

A comfortable silence develops between us, and we stare at each other.

Scottie rises to his big ole feet. He gently grabs my hand and whisks me out of my seat. "I love talking to you, darling, but we need to get back."

"That's okay. I'm cool." I slide my feet into my flip-flops and stand up.

By the time we get back to the Meadows setup, I can tell the area is nearly filled to capacity. Elderly gray-haired ladies are slumped in wheelchairs. Middle-aged men are slapping dominoes on the table and yelling. And fast-ass teenage girls are wearing skintight jeans, twisting their lips, putting their hands on their hips, and yelling, all at the same time.

I continue looking around at all the people, wondering which table I'm going to sit at, when I realize it's been a half hour since my son went to the wildlife habitat. He's probably getting hungry like me. I need to pick him up.

I excuse myself from Scottie and take quick steps toward the sound of children's voices. My tits nearly bounce out of my bikini top. I can feel the disapproving stares of senior women when I move past them. And although by my serious facial expression, it should be obvious I've got something important to do, all these grandmas can focus on is my appearance. But Dani's got to be Dani, no matter what. And being sexy and desirable is the very essence of who I am.

"What y'all old bitches looking at?" I say to several

bifocal-wearing women. I hope their hearing aids aren't working.

"Hey, Dani, where are you headed?"

I'd recognize that voice anywhere—Sharvette, aka Vette, Neil's lovely younger sister. I'm focused on picking up my son, so I'm in no mood to talk. I try to ignore Vette, but she screams louder, "Hey, Dani, over here."

I whirl around, ready to tell her I'll get with her later, but when I see her holding Brax on her hip, the fight goes out of me.

"Awww, there's my babyyy!" I step to him and plant a wet kiss on one of his fat, soft cheeks.

Vette explains. "I saw him with the other kids and couldn't resist bringing him with me. I made him a plate of food, so he's already eaten. Hope you don't mind."

"Nope, I don't mind. Thanks, Vette. Speaking of food, I'm going to get me some right now. Will you find us a spot near the deejay booth? I'll be right back."

I stand in line and load my plate with barbecued brisket, baked beans, chilled veggie salad, and an ice-cold cup of lemonade.

Vette and Brax are sitting at a rectangular table inside the pavilion, which is only a few feet away from where the latest jams are being played. Scottie is stationed back at the music booth, spinning records and swaying to the beat.

"Glad you found us a good seat," I tell her before settling down. I say my grace and dig in.

"Hmm, from the way you're dressed, it looks like you want to find a *man*."

"Vette, please. You don't know what you're talking about."

"Dani, you're dressed like you should be at the beach, not a family picnic where you know some of these folks are preachers and deacons and mothers of the church. I'm telling you, they do not want to see all that."

"Oops, well, *excuse me.* If I would have known this is a sanctified church convention, I would have worn my *Little House on the Prairie* dress and brought my three-inch Bible in case someone wants to hear a sermon. Get real, Vette. Most of these people don't give a damn about me. They don't even know me."

"Oh, they know you all right. Some of them are just too classy to say anything. Better pray you don't cross paths with the loud, opinionated ghetto side of our fam."

All of a sudden, an elderly dark-skinned man wearing a clergyman's shirt passes by.

"Good afternoon, sisters," he says politely and waves, but he doesn't stop.

"How you doing, sir?" I greet him and fold my arms over my breasts even though he's just moved past us.

"See what I'm talking about?" Vette hisses at me. "That man shouldn't be seeing your body parts. I don't care how much of an adult he is. And you can bet most of my other relatives feel the same way."

I scan the crowd. Watching so many unfamiliar people happily socializing and hugging makes me feel utterly alone—like I'm invisible, but I know I'm not because every few seconds, I notice a few folks checking me out on the sly. They're probably wondering what I'm doing here, the former "other woman." And I'll bet they can't wait to see what may happen when Neil's wife and I cross paths. There're often fireworks between me and Anya since our history is so emotionally raw.

Several years ago, Anya suffered from a hormonal disorder that left her with such a low sex drive she never wanted to make love. She felt guilty for denying Neil sex and told her hubby it was okay by her if he found a mistress. At first, Neil was reluctant to find another partner. But then, being a man, he went for it. I was his cute, spirited coworker who had the hots for him. Back then, the man was everything I wanted. So we hooked up every time we could, anywhere we could, and enjoyed some of the most passionate, experimental sex I'd ever had. He fell in love. I did, too. Our son, Brax, was the "shocking" outcome.

I'm lost in deep thought until I hear someone say my name.

"And this next joint goes out to the gorgeous Ms. Dani F." The voice is loud, excited.

I hear the thumping bass line of a Lil Wayne song. I slowly turn my head around until I get an unobstructed view of the deejay booth. Scottie grins in my direction.

Several couples spill onto the dance floor, singing and doing some funky hip-hop moves.

"My brother is giving you serious attention," Vette says, winking. "What's up with that?"

"We met, instantly clicked, exchanged numbers. I think he's kind of cool," I reply. Scottie and I lock eyes. I can feel Vette staring at us.

"Vette," I beg. "Will you watch the baby for me?"

"Girl, go ahead and do your thing." I thank her, then leap from my seat to the dance floor. I gyrate my hips and sing along to Lil Wayne's rhymes. I love it that Scottie dedicated a song to me. I want to enjoy the moment and begin to dance like I'm performing onstage at the freaking Toyota Center.

"I don't believe this shit!" LaNecia appears from nowhere, shouting at me as she approaches. This chick has the nerve to stand in front of me, competing with me for Scottie's attention.

"Who invited you here?" she asks.

What's with her? Can't she see I'm busy?

"Excuse me?" I ask, still rocking to the beat and shaking my ass. "Do I know you?"

"You may not know me now . . . but you will." She rudely narrows her eyes on my outfit. "Why are you dressed like that? You know what they say about people who dress all skimpy like you?"

"No, I don't know what they say. But fill me in."

"You're dressed like a whore. No, not *like* a whore . . ."

I stop dancing. "I *am* a whore? Is that what you're trying to say?"

"Yep."

"Look, little girl, whoever you are," I say sarcastically.

"I'm LaNecia." She points at a wooden necklace she's wearing that spells out the sentence "LaNecia is the SH#&." Obviously monogrammed. "Can't you read?"

"I am a grown-ass woman, Miss LaNecia. I don't know why you gots to be all up in my face. I was invited, if you don't mind, and I'm about to finish dancing. The good part is about to come on." I start rocking back and forth to the music again.

"You're too old to be dancing to Lil Wayne anyway."

"And how in the hell do you know how old I am?" I jiggle my butt and gyrate my hips.

LaNecia opens her mouth again like she's about to go off on me. The clergyman returns and steps past us to talk to Scottie at the deejay booth. I do a bunny-hopping dance move and bounce over a few spaces past LaNecia so I can discreetly check out the happenings. The clergyman gestures at Scottie like he wants him to please stop the music. Scottie shakes his head. Turns the music up louder. *Boom, boom, boom!* I can feel the cement floor vibrate like aftershocks rumbling under my feet.

Clergyman frowns and cups his hands over his mouth, yells something at Scottie. LaNecia swings her head around and storms over to the deejay booth, leaving me by myself. Soon she and the clergyman begin arguing.

I put two and two together. The way that she listens to the preacher, then points a hard finger at Scottie, I can tell she's defending him. The question is, Why is she taking up for Scottie over a man of the cloth? And I want to know why she's given me a lot of attitude when she doesn't so much as know my name.

Meanwhile, I notice that people are now craning their necks and staring more at LaNecia's antics than at me and my fancy dance moves. I slow things down a notch until I'm standing still. Thankfully, I hear my name being called and turn around to see Brax sitting on Vette's lap. He waves happily at me. I wave back, then return to our table, take a seat next to them, and scoop Brax into my arms. I give him a loving hug. He squirms and yells, "No, Mommy, too tight!" I laugh, because I'm positive he knows I didn't squeeze him *that* hard.

"All right then, fine. Be that way," I say and cover my face with my hands and start sniffing loudly and moaning. "Ahhh," I cry. I peek at Brax through my fingers. His mouth is wide open as he gapes at me with his big ole pretty eyes.

"Mama, don't cry. Sorry."

I look up, laugh, and squeeze his cheek. "Got ya, Brax."

He laughs, too, giving me a toothy grin.

"Y'all so crazy, Dani. You are still the same, girl." Vette

shakes her head and starts sipping on a clear plastic cup filled with lemonade and ice chips. "And that's exactly why my cousin LaNecia feels threatened."

I lean in closer. "I've noticed her bad attitude. What's up with her?"

"I'm not sure you're ready for this part of our family history."

"C'mon Vette, quit messing around. I'm sick of this girl acting crazy with me, so go ahead and tell me. I can take it."

"Here it goes. If you sense something is up between Scottie and LaNecia, you're not imagining things. Um, they kind of took the 'kissing cousin' concept to the extreme a while ago. . . ."

"Stop." I cover my ears. "I don't wanna hear it."

Vette pulls down my hands. "If you plan on being involved with my brother, you need to hear this, trust." She continues. "Scottie sometimes has poor judgment. He acts first, thinks later. That method has gotten him in tons of trouble. Don't get me wrong. Scottie has a good heart. He tries very hard . . . but sometimes all that good is overtaken by the bad."

"And where does that girl come in?"

"He got her pregnant. . . ."

"I can't take this!"

"Calm down. They lost the baby, and they've *been* over, but she thinks she's in love with him." Vette pauses. "And that confrontation y'all went through on the dance floor . . . prepare to go through much more than that if you're interested in Scottie Meadows. LaNecia is the type to take you to hell and back."

I sigh heavily and try to process what Vette has told me. Sounds like LaNecia is a crazy young lady that I may have to introduce to my other side—the part of me that comes out to prove that I am more than just a pretty face. This pretty face can get downright ugly when it has to.

Suddenly Vette looks up and yells excitedly. This dark-skinned chubby girl parades to our table.

"What up, Karetha?" Vette greets her.

"Ain't nothing up," the girl responds. She looks like she's in her early twenties. Although I try to make eye contact to say hello, she totally blows me off as if I'm not sitting right next to Vette. No biggie. I'm accustomed to all kinds of women ignoring me like they can't stand the sight of me even though technically I've done nothing to deserve their attitude.

"Oops, I am being rude. Dani," Vette says, "let me introduce you to Karetha, my cousin LaNecia's best friend. When those two get together, don't pay them any mind. They're young and wild like the rest of the fam. Ka may as well be in the fam as much as she hangs around."

Karetha produces a forced smile, and I want to throw up a hand and tell her, "Save the phoniness. Don't bother." But I swallow my pride and grin, extending my fingers for a handshake. "Pleasure to meet you. Hey, Vette, you don't have to explain. I was their age once."

Karetha starts snickering right in my face.

"Um," I say coolly, "I don't know why you think that statement is so funny. . . ."

"Damn, Dani, please don't start. You don't have to turn every incident into an argument." Vette smiles and rolls her eyes. "There's already enough of that going on."

Karetha laughs and glances briefly at Scottie, LaNecia, and the clergyman.

"That man of God doesn't care too much for rap music," Vette says. "But Scottie feels since he's the deejay, he can play whoever he wants. And poor LaNecia, of course, she's gonna back Scottie. But I think they're all trying to work things out. Some things just aren't worth an argument."

Several minutes pass as Vette and Karetha gossip while I spend time playing peekaboo with Brax.

We're interrupted when Scottie and LaNecia wander over to our table. He apologizes for the commotion about the music and suggests we strike up a spades game while he takes a break. LaNecia immediately grabs his arm, pleading to be his partner, and he says okay. I look at Vette, but she shakes her head like she's not interested. I decide to wave at Neil, who is seated two tables over. He quickly comes to see what I want and agrees to team up: me and Neil against LaNecia and his brother.

Vette holds Brax in her lap so they can watch us play. Neil is seated across from me, and Scottie is on my right side, with Vette and Brax on my left. LaNecia sits across from Scottie, and Ka is seated next to Neil.

"I'll shuffle," Neil offers, and he deals the first deck.

"First hand bids itself. No bidding," Scottie instructs us.

I try to concentrate on my hand but find myself blushing when Neil offers me warm gazes from across the table.

"You bothered by something?" I ask Neil as he places a card on the table.

"What are you talking about?" Neil asks as LaNecia tosses her card.

"You keep giving me these peculiar looks. Watching me like a hawk."

Neil studies Scottie and says, "Just making sure you're not cheating."

"Whoops, sorry, boyfriend," I say to Scottie, as a warning that my card is about to beat his.

"He's *not* your boyfriend." LaNecia stands up and glares at me, then sits back down.

"Excuse me. Have you forgotten you're just his little cousin?" I ask, just to antagonize her.

"Dani, not now," Neil pleads. "Ignore LaNecia. It's your turn."

"Here, how's that?" I slap down a king of hearts.

"Play ya game, baby. I ain't mad atcha," Scottie says.

I proudly scoop up the cards. We continue to play, and I'm trying to have fun. It feels good to know that, surprisingly, Neil and I are winning, earning more books than Scottie and LaNecia. Winning makes me feel good and powerful. Especially since my competition is clearly a woman who has eyes for Scottie Meadows.

"Neil? Dani?" Uh-oh. It's Anya Meadows. Fine time for her to show up.

I take a long, hard look at Neil's wife, a woman who sometimes acts catty with me for obvious reasons. Anya's shoulder-length hair is filled with new auburn and blond highlights. Her slightly puffy stomach makes her resemble a kangaroo. And look at how she's dressed. Her outfit consists of a multicolored hoodie (of all things) with a matching do-rag covering the crown of her head, a pair of gold macramé Egyptian sandals, and some extremely tight blue jean shorts. She's standing at the card table next to Neil. Reese, their eight-year-old daughter, races by laughing as she's being chased by a couple of rowdy boys.

"Well," I reply. "Hmm. Is that Anya Meadows?" I say jokingly.

"You got that right, Dani," she fires back. "I *am* a Meadows."

I am a pro at reading between the lines. She's a Meadows. I'm a Frazier. Point taken.

I ignore her rude stares and focus on playing the game. We continue talking trash and slamming cards. And when Scottie calls over a young relative and offers him a dollar to bring me a big cup of lemonade, then openly shares it with me by sipping on my straw, I don't know whether to act happy or annoyed when both LaNecia and Anya look stunned.

Neil and I win by three books and celebrate with a high five. Anya gapes at Neil like he's lost his mind, then abruptly turns around and leaves. But Neil barely blinks an eye.

I rise to my feet and take Brax in my arms. Vette stands up, too.

Suddenly, LaNecia verbally attacks Scottie, who's still sitting at the card table.

"Why the fuck won't you answer my question, dammit? When you were eating my pussy and going raw dog in me, you wanted to hear every little thing I had to say. . . ."

"Oh, God," I say, covering Brax's ears. "I feel sick."

Vette steadily watches LaNecia. "Humph, you and probably everyone else."

I take one final look at the man who made me feel like a princess today and decide I've had enough. I grab Brax's hand and head for my car. Vette follows me.

"I'm ready to go. Do me a favor and find my little red cooler and set it aside for me, okay? But even if you can't find it, whatever."

"Sure, I'll get your cooler for you, and I totally understand if you don't feel like staying any longer. It's been a heck of a day, girl."

"Hasn't it, though? I mean," I say wistfully, "I enjoyed myself for the most part. I–I think Scottie is considerate and intriguing," I tell her, my voice rising with emotion. "His approach was adorable, and I love how he was into me, but all this drama . . ." I laugh abruptly, then stop. "I ain't trying to go backward. Trying to move forward."

I wave 'bye to Vette and thoughtfully observe Scottie and LaNecia from the safe distance of the parking lot.

2

ANYA

My Reality Is Far Different from My Dream

It's moments like these that make me wonder if time really heals all wounds. In some ways, I'd say that time does heal. You definitely cannot compare the way I feel about Dani now to how I used to feel about her. In the past I could imagine myself taking a butcher knife and slicing it across this pretty young thing's face.

Yet some folks advise, "Don't give your energy to the 'other woman.' You should take out your anger on Neil. After all, he's the one who made those vows to you, not the other woman." And I'd shoot back, "Yeah, yeah, yeah, yeah. I know what you're trying to say. Beat *his* behind. Leave *hers* alone." Everyone in the world knows this type of thing is a lot easier to say than do. Even if my hubby broke his vows, he had assistance. And a woman who helps a married man stumble and fall must shoulder some of the blame. She's an accomplice, and we all know what the law says about accomplices.

This afternoon, watching Danielle Frazier prance and dance at our family reunion is enough to make my blood boil. Why can't she just disappear? But because of Brax, it's impossible for Dani to ever be out of the picture. So I am forced to deal with things I'd rather forget.

No matter how much I try to get a solid grip on my life, I can't. For me, control is like trying to hold something valuable in your hand, but your hand is covered with sudsy soap and water, so the thing you try to clutch on to always slips out of your grasp.

The spades game is a perfect example of my not being in control. Instead of playing it cool and patiently watching my husband and the others play the game, I make disapproving faces and eventually storm away to sulk at a nearby table.

After the card game ends, I notice Dani leaving with Vette. LaNecia's loud mouth can be heard even from where I am. She's shouting profanities at Scottie, and from the look on his face, he wants to yell back. A small crowd has gathered. I think I should intervene. I join the crowd and stand next to Scottie, LaNecia, and Karetha.

"What's going on over here?"

LaNecia shakes her head like she doesn't want to talk about it.

To try to ease the tension between them, I offer a hopeful smile.

"Hey, brother-in-law, you're truly looking good these days. I mean that," I tell Scottie. "And you'd look even better if you can stop showing off in front of family," I say jokingly, referring to their public spat a couple of minutes ago.

"You need to talk to *her* about that," Scottie says and points at LaNecia.

"If you don't mind," I reply. "I'd love to talk to both of you about things."

"Women sure love to talk, talk, talk," Scottie complains.

I laugh and nod. In my opinion, Scottie is good people. He's never done any harm to me, so I've taken a liking to him even though other family members view him as a problem.

"All right, Ms. Anya, give me a minute," LaNecia replies as Karetha fans her sweaty face with a magazine.

"Girl, calm down. Listen to Ms. Anya. I thought you two had made up. Yet you're clowning in front of everybody. Screaming and advertising y'all's business. They're going to be talking about this for weeks," Karetha cautions LaNecia as she watches the crowd disperse.

"I don't care!"

"Yes, you do."

"Do not."

"LaNecia," I cut in, "your friend is right on this one. You don't need to have people talking against you after all you've been through with Scottie. Trust me. I know how horrible that kind of thing feels."

"Yeah, but, sometimes I don't care what these Negroes think because they can't live my life for me," LaNecia tells me.

Karetha says, "I wish they could. Maybe that's the only way you'll get it in your head when it's time to back off. . . ."

LaNecia sharply interrupts. "C'mon girl, even if you don't agree with my choices, as my best friend you're supposed to have my back."

"Having your back doesn't mean I can't tell you the truth."

"I don't wanna hear it," LaNecia sputters. "When I'm upset, I can't hear anything anyone says. *Anyone.*"

"LaNecia, believe it or not, Karetha has your best interests at heart. You don't always have to do what other people say, but it's good to listen. We see what you don't see. Okay?" I grab her around the waist and give her a solid hug, something I know she needs. I want to give her the emotional support I wanted when Neil's family heard he and Dani were having a baby.

When I see how young and innocent she is underneath her tough shell, I believe LaNecia's true potential is within reach. In some ways, I wish I were still LaNecia's age.

If I had known then what I know now, I'd have taken the world by its horns and set it on fire. I definitely would have done more with my life than be a housewife, or a woman who briefly held a position in the travel industry. No, I would have loved to earn a degree in international business, globe-trot around the world, and help make an impact on society. But my reality is far different from my dream. Right now, I just want to keep my marriage together and raise my daughter, Reesy, to be responsible and emotionally mature. Life's just too damned short. About as long as it takes to blink an eye, you look up and life is over. As I inch closer to middle age, I know I want my life to count for something.

LaNecia and I finish our hug. Scottie looks impatiently at his watch.

"We can talk over there." I point at a wooden picnic table several yards away. All of us, including Karetha, take a seat around the table.

"Scottie, it's so good to see you. It truly is. I've been worried about you, wondering if you're making out okay since you went to Detroit. How you liking the weather?"

"Sister-in-law, Motown's freezing temperatures ain't no joke. Winter lasts more than six months up there. I love the snow and snowballs and Frosty the Snowman and all that, but damn, you know what I'm saying?"

"Does that mean you're coming back home?" LaNecia says.

He coughs and shrugs. "Don't know. The economy sucks ass up there with businesses closing left and right. It looks like a ghost town in some parts. Truth be told, my uncle James's construction business may not be making as much money as it used to."

"That's understandable," I say sympathetically. "You're always welcome to come live with us."

"Ha!" Scottie laughs. "I don't think Neil feels that way."

"We never know how Neil is going to feel. But you'd be surprised to know your brother loves you more than you think."

"Yeah, right."

"He does. He just has a weird way of showing it."

"Yeah, well, anyway. I know I'd have to get a job right away . . . if I do end up staying with y'all. Neil used to say all the time, 'People who don't work, steal.'"

"That sounds like Neil."

"I wouldn't want to be under your roof, living off his money, and have him assuming I'm in his house being a moocher. That ain't my style."

I'm noticing how LaNecia dreamily stares at Scottie. Watching how she acts around him is kind of disturbing. She should learn how to let go of Scottie because she's never going to have it her way. Even when I first heard about these two, that they were going out and hanging around each other all hours of the night, I didn't think much of it. But when I'd go over to Sola's, my mother-in-law, and they'd come around, too, I'd notice how LaNecia would act really possessive over Scottie. A blind person could sense they were screwing. A woman can always tell when another woman is having sex with a man. Body language. How comfy the man and woman look when they sit next to each other, how they stare into each other's eyes as if no one else exists. Yep, my experiences with Neil and Dani have taught me much more than I've ever wanted to know.

Maybe the lessons I've learned can be shared with LaNecia and Scottie. I hate to say it, but I think that had their child survived, it might have grown up confused, mocked, and rejected.

"So, about that little confrontation you two just had. Is everything okay now?"

"Yeah, I regret that things got a little out of hand," he replies, eyeing LaNecia. "But we'll be okay in time."

"How can that happen when you barely talk to me right now?"

"Scottie, I think she's asking a legitimate question. I'm not trying to get deep in your business, but I can act as a mediator...."

"Hell, I could've done that." Karetha looks offended.

"I'm not trying to take your place, Karetha. But you are so close to the situation.... Maybe I could be a little bit more objective."

"The fact is, LaNecia and I needed to have a private conversation right after the card game, and I was trying to tell her that we were through," Scottie says.

"No, Scottie, *you* were. I'm not."

"What do you want?" he asks.

"Another chance."

"Fine, it's out on the table," I say. "LaNecia knows what *she* wants. Now what does Scottie want?"

He pauses. "I wanted to hang out with someone else, to be honest." He looks back toward the family reunion. "But I don't see her anymore." He hops up to his feet and squints. A worried expression flashes across his face.

"Oh, so it's obvious you're feeling something for her?" I ask, knowing he's referring to Dani.

"I hope she knows . . . ," he says, but stops himself.

"She's gone," I tell him. "Maybe she has stuff to do."

"She could have at least . . . dammit." Looking defeated, he slowly sits down. "What can you tell me about . . . ?"

"She's a handful, but knowing what I know about both of you, y'all might make an interesting couple."

"How can you say that to Scottie with me sitting right here?" LaNecia sputters. "Scottie, don't you know that woman is just a tramp whore who thinks she's better than everybody. I don't like the bitch."

"Don't be calling folks out their name."

"Scottie, don't be trying to push up on another woman in front of my face. That's *very* disrespectful."

"Are you always respectful, LaNecia? Are you?"

"She's been hurt, Scottie," I explain.

"I have, too," he says sadly.

"Not more than me, though," LaNecia says. "I think you owe me."

"Look, LaNecia, I'm trying to be nice, but you don't run me. Give me some space. You're pressuring a brotha. I have decisions to make, a life to live. And that's all I have to say."

I decide to jump in to ease tensions. "LaNecia, what if something happened to Scottie and he decided to return to Michigan and never come back? Could you handle that and move on with your life?"

"I–I don't know, Anya. It's hard to think about that when I can see Scottie right in front of me. I mean, damn, how you expect me to act when it's my first time seeing him since he hauled ass and left me."

Scottie stands and looks like he wants to comment, but he spins around and faces the family reunion. "I gotta go."

"Girl, he's not thinking about you, LaNecia," Karetha states in a weary, pleading tone. "So you shouldn't be thinking about him. If you believe you're going to wear the man down and he'll eventually give in to you, it ain't happening."

"Hey, tell you what!" I say with excitement, trying to come up with a positive spin on this sad situation. "LaNecia, remember back in the day when you had a dream? You used to talk about being the next Gina Prince-Bythewood and would run your mouth nonstop about going to Houston Community College to study filmmaking. Are you still into that?"

She nods halfheartedly.

"I know you didn't get a chance to enroll in school last year. But that isn't any excuse. Why not try to get in this year? I can help you."

"You don't have to do that, Anya."

"I know, but I'd like to. You need an intervention and I can handle things. That way you can focus on doing something positive for yourself. I mean it, LaNecia. Don't give up your dreams trying to chase after someone else."

"I—I dunno."

"You'll never know if you don't try What if you end up being a producer?"

"Ha!" She laughs, as if it's a ridiculous idea. "What am I going to produce?"

"You can start with me," I tell her. "Come up with a good story idea and I'll let you film me."

"*You?* I think I can find a more interesting subject than you."

"Well, excuse me, miss. I guess you feel like my life is

dull and uneventful compared to yours, but let me assure you, there's always something going on in the Meadows household."

I stand up, face the girls, and describe the drama I've faced being the wife of a man who has a child with another woman. In the middle of my juicy story, I suddenly feel a big gush that makes my pants soaked and warm. I grow uncomfortable. I take a deep breath, and feeling very embarrassed, I squeeze my legs together. I ask Karetha and LaNecia if I may be excused. "I'll catch up with you later," I say. I walk stiffly yet briskly toward the nearest women's restroom, hoping no one sees the funny way that I'm moving.

As soon as I reach the restroom, I lock myself in an empty stall and quickly pull down my panties. My maxipad is soaking wet. Blotches of blood stain my underwear.

"Why is my period so freaking heavy?" The fear and dread is so great, I feel like bursting into tears. I've experienced heavy bleeding this past April, May, and June. Last month I woke up in bed and noticed a foul smell. I turned on the lamp and saw blood soaking through our sheets. Thank God Neil had already gone to work, so I got a chance to strip the bed and wash the sheets in bleach water. Last month I didn't worry about what was happening. But now I can't avoid the problem. I'm not in the mood to be around people anymore. And unfortunately I don't have a fresh maxipad. I grab my cell phone from my jacket pocket and am relieved when Vette answers on the first ring.

"Hi, Anya, where are you?"

"Um, I had to use the ladies room. Hey, I need a favor."

"What's up?"

"Do you have a maxipad?"

"No, did you check the machine in the restroom?"

"They're all out. Dammit."

"You want me to ask around?"

"Yes, please do. Thanks Vette."

She says okay and hangs up. I hang out in the ladies room until Vette enters.

Fifteen minutes pass before I hear my name being called and the sound of footsteps across the restroom floor. "Anya, you still in here? I have something for you."

"I'm in the last stall. Hand it to me under the door, please."

Thank God she does just what I told her to do and is sensitive enough to not ask me any questions.

Questions I want answers to myself.

3

SCOTTIE

An Afternoon with Scottie

Scottie Meadows *decided to* let Dani have one night to herself. He resisted the urge to call her the first day they met. But when he wakes up early the next morning, as he lies in bed, he knows he can't let the day end without calling the woman who's on his mind.

For the time being, he's staying in the Westchase area of town at a Studio 6 Extended Stay. Although he appreciates having a fully equipped kitchen, he hates the cramped quarters, but a hotel is the best he can do until he comes up with a better plan.

"Yesterday is history," he sings to himself. "Today is a new day, and it's gonna be a lovely day-y-y."

After he gets up, he eats breakfast and watches television to pass time. But he can't take the suspense anymore. He waits until eleven-thirty before he grabs his cell phone. He scrolls down his address book until he gets to the newest entry and thoughtfully stares at her digits. He takes a deep breath and presses the call button. When the number rings several times without an answer, he immediately places a different call.

"Hey, there, brother-in-law," Anya coos into the phone.

"What up? Um, you busy?"

"What do you need?"

Scottie laughs and explains in detail what he wants and how Anya could help. He grabs a pen and some paper to jot down her advice. He listens to her chirp for a couple of minutes, then happily disconnects the call.

Scottie steps out of the shower, dries off, puts on deodorant, and rummages through his suitcase until he finds a Hurley black graphic tee and slacks, which he takes time to iron. After Scottie gets carefully dressed, he heads out the door and takes off in his car to the mall. By the time he's finished shopping an hour later, he feels lighthearted, joyous, and bursting with anticipation.

But his excitement turns to complete jitters the second he's outside the entrance gate of Dani's apartment complex.

"What am I, a stalker?" he asks himself. "This ain't my style at all."

He's driving a five-year-old Cadillac Escalade, a vehicle his uncle James bought for him when he moved to Michigan. Scottie puts the Escalade in park with the motor still running while he waits for someone who knows the code to show up at the gate so he can follow in behind them. Once he's inside, his hands become wet with perspiration as he finds an empty parking space in the visitors' section.

"Here goes," he says. Carrying a plastic bag filled with goodies, he walks to Dani's apartment. Two plant holders sit on the ground right beside her door, and a brown mat with white letters saying Welcome greets him.

When she answers his knock, her hair is uncombed and she's wearing no makeup.

"Oh my God, what are you doing here, Scottie?"

"Hey! I'm sorry. I–I had to see you."

"About what?"

Scottie hates how her words sound, but he plows on. "You and me . . . we have a pact." He grins, boyishlike. "We must talk every day. We must stay connected. Plus I have some very special things for you. So when you gonna ask me in?"

Unable to contain her smile, Dani shakes her head in amazement and opens the door wider for him to enter.

"Man, you are a trip! You could've given me a warning."

"I called, but you didn't answer," he replies, following her inside her quaint and spotless apartment.

"You did?" Dani digs in her purse, which is sitting in a corner of the sofa. "Oh, I see I have a couple of missed calls, but you still should have kept trying until I answered. It just works better that way. Remember that next time." Instead of waiting for Scottie to respond, she reaches inside the purse, pulls out a brush. She sweeps her hair into a ponytail and swipes her lips with ChapStick.

"I'll be right back. Gotta go check on Brax. I laid him down for his nap a little while ago," she says and disappears down the hall.

Scottie takes a few steps inside the apartment, soaking in his surroundings. He inhales the scent of fresh flowers in a red ceramic vase in the center of the dining room table. Several decorative rugs line the plush carpet. He is impressed by the large brown leather sofa set and notices a tan body pillow resting on the floor in front of the entertainment center.

Ah, he thinks, *she loves music and movies just like me.* Dani's collection includes hundreds of organized CDs and DVDs that sit next to a wide-screen television. A couple of fluffy teddy bears and some toy fire trucks sit on top of a toy chest. And three blown-up framed portraits of Brax grinning and sitting snugly on Dani's lap are mounted on the living room wall.

The more he looks around, the more he likes what he sees.

"My little man is knocked out and clutching his pillow," Dani says as she returns to the living room. "Thank God he's asleep, because although I'm glad you're here, I had no idea you were coming, and when you knocked on the door it scared me because I wasn't expecting anyone. We've had a few break-ins around here."

"Hey," he says seriously. "I do understand and I'm sorry. Should I leave?" he says, feeling nervous about her reaction.

"Don't go. It'll be fine. To be honest, I was bored and I could use some company." She grins.

Feeling a little more confident, he says, "I think you'd better learn to accept all this spontaneity, get used to seeing the kid." He points to himself. "Don't you know I'm your man? At least I'm trying to be. . . ."

Dani takes a deep breath and lowers her eyes before peering up at him again.

"You make me feel so . . . I dunno. Scottie, I don't know if I should tell you this," she admits and plops down on the sofa. She delicately pats the space beside her so he can sit. "Man, the oddest thing happened to me. You were in my dream last night. . . ."

"Aha! Ye-oh!" He wants to be in her every thought just like she's in his.

"No, wait, silly. I mean it was cool, but I'm blown away that it happened so soon after meeting you."

"What happened? Tell me!"

"You and I were in this great big house, like a mansion," she explains. "We were just going from room to room, chatting and whatnot. You were talking my ears off, as a matter of fact. I just don't remember everything you were saying."

"How'd you feel when you woke up?"

"Sad." She nods. "Sad."

"Why?"

"Because I realized I didn't finish talking with you the way I wanted to yesterday. So much happened during the reunion, I decided I'd had enough, and I up and left."

"That's what I heard," he says, sounding hurt.

"And . . ." She begins nervously playing with her hands. "Well, Scottie, I didn't expect you to actually call me last night. . . . You know, I mean, you never know how these things go. . . . Yet when you . . . when you *didn't* call me, well, it's silly. . . ."

"Tell me!"

"I wanted to hear the sound of your voice again. I tried to picture you and remember how great things felt when we met. I kind of wanted that again but couldn't predict when it would happen. And now you're here."

"I'm here, Dani. I'm here."

Scottie sits back, growing more relaxed, and begins telling her what he did after the reunion, how he hung out with some of his male cousins, drinking beer, watching TV, bonding and catching up. She quietly listens to him talk. He loves that she's hanging on to his every word.

He decides to spring his surprise on her and reaches inside a plastic bag. The first gift to emerge is a simple clear glass vase filled with five yellow roses that smell deliciously sweet.

"Scottie, I love anything yellow. How'd you know?"

He just winks at her knowingly and reaches inside the bag and presents the next gift.

"What the hell?" Dani squeals. "Who told you I adore Coco Mademoiselle bath and body products? Oh my goodness, I could use this good-smelling stuff every day. And I was running low on the twist and spray. . . . How'd you know, Scottie? Please tell me."

"No, it's my little secret."

"I hate secrets." She pouts.

"Why?"

"Because I have a need to know things."

He just laughs at her when she pleads with him to tell.

"No way. I'm having too much fun."

"Actually," she says, "so am I."

The more his nervousness lessens, the more he's determined to show her that he is for real. He wants to prove to himself that he can start a positive relationship and build it into something substantial.

The afternoon is filled with more unexpected surprises. When she isn't looking, he whips out a Tickle Me Elmo talking doll.

"You've gotta be joking."

"I'll bet Brax won't think it's a joke!" He plants the doll on her lap and plays with its stomach. Both Dani and Scottie erupt in laughter when Elmo makes squeaking sounds and shouts, "That tickles!"

"You're amazing! Elmo dolls aren't cheap, either. Thanks, Scottie!"

"Just looking out for . . . for my nephew," he says in a whisper. When he hears himself say these words out loud, he feels awkward. It's the first time he realizes that the woman he's trying to get with is the mother of his relative. It feels sobering to acknowledge that the baby he almost had with LaNecia would have been his son and his cousin. He tentatively looks up at the photos of Dani and Brax. It pains him to see that Brax shares many of Neil's facial features. *If things between me and her go the way I want, how will I handle the child issue?* Instantly he feels himself getting stressed; this isn't what he wants to think about. The most important thing he's concerned with is trying to make an impression.

"Brax is going to have so much fun playing with Elmo. How'd you know he loves . . . ?"

"That's classified info. Don't you listen?" he says, trying to keep his mood light.

He and Dani fiddle with the toy a little longer until she sets it aside and looks expectantly at him.

Then she excuses herself to put her gifts in the bedroom. The second she leaves, Scottie starts snooping around. He wanders into her contemporary kitchen filled with black appliances and tall oak cabinets. He opens the refrigerator door and checks out the groceries and thoroughly investigates the cupboards. When she returns to the living room and notices him standing in the kitchen, she puts her hands on her hips. She watches him wrap a tan apron around his waist. It barely fits.

"Mister Meadows, what in the hell do you think you're doing?"

"Just call me the gangster chef," he says, pointing at the black bandanna wrapped around his head.

"The who?"

"I'm acting like the type of man that I hope to be."

"You're a great actor," she teases and goes to take a seat at the breakfast bar.

Scottie enjoys taking over her kitchen, acting as if he's cooked meals on her stove for years.

"Need any help?" she asks.

"No, Mariah."

"I'm not . . . never mind. The onion powder and lemon pepper . . ."

"Shhh. I know where everything is."

"Scottie, you're scaring me."

"You won't stay scared if you have faith in me."

He prepares double-decker cheeseburgers and a garden salad with all the works. A half hour later he sets the table for her, scolding her for getting up for even a second when she offers to help.

"This is all on me. You sit. I work. You watch. You learn."

"Yes, sir," she says, smirking.

When Scottie is done cooking, he cuts off the burner, carefully fixes her a plate and brings it to the dining room table, where she goes to take a seat.

"Here ya go," he says and hands her a can of Coca-Cola Zero. "I popped the top for you so you won't have to break one of those pretty fingernails."

"Scottie, you don't have to go that far. I can do these things for myself, ya know."

"I know, but I don't want you to. I got you!"

Scottie's as anxious as he would be on an all-day job interview.

In some ways, Scottie believes he can handle Dani. He's dated enough women to know what they like and want. But what if he goes all out to impress her and she gets bored with his ways and accuses him of trying to buy her? How can he also show her that he simply enjoys being around her, too?

Scottie decides he needs to calm himself down and take a seat.

"How's it taste?"

"Not half bad."

Immediately after she finishes her meal, he sets the dirty dishes in the dishwasher, takes her by the hand into the living room to sit on the sofa, props her feet on top of the coffee table, removes her sexy little sandals from her feet, and sticks a throw pillow behind her back.

He looks around the living room until he locates the remote control for the cable, hands it over to her, and lets her take charge.

She speeds through the menu until she locates a program on TV One.

"This feels kinda nice," he murmurs. It's all he can do to keep from resting his chin on top of her head. He wants to reach out and let his fingers play in her hair. *What does her hair smell like? Does she smell as good as she looks?* To Scottie, Dani is a princess who's honored him with her presence. The thought of that makes him want to be worthy.

"I want to ask you something, but I'm not ready to know the answer," he says. He wants to ask her about her relationship with Neil but is having second thoughts about possibly spoiling their moment by discussing such a serious issue.

"Oh, please don't do that. You can ask," she says.

"Tell you what, when the time is right, I'll ask you lots of questions. I just want to chill with you and enjoy myself. That is, if you don't mind."

"Dammit, Scottie," she scolds. "I knew you were the smooth type, and that's fine, but next time you need to just spit it out." She looks agitated.

"Dani, I didn't mean to offend you."

"I'm not offended. I just hate when people do that. It–it's no biggie, though. Let's watch TV." She picks up the remote and increases the volume.

Oh, hell, he thinks. *I've messed up. I gotta do something.*

"Young lady, pay attention to the show. I'm going to give you a pop quiz once it's over, okay?"

Dani and Scottie sit cozily together for several minutes. The quietness ushers in a peace that Scottie hasn't experienced in a long time.

Suddenly, Scottie's cell phone screams loudly, like a wailing siren from several police cars.

"Who the hell is this calling . . . ?" he mumbles. "I ain't answering it." He retrieves his phone from the clip off his belt and glances at the caller ID. "Damn, how in the fuck . . . ?"

"What's the matter?" Dani asks.

Darkness flickers across his face. But he doesn't say a word. They continue to pick up where they left off, watching television. He absentmindedly strokes her bare arm with the tips of his fingers.

"Scottie!" screams a voice.

Alarmed, Dani tosses Scottie's arm off her shoulders. She sits up straight like a dog sensing danger.

"You hear that?"

"Hear what?"

"That?"

More screams of Scottie's name ring out, then a loud, persistent banging at her door. Her doorknob even rattles.

"Aw, hell nah." Dani jumps to her feet and zips to the door to peer through the peephole. "Shit," she grumbles and steps back. She just stands there, frozen in place, wondering why LaNecia is standing in her doorway.

Scottie then comes over to look.

"Um, wait a second." He opens the front door and disappears behind it.

"What the fuck you doing here?"

"I should be asking you the same thing."

"You don't have the right to ask me shit. . . ."

"Scottie," she yelps, "don't talk to me like that. . . ."

"LaNecia, I swear this is not how I want to be, but what choice do I have?"

"Choose to be nice to me."

"You're going to have to act different if you want me to respect you, or else . . ." He pauses. "Or else I'm going back to Michigan."

LaNecia gasps. "You serious? Okay, fine. What do you want me to do?"

"You cannot be rolling up at Dani's spot like you have the right to be here. Not cool."

He thinks about how he actually did the same thing, coming over without Dani knowing in advance, but he knows he's more welcome than crazy-ass LaNecia.

"How'd you know where she lives? You followed me?"

"Mmm hmmm."

"See, that ain't gonna work. You can't be harassing this woman. You understand?"

"Hmm, okay, Scottie." LaNecia sighs. "I'll do it your way."

Scottie exhales. "Because I know you very well, if you want me to talk to you in a way that's respectful, you need to completely leave Dani alone. Don't call. Nothing."

"What you gonna do for me if I do what you say?"

"What do you want?"

"Promise me you'll take me out one last time, for old times' sake."

His eyes glaze over. "Promise."

Satisfied, LaNecia extends her arms toward his waist. "Hug?"

She places her head on his chest, closes her eyes, and squeezes her arms around him so tight that he can feel her breasts. For a second, Scottie's mind leaps back in time. Back then, he savored how it felt to caress LaNecia's young, hot curves—a feeling so good it made him forget where he was sometimes.

He coughs and loosens himself from LaNecia's grip. "I'll holler at you later. I think it's easier for me to go ahead and listen to what you have to say than it is to have to watch my back and wonder when you gonna jump out the bushes like the damned Bigfoot."

"Ha-ha. That's the Scottie I know. That's all I want," she says in a barely audible voice. "I want to see and still hang out with the man I used to know."

"Um, yeah. Anyway, I'll call you." Scottie waves at La-Necia, then slips back inside Dani's apartment.

He returns to the living room to find Dani sitting on the sofa, blankly staring at a Viagra commercial.

"Everything okay?" she asks.

"Everything is A-okay. You all right? You need something else to drink?"

"What did she want?"

"What do you think?"

"What did you say to her?"

"It's too damn long of a story."

"It is *not.* You weren't outside long, Scottie Meadows."

"Long enough to get the job done."

Dani gasps, then giggles. "You didn't kill the bitch, did you?" she says jokingly.

"You're silly, you know that? You really think I'd kill for you, Mariah?"

"Word on the street is that you're a bad boy. . . ."

"I'd love to show you how bad I am once you become mine. You know that's gonna happen, don't you?"

Dani's cheeks flush red and she doesn't respond.

Scottie continues talking as Dani leans against his broad chest while he tells her stories of his life. How his mother, Sola Meadows, met his father, George Foster, when she'd already had Neil by another man, a man she never married.

"We grew up in a single household. My mom got jerked around by her boyfriends, but she raised me and Neil to treat a woman with love, respect, kindness. That didn't always happen, of course."

Scottie admits to Dani that as a young boy, he felt lonely at times, because his only brother was quite a few years older. Sometimes Neil would let him tag along; other times he didn't want to be bothered.

"Did you wish your mom would've had another little boy and not just Vette? Someone you could play with?"

"You can't miss what you've never had, Dani. But I missed you from the second I laid eyes on you."

"Eww, sounds like someone is running game on me."

"Not running game. I'm the real deal, Mariah."

"I wish you'd stop calling me that."

"Okay, future Mrs. Meadows."

"Ha-ha." Dani laughs. "I never thought I'd hear anyone refer to me as *that*."

"You weren't supposed to hear that until you hooked up with me, lovely one."

"Scottie, you don't have to lie to kick it with me."

"Oh, so you doubt me? Where's your faith? You gotta have faith to be with me."

Dani doesn't say anything.

"I'm not hearing anything," Scottie says softly.

"I'm not saying anything."

"Then do something. You don't have to say a word. Do something."

"Do what?" She frowns.

"Wait a second." Scottie lifts himself up from the couch and strolls over to the music. He knows music and the spines of CD cases so well, it only takes him seconds to find what he wants.

He slides the CD case from the tiny shelf and pulls out the disc, carefully placing it in the CD player and searching until he sees the track he wants to hear.

He turns off the television, then walks over to Dani and lifts her to her feet.

"May I have this dance?"

"Oh, Lord."

"Too late to pray now, baby."

Dani lets out a sigh while Scottie gives her a bear hug and embraces her around the waist. His heart leaps forward when she starts moving with him to the music. They slow-dance to a Stevie Wonder song, an artist who happens to be one of Dani's all-time favorites.

Does she have faith in me? Can she picture us doing this more and more? She lets him fold her sensuous body into his arms. She closes her eyes and rocks with him, slowly rotating around the room.

After a while, Scottie can't even hear Stevie Wonder singing anymore. He's too busy getting lost inside his thoughts.

I don't know how long this is going to last, or where it's headed, but damn it feels so good to be with this woman right now.

4

DANI

Neil Still Loves Me

It's early August, a few weeks after Scottie returned to Houston and decided to stay for good.

"I'm about to pull up in your driveway right now. Are you ready for Brax?" I'm down the street from Neil's house in my truck, babbling with him on my cell phone. According to our child support arrangement, it's his weekend with Brax. So every other Thursday, Brax cries for a good ten minutes and wildly kicks his feet when he's strapped in his car seat. It's not that he doesn't want to spend time with his daddy; it's just that whenever I drop him off, he has a hard time letting go. Today is one of those days.

"Aw, is that my little man pitching a fit again?"

"Yes, I think it's because your little man was deep into his favorite cartoon. And it seems we always have to leave just when the good part is coming on."

"I hate hearing him cry."

"You aren't alone. I keep explaining that our DVR will pause and wait for him until he comes home, but it's kind of hard for a three-year-old to completely understand."

"I'll make him forget all about that cartoon."

It feels refreshing to hear Neil sound more chilled out

than he was at the reunion. Since then, we've made somewhat of a pact. It's important for us to get along for Brax.

I turn the truck onto Neil's driveway and park. He's waiting for us under the covered entrance that leads from his sidewalk to the front door of his two-story brick home. The concrete walkway is bordered with three-feet-high bridal wreaths accented by decorative gravel stones that Neil scattered and arranged last summer. As soon as the engine of my pickup sputters into silence, Neil rushes over, barely looking at me he's so busy trying to fling open the rear door of the double cab to unstrap his son.

"Daddyyy!" Brax happily shrieks, wiggling in his baby seat.

Neil smiles and kisses Brax on the center of his forehead.

"Are you gonna miss me?" I ask Brax and extend my knuckles so we can do a fist bump.

"Mommy, you stay here, too. Okay?"

"No, honey bun, I gotta go grocery shopping. We're getting low on milk and eggs and bottled water and bacon."

"Figures." Neil smiles as he hoists Brax into his arms.

Before I can continue explaining my shopping plans to Brax, we're interrupted by the noise of a car that turns into the driveway and comes to a stop behind my Toyota.

The music in Scottie's Escalade is playing so loud it pulsates like the sound of a washing machine.

While holding Brax, Neil covers his ear and shouts at Scottie to turn off his music. Instantly the thumping music goes silent, and Scottie slowly steps out of the car.

I avert my eyes and start barking instructions to Neil. "Anyway, everything he needs is in his day bag as usual. Please do not let him have any sweets. I don't care how much he begs. And make sure he goes to bed at a decent time."

Neil lowers his questioning eyes at me. Scottie's car door slams. Soon I can feel his body standing inches behind me. He's so close I can smell his cologne. Since that day he popped over unannounced a couple of weeks ago, we've been hanging out more and more. But this is the first time we've been at Neil's house at the same time. I can tell Scottie's growing more comfortable with me, but I haven't exactly wanted Neil to know just yet, especially now that Scottie's living with Neil.

"You come by to see me?" he whispers. The heat of his minty breath tickles my ear. Neil flashes us a suspicious look.

"Um, hey Scottie, what's up?" I ask, feigning surprise.

"You want to go up to my room?"

"What's going on here?" Neil asks. Brax is now tugging his daddy's shirtsleeve and ordering him to carry him inside the house, but Neil barely pays attention. With Neil's eyes locked on mine, I hear him mentally asking, *What do you think you're doing?*

"Let's go inside," Scottie says to me. Neil is holding Brax and his day bag in one arm. He grabs me with his free arm and pulls me along with him. I stumble on the walkway but don't say a word.

"Hey, bro, you're trying to do too much. I can handle Dani." Scottie removes Neil's hand from my arm and places his hand in mine. We follow Neil into the house, and I can't help but wonder what Neil is thinking.

Neil sets down Brax and his day bag once we are inside his foyer. It's a wide, open space that gives a full view of the staircase. A tiny office with French doors is located right off the foyer. The stained concrete flooring gives Neil's house a homey feel.

Brax dashes away, running in a circle and screaming, "I want some chocolate. I want some chocolate."

"What's he talking about?" I ask.

"Not real chocolate," Neil explains. "Hot chocolate. I don't understand how he can stand to drink something that hot when it's probably a hundred degrees outside."

"When Brax wants what he wants, you know he doesn't care."

Brax screams, "I want my choc-late."

"Well," I laugh, "are you going to go make him some?"

"No, *you* are."

"Neil," I plead, feeling like my sticking around right now is not the best thing to do. Earlier Scottie and I made tentative plans to see each other. But I thought he could meet me at the gas station around the corner, definitely not here at the house. "I–I really gotta be going."

"She sure does. Follow me," Scottie says. He strides past me with his head held high, then patiently stands at the foot of the stairs.

"She's not going anywhere, Scottie. I *knew* this was going to happen. Just because I let you stay with us d–doesn't mean you can have c–company."

Neil's voice is strong yet weak; he's babbling like a punk.

"Where's your wife?" Scottie asks. "Let's hear what your wife has to say about me having company."

"Okay, you two," I cut in. "This is nuts. We don't have to be like this. I'm trying hard to maintain my composure. And more importantly, we shouldn't be a-r-g-u-i-n-g in front of the baby."

"Where's my little brother?" Reese joins us from upstairs,

her big feet stomping all the way till she reaches the bottom. Grinning so wide that all her teeth are showing, she squats till she's eye-level with her brother, then hugs Brax around his little shoulders. He pushes her off and continues to run in a circle. Just watching him makes me feel dizzy, like I need to sit down.

"You want to go outside and play kickball? I'll let you win this time. Come on, Brax."

I watch as the kids race through the rear door in the kitchen that leads to the enclosed patio and backyard.

The tension feels so thick I can barely think. Although I have entertained thoughts of what would happen if I dated Scottie, I've tried hard not to overthink things. And right now it seems Neil, Scottie, and I need to have a conversation I'm not ready to have.

Sighing, I go into the den, the room in which the family usually gathers to watch TV and eat. I take a seat on the plush leather love seat, a piece of furniture I've sat on many times in the past, back when I first gave birth to Brax. In the early days, I was welcome to stop by the Meadowses' house. I'd come by, relax on the couch when Anya was here so we could discuss babysitting arrangements whenever I needed help.

But when Brax turned one, Anya convinced Neil that I shouldn't be the one to drop Brax off. I got carried away one day and came by their house dressed like a porn star. Anya pitched a fit and didn't want me around anymore. At first we used Riley Dobson, the next-door neighbor, as the go-between for me and Neil. She was safe, supportive, the ultimate peacemaker. But when her schedule changed and she couldn't drive Brax to my place, we decided that my girlfriend Summer Holiday would take over. That plan worked at first for an entire year. But earlier this spring, Summer got a new man named Andre, no one else was available to step in, and lately I've been the one who finds herself back at the Meadowses' house. And now that Scottie is living with his brother, the pressure has tripled.

According to what Scottie told me, Neil reluctantly agreed to let his brother live with them last week. Scottie argued that it was better for everyone if he gives Neil money than to fork over four hundred dollars a week to a hotel.

Anya was all for the arrangement. "I can use that money," she told Neil. And that settled it.

"Well," I say to the guys, "since I'm going be here for a little while even though I hadn't planned on it, can some nice gentleman bring me something to drink?"

Scottie trudges to the large, open kitchen, which is visible from the den. Neil is right on his heels. Scottie opens the refrigerator and scans the contents. He reaches for a can of ginger ale. Neil slaps the can from Scottie's hand. It crashes to the floor and rolls until it hits a baseboard, then comes to a stop.

"She has diabetes and can't drink that, dummy. She needs to drink something . . ." Exasperated, Neil stops talking and pulls out a can of Coke Zero and stares knowingly at Scottie.

"Oh, I get it. I'm taking notes, my brother." Scottie tries to snatch the soda from Neil's hand, but he chuckles and waves him off.

"If you gonna take notes, then take 'em."

They return to the den. Neil holds my soda and stands in front of me, still quarreling with Scottie like a boy.

I sit back amazed and watch these two men in action.

Here you have Neil. He's dressed in a white unbuttoned dress shirt with no tie. He's just gotten off work from his job as a finance manager at the Texas Medical Center. I love how he's wearing a ribbed wife beater tank top. Mmmm . . . I can remember the times I'd be in bed with Neil, lying on that man's chest. He'd hold me in his arms and we'd fall asleep with my head on his shoulder. It rarely happened, but the few times it did made me wish I could experience lying next to him every night. Of course, Anya got that privilege even though she rarely took advantage of it—they slept in separate rooms. What a waste!

Neil looks steadily in my eyes and hands me the drink.

"Thanks, Neil. That's so nice of you."

"Hey, let me pop it open for you, Mariah."

"What you call her?"

"She's beautiful, fun to be around, a little spitfire, so that's my nickname for her."

"That sounds so stupid."

"Neil." I giggle. "That's not nice."

"And?"

Scottie sits next to me on the love seat.

"There's plenty of room on that sofa over there, boy."

"Boy?"

"You two are so adorable. Is this how you acted when you were younger?"

"Scottie has always acted like a fool!"

"Oh, really, Neil?"

Scottie ignores Neil's comments and opens my drink, then places the can against my mouth.

"This is so disgusting. I can't take it anymore."

"Okay," Scottie sings. "Byeeee."

Neil grunts, then abruptly turns and leaves.

"You are sooo naughty, Scottie. Jeez, that rhymes doesn't it?"

Scottie tilts the soda can to my mouth again even though I've just taken a sip. He raises the can so high that some soda spills all over the top of my lips.

"Hey, let me get that off for you."

He removes a piece of tissue from a box that's sitting on the coffee table. With the paper clutched in his fingers, he leans over, then presses his lips against mine.

"Oh," I try to say, and squirm in my seat.

Scottie's eyes are closed, and he continues to kiss me. His lips are warm and soft. I relax and let the man kiss me for a few seconds.

"Did you like that? Did I offend you?"

"Oh Scottie, this is a bit much for me."

"Aw, damn, I'm sorry. I don't want to pressure you."

"We are in your brother's house. What if he walked in on us?"

"He needs to know that I'm trying to date you. He's going to have to grow up."

"Yeah, but . . ."

"But nothing. We've been kicking it since I was at your crib. And for a minute, it seemed you didn't care what Neil thought. Now you act like you shy or something. Where's my little spitfire, my little I-don't-give-a-damn woman?"

"She's still here."

"Show me!"

"This isn't the time or the place."

"You want to go to my room?"

"Be serious, Scottie." I laugh. "You're so different from your brother."

"And do not compare me to him. I've been through a lot. You're probably the most illegal thing Neil has ever gotten himself into. Shit, I'm shocked that y'all hooked up, knowing my brother."

"Um, yeah," I say feeling uncomfortable. This house brings back so many memories of when we'd have the hots for each other but couldn't do much since it felt like Anya's eyes were on us even when she wasn't home. And although it's been over three years since Neil and I were messing around, it feels weird to discuss what happened with Scottie. But since it's true that the guy definitely ain't married to me, I should try and be more forthcoming.

"I think it was mostly on my part, the reason we hooked up."

"Do tell."

"It's too damned long of a story."

Scottie laughs and squeezes my hand. "So you *do* listen to me. Trying to steal my lines."

"You trying to steal my woman." Scottie and I both look up. Neil is standing in front of us. He's no longer dressed in his work clothes. He is wearing a blue tank top and some black workout shorts. His legs are so muscular. I stare harder and notice a bulge in his shorts. Incredible. I want to laugh out loud, but that would be too rude.

So I sit and observe like I'm at a tennis match.

"She *was* your woman. Not anymore."

"This is the mother of my child. Nothing can change that."

"Yeah, well, that's all she is to you, Neil. Y'all not about to go back in the past."

"You don't know what we do," he says a little too loudly.

I gasp. Neil's just trying to pretend like we're messing around, even though we're not.

"You're lying, Neil."

"And if it weren't for me, you wouldn't have a place to stay. As a matter of fact, when you gonna throw down for some rent? You always in the refrigerator. You always playing music all night long, using up electricity."

"You make the big bucks down there at the great medical center."

"I'm a real man. That's what real men do."

"Man, hold up now." Scottie stands up and faces Neil. "I'm a man, too. I work hard; it's just that I'm waiting to hear back from some companies. I've been on at least six interviews."

When Scottie decided he was staying in town, he said he missed Texas and wanted to take his chances here and see if he could get a job and not have to move back to Detroit. In the daily telephone conversations that we've held since meeting, Scottie's told me how he's doing everything he can to make sure his return to Houston is permanent.

"And what have you been doing the rest of the time, huh, Scottie? Looking for work is a full-time job. You can't go on two interviews a couple of times a week and expect to get a good job."

"You don't need to lecture me, man. I ain't trying to hear all that."

"You need to listen to somebody. It's when you don't listen that your life gets screwed up."

"Here we go. You ain't my daddy." Scottie's voice breaks. I can hear the hurt in his words. His eyes look so sad, I want to hug him. But he throws his hands in the air.

"I'm done, Neil. Hey, Mariah, you follow me. We can go to my room."

Scottie looks at me like he expects me to obey.

I grab my purse and stand. He extends his hand and leads me from the den.

But I walk toward the front door and not upstairs like he wants.

"This is too awkward. I'd rather hang out at my place," I whisper to Scottie.

"That's cool. I'm gonna go upstairs and get some music I want you to hear. Be right back."

I go stand next to the door so I can wait and think. But Neil enters the foyer and pulls no punches.

"Dani, what do you think you're doing?"

"Do you really have the right to question me?"

Neil is eerily silent. Even though it's obvious Neil still loves me, I can't help but feel upset about everything. Let's face it, Neil chose and has the woman he wants. I'm still waiting to get everything I want.

And now I want to be the one who gets chosen in the end. I want to be somebody's wife one day.

5

LaNecia

Gotta Get My Face Time

It's the last weekend in August, an entire month since Scottie made LaNecia a promise. Ever since then, she's waited for Scottie to call and set up a date, but she's sick of wondering what's the big holdup.

On this Tuesday morning right before the lunch hour, the skies are so clear it looks like an endless stretch of blue. The sun sparkles with a brilliance that makes the day feel perfect.

A new multimillion-dollar elementary school is being built on the north side of Houston. It's almost noon by the time LaNecia and her best friend, Karetha, arrive at the construction site of the upcoming school. The last time LaNecia was lucky to catch Scottie on the phone, they spoke briefly; he mentioned how busy he'd been because he'd finally secured a new job as a construction foreman for the school district. He's been on the job a little over a week and sometimes works ten hours a day. By the time he gets home he's tired and funky, and that's the excuse he's given LaNecia about why he hasn't been able to hang out with her. LaNecia figures that since he can't come to her, she'll go to him.

LaNecia's wearing a colorful floral-designed maxidress.

Because funds are often low, she's been spending time painting her own toes and nails and has gotten pretty good at it. Today she feels she looks her best, and she wants Scottie to notice.

LaNecia frantically knocks on Scottie's construction trailer door, but no one answers.

"Step away from the peephole, fool," Karetha warns.

"Shut up," LaNecia says, and keeps tapping loud.

"Girl, why did I ever listen to you? It isn't a good idea to just show up on this man's job. Nobody's here, plus we're supposed to be registering your ass for school. And on top of that, need I remind you I'm on my lunch break. An *hour* lunch . . ."

"If you were my real friend you'd . . ."

Karetha rolls her eyes even though she doubts LaNecia can see her, because the girl is too busy banging her fist against the door. They're huddled together in front of the Bayou Town Construction trailer and LaNecia is getting angry.

"Is he trying to hide from me?" she asks Karetha. "I see his car big as day sitting there," she says, keeping watch on the tiny gravel parking lot.

"Hold up a second." LaNecia leaves Karetha standing next to the trailer while she rushes over to Scottie's SUV. She touches the hood of the Escalade, then walks back to LaNecia.

"It's colder than a subzero freezer."

"Humph, he's not answering my knock, but his car is here. I wonder where he is."

"Girl, he's a grown-ass man and, face it, he's not exactly keeping you in his loop."

"Yes he is. We talked on the phone a week ago. I called

him. He told me what he was up to. Promised he'd get back with me. I'm just helping him out a little bit."

"Ugh, there you go. How do I let myself get involved in this?" Karetha groans, looking frustrated. "If a man is truly interested, he'll call a chick on a regular basis, and even if he's busy, he'll make time for the woman he wants to see."

"And if a woman is going to have a man, she has to step up her game and show him that she's down for him, no matter how long it takes. Cookie waited for Magic Johnson umpteen years. I've only been waiting on Scottie for a year."

"Girl, you are such a fool. Scottie is no Magic Johnson," Karetha responds.

"Shoot, we need to get back on the freeway before traffic builds up. I can drop you off at HCC so you can register. And I want to stop by Popeye's drive-through and get me the Tuesday special. C'mon, Necia, later for Scottie."

"Anya will take me to register."

"Then what you need me for?"

"'Cause I want you here, plus you're my girl."

"I'm your fool."

"Shhh, I hear a car coming."

Karetha suddenly gets shoved to the side as LaNecia rushes past her. She runs to the other side of the lot and hides behind some bushes so she can peek through the branches. Karetha scurries after LaNecia and crouches beside her.

The second LaNecia spots Scottie with Dani in "Ugmo's" truck, she seethes inside. Ugmo, short for "ugly mofo," is the nickname LaNecia gave to Dani the minute she sensed that Scottie was attracted to the chick he met at the family reunion. Even from a short distance, she can see Scottie wearing a broad smile on his face as he pulls into the parking lot.

"Oh, hell no. There's Ugmo's pickup. You see Scottie

getting out of the driver's seat? Did that bitch let him drive her old beat-up hooptie?"

"Her car isn't that old, Ne . . ."

"Shut up. You talk too loud. What if he hears us?"

"Huh? If your original plans stay the same, Scottie's gonna hear us eventually since you're coming by unannounced."

"We haven't crossed that bridge yet, Ka. We haven't crossed that bridge. Now hush."

Before Karetha clamps her mouth shut, she whispers to LaNecia, "Remind me to curse you out as soon as we leave the premises."

LaNecia quietly watches Scottie as he takes a few slow steps toward the front of Dani's truck. But it takes every ounce of strength to remain still when she observes her cousin stride over to the passenger door and open it. Dani hops out wearing a pair of four-inch heels, some tight jeans, and a yellow tube top. She's struggling to hold a couple of huge sacks from Luby's restaurant, plus a plastic Kroger bag. Scottie offers to hold the bags for her. Dani smiles and hands all the packages to him.

"What?" LaNecia hisses underneath her breath. "That is not gangster right there at all. He better be glad he doesn't know I'm spying on his ass."

"Wow, it looks like they're about to have a nice romantic lunch alone in the trailer. I hope they bought enough to feed us, too. I love me some Luby's. . . ."

LaNecia gives Karetha the evil eye and resumes watching the action.

Scottie and Dani continue quietly chatting as they slowly walk up the stairs that lead to the construction trailer door. They stare into each other's eyes and slip inside.

"I can't believe this! What should I do, Ka, tell me!"

"Get. Out. Now."

"Who asked your advice, anyway? Damn, I need something to drink."

"We still have bottled water in the cooler in my car."

"I'm not talking about that kind of drink. Damn, Ka, you're not being any real help at all today."

"Um, can we please stop bending over and hiding in the bushes? My back is starting to hurt."

LaNecia can't help but grin and shake her head. Seeing Karetha bent over is the only funny thing that's happened today. But LaNecia's smile lasts for a brief moment. If she had known that her plans of dropping by on Scottie and asking him to commit to a date night would result in her seeing him and Ugmo together, she would have come up with a plan B.

"Damn, damn, damn. I can't believe he's spending time with her . . . again."

Unable to help herself, last night LaNecia snuck and parked her car near Dani's apartment and almost vomited when she saw Scottie drive up around ten. "That's too damned late to be going over to someone's house," she said at the time. Although she was dying to wait and see how long Scottie stayed, her eyelids began to drop from sleepiness, and she was forced to go home.

"Okay, Miss Fatal Attraction. Now what?" Karetha asks.

"I dunno." LaNecia sighs.

"Well, I do. Give Scottie a chance to do things his way. And until then, you should take your life in your own hands. Call Ms. Anya and do the college thing since she's so willing to help you out. She sounds like she truly cares about you, girl. Not too many other folks running after you to help you like she is."

"Yeah, I just wish I could take Ms. Anya's heart and place it inside Scottie. That would make me feel so good."

"You need mental help, LaNecia."

"What I need is inside that trailer. What on Earth are they doing in there all alone? Where are the rest of the workers? What kind of foreman lets his employees goof off and not be at work?"

"The same kind of supervisor that may fire us if we miss work. And I'm telling you, you shouldn't have called in sick today at Pappadeaux's just to follow behind Scottie's ass. You can at least take the rest of your day and do something productive. Try and get a good night's sleep, and tomorrow you can return to work and bag those to-go orders." Ka giggles.

LaNecia ignores Karetha's comment. She stares down at the ground and paces in a small circle. "It's all Ugmo's fault. Scottie wouldn't be acting this way if it weren't for her. What does he see in her? Why did I ever have to get pregnant? I know he's acting out because we lost our baby. Little Scottie."

"Girl, please. You don't know the gender."

"I do too know. It was a boy. Our son. He'd be about seven months by now. And I love when kids are that age. They play with their toes and talk baby talk and . . ."

LaNecia's longing for her dead son is interrupted. The door of the trailer swings open and Dani emerges first, followed by Scottie.

"Thanks for hanging out with me at lunch. Gotta get back to work, though. The rest of the crew should be back here any minute," Scottie says to Dani while walking her to her truck.

"I enjoyed the food."

"Is that all?"

"And you, of course. You always make me laugh, Scottie. Now I better head on back. Gallery Furniture is scheduled to deliver the new bed this afternoon and I don't want to miss them."

"Hmm, I can't wait to see your new bed."

"Oh, Scottie, try and be good."

"Why you say that? It's not like anyone can hear or see us."

He leans over and plants a solid kiss on Dani's lips. She waves good-bye, gets in her pickup, and drives off.

Scottie watches her until she turns the corner, then heads back inside the trailer.

"Damn, I just can't believe this."

"Maybe you should try," Karetha says.

"I think I'll have a little talk with him. Do you know we haven't seen each other in weeks, since I showed up at Ugmo's? I know once he sees me in a good setting, he'll realize he hasn't treated me all that well. I just gotta get my face time, Ka. Wait for me in the car."

LaNecia boldly walks up the little stairs and taps lightly on the trailer door. When Scottie doesn't answer, she turns the knob and steps inside. The room is deserted. She notices several construction drawings spread across the surface of some portable tables. The walls are filled with colorful renderings of the upcoming elementary school.

"Damn, this doesn't look like a school for little kids," she says to herself. "It looks like a fucking college campus."

LaNecia hears the sounds of a toilet flushing. Then the door of the tiny bathroom opens.

"LaNecia?"

"Hey there, Scottie," she says reminding herself not to

refer to him as cousin anymore. She wants him to see her as a woman, not as his flesh and blood.

"How'd you get in?"

"The door was unlocked. I knocked, but you didn't answer, and I knew you were here because your car is."

"Cousin, my staff will be here any minute. They all went out to lunch together. You got three minutes."

"Okay, okay, okay." LaNecia, who only minutes ago had mentally rehearsed what she would say, is now just staring at Scottie as if she's stumped. *What in the fuck is my problem? If he starts to think I'm losing it, can I blame him? Get it together, girl.*

"What time do you get off today, Scottie?"

"Three-thirty."

"Good. How about we catch an early movie? That way you feel no pressure. We can just chill tonight."

"What is the purpose of this?"

"Remember you said you'd do one more date with me and then that would be it? Once you get it out of the way, you won't have to worry about me anymore."

"For some reason I find that hard to believe."

"You won't know unless you give it a try. So let's meet up. I can drive myself. We can go to Alamo Drafthouse. That movie *Wanted* is still showing, and I love movies about assassins."

She notices the lines softening in Scottie's forehead. "Damn, I keep hearing how good *Wanted* is and I haven't had time to go check it out. You know what? Let's roll. Now go on and get back in that car of yours. I can see some of the guys pulling up now. They're late!"

"Okay, boss man." She laughs. "I'm so glad that you got the job, Scottie. It seems like your life is going to turn out okay. I just want the same things for my own life."

He ignores her comment and watches six members of his construction crew file past LaNecia, up the steps, and into the trailer.

"So, how'd it go?" Karetha asks the second LaNecia returns to the car. "You had me waiting in here so long I started to drive off."

"Girl, don't worry about what those folks at work think. Just tell 'em you got sick during your lunch hour. It does happen, ya know."

"Hmm, in a way it's true because I'm so sick of you and Scottie I could scream."

"Well, start screaming, Ka. Go on and scream."

Later that evening, LaNecia paces outside the Alamo Drafthouse. She decided to wear an eye-popping hot pink halter top and her favorite pair of skinny jeans. Karetha volunteered to style her hair, and LaNecia feels that the bangs that partially cover her right eye makes her feel sexy and mysterious.

Damn, I hope he's not playing me. But I know how much he loves movies, and it's been so long since we've watched a flick together, I don't see why he'd be tripping out over this tiny little so-called date. I'm driving myself. I'm paying my own way. Maybe he can spring for the food.

From the corner of her eye, LaNecia notices an image that perfectly fits Scottie. But she continues pacing back and forth like she isn't desperately waiting on his arrival. When she feels a hand tap her shoulder, she swings around and purposely enlarges her eyes.

"You scared me."

"Sorry 'bout that, cousin."

"LaNecia will do."

"Okay, LaNecia."

"You look nice as usual." She checks him out from head to toe and admires his fresh pair of jeans and partially opened button-down shirt. "That's sexy. Is it new?" she asks, blushing. Scottie has a way of making her feel girlish and special. And the fact that he finally made good on his promise makes her feel like he is starting to miss what they used to share.

"Matter of fact, it *is* new. New shirt, new shoes. Hell, I'm wearing new boxers, too."

"Mmm, I heard that. Well, how do I look?" She twirls around in a circle.

"*Nice.* Okay. You get your ticket yet?"

"No," she says mildly hurt. "I waited for you." She wishes he could have gone into more detail about her appearance. *I spent a lot of time making sure I look good and he barely notices.*

"That's just as well. Go ahead and get your ticket. I'm right behind you."

Jaw rigid, LaNecia goes to the box office and buys a single ticket, then glances at Scottie. "Go on," he calls to her. "I'll be there in a minute."

Well, fuck, I might as well come to the movies by my damn self. Disappointed, yet happy that Scottie showed up, LaNecia reasons, *If things go my way, by the time the movie is over, I can put it on him the way I know he likes it. Seduction is one of my strong points, if only he'd let me seduce him.*

LaNecia forgets about Scottie and rushes to go sit inside the last theater, located at the end of a long, dim hallway. The auditorium is one-quarter full, and the previews haven't begun. LaNecia takes a seat in the first chair on the row closest to the back of the theater. *That way he can't help but see me when he finally gets his ass on in here.*

On each row throughout the theater, several eight-foot-long wooden tables are mounted in front of the theater chairs, giving all the moviegoers space to write down their order, plus eat and drink. LaNecia picks up her menu and squints as she browses the selection of finger foods, salads, sandwiches, and beverages.

"Hey there. Sorry," Scottie says. He squeezes past her knees and sits in the empty chair on her left. "You order for me yet, kiddo?"

"Yeah, right. In case you forgot, we're going dutch tonight. But next time, guess who's paying for my ticket and food?"

Instead of answering, Scottie quickly scans the menu and picks up a pencil to scribble his selection. He slides the tiny sheet of paper between a thin metal bar so the waiter can see that he's ready to order.

Curious, LaNecia snatches the paper from the metal slot and reads his writing:

1 Diet Coke

1 chardonnay

1 large popcorn

1 fried pickles

1 Philly cheesesteak w/waffle fries

"Dang, you are one greedy-ass bastard. No wonder you don't have enough money to pay my way." She starts cackling. He doesn't.

"Hey, psst!"

Startled, LaNecia turns around in her seat and sees Dani entering the theater with her leather satchel flung over her shoulder. She stops in the aisle right next to LaNecia.

"Um, excuse me; I need to squeeze past you."

"W–why are you here?"

"Are you going to let me by or what?"

Stunned, LaNecia moves her legs to the side and Dani says thanks. She smirks and glances down at LaNecia's chest protruding from her halter top. "Girl, it's cold as fuck in here and I don't know why you'd dress in that skimpy shirt." She takes a seat on Scottie's other side and squeezes his hand.

"What took you so long?" he asks.

"Ladies room. Fashion emergency. My button popped off my shirt and I had to ask someone for a safety pin."

LaNecia stares straight ahead, her face burning with anger and humiliation. *How can he do this to me? He doesn't know who he's fucking with. He promised me a date, and, dammit, I'm going to have me a date.*

6

SCOTTIE

Hurricane LaNecia

In the second week of September, the National Weather Service predicts that a hurricane may hit the Gulf of Mexico. So far, the effects of Ike have been devastating, leaving millions of dollars of damages and dead bodies along the way. Haiti was hit hard, the storm causing over seventy deaths, a third of them children. Houston hopes to avoid the same fate, but the Category 4 hurricane seems bent on doing more destruction.

Neil begins preparing for the unknown by wasting precious gas driving to every Home Depot around, trying to find plywood in case he needs to board up the windows on his two-story home.

That Wednesday evening, he asks Scottie to go to the Walmart Supercenter for him and stock up on more hurricane preparedness supplies. Scottie calls Dani and tells her he's coming to pick her up so they can go shopping.

They arrive at the store located in Stafford on West Airport. Once they park, Scottie feels lucky to find an empty cart that's lodged between two parked cars.

"Damn, check out all these people," Dani gushes. "It looks like the day after Thanksgiving sales."

"Let's just grab whatever we can and put it in the basket. I hate crowds, and I don't plan on being here all night," Scottie growls.

Once they set foot inside the store, a chorus of voices rises to the ceiling as customers chitchat about what they need to buy. Dani grips the handle of her cart and pushes it past crowds of shoppers who block every part of the main aisle. Women with worry lines etched in their forehead yell at kids to keep up. Super Walmart is superbusy today.

"Hey, you seem lost in thought. What are you thinking about?"

"Thinkin' about you and your delicious lips."

"Don't even try it, Scottie. C'mon, what's on your mind?"

"Naw, Mariah, I'm kinda thinking that this time last year, I was in Motown. Trying to adjust to the fact that the leaves up there turn colors, cool-looking orange and red colors. Then before I knew it, winter came. And cold. And lots of snow."

"And now you're back home, huh," Dani says.

"All I'm saying is sometimes I'm shocked at where life takes you."

"I feel the same. I've been in H-town for a while now, but I never forget my hometown, Long Beach. Shoot." She shivers and examines a dented can of tuna fish. "I still can't get used to this hurricane warning stuff."

"Mayor Bill says this is the big one," replies a gray-haired white woman who is listening to Dani's conversation. "I've been looking at the news constantly. I want to leave town but don't have enough money to fly outta here. Plus ticket counter lines at Hobby and Bush airports are insane."

Scottie laughs and drags the cart away from Dani. He's trying to keep her from saying anything sarcastic to the nice old lady.

They turn down the bread aisle.

"I guess Brax and I will be staying with you and Neil if this storm hits."

"Of course you're staying with us. No doubt," Scottie replies. "Don't worry, Dani. I'm here for you, no matter what."

"Scottie, you are good. You really are a good man."

Scottie and Dani end up buying four bags of nonperishable items and three cases of bottled water in preparation for the hurricane. Two days later, on Friday morning, the city of Houston releases an official warning for everyone in Galveston to vacate the island. The storm surge is predicted to reach fifteen to twenty feet, with winds gusting to over a hundred miles per hour; massive damage is imminent.

"If you don't leave, it means certain death," say the emergency officials.

"Houston, we've got problems," Scottie says in a singsong voice.

Earlier, when Scottie begged Neil to let Dani and Brax hunker down with them, Neil took one look at the Weather Channel and said okay.

Scottie, Dani, Neil, Anya, and Vette are congregated in front of the jumbo TV screen in Neil's den. Reese and Brax are playing on the floor with some toy fire engines and police cars.

"Well, damn, if that's not a hint for those island folks to get the hell out, I don't know what is," Scottie says aloud to the television.

Yesterday Neil removed items from outside the house that might cause harm in the event of the storm. He suggested storing potted plants, metal garbage cans, Brax's Big

Wheel, lawn chairs, and a steel-framed picnic table in the first-floor library, a simple office filled with hundreds of books stored in bookcases.

After peeking out the window to see how dark it is, Scottie sits next to Dani. He wraps one arm around her. She whispers, "Thanks." Not even a tiny smile is on her face.

Anya makes it a point to say, "If I haven't mentioned this already, I'm glad Scottie decided to stay in H-town. I'm so proud of you. You've adjusted to the new job. You're like a changed man."

"No, he's not," Neil snaps.

"Thanks for your support, sister-in-law. That means a lot to me."

A few minutes later, Scottie motions at his brother so they can step into the kitchen and chat. Like typical siblings, they argue one minute and act civilized the next.

"Hey, man, I haven't properly thanked you for taking me in and letting me get myself together."

"In a way you've been lucky. When you think about it, it's taken other people much longer than you to land a good job."

"It's a trip, man. I think Anya is right. Seems like everything in my life is falling into place."

"I guess that includes Dani, huh?"

Scottie grins and asks Neil, "Lucky me, huh? I can't believe you not with that anymore."

Neil plunges headfirst into Scottie. Scottie gets Neil in a headlock. They both crash to the ground and exchange blows while wrestling on the floor. Anya hears the commotion and runs into the kitchen. Vette and Dani follow behind her.

Vette says to the women, "Let me handle this. My brothers can be such big babies."

Anya and Dani observe for a moment, then return to the den.

"Why are you guys acting like this?"

No one answers, so Vette reaches down and tries to pull Neil off Scottie.

"If you don't stop, I'm calling Mama. She'll get y'all straight."

Neil rises to his feet. "We're just talking. Leave us alone. Go on, get out of here."

Vette turns around in disgust and leaves the kitchen.

Neil grips Scottie around his shoulders. "I don't appreciate you talking about her like she's one of your . . ."

Scottie says firmly, "Get it straight. She's not one of yours anymore; that's what this is about. And get your hands off me right now before I really do something that makes you mad."

Neil releases Scottie, shakes his head. "I can't control what you do."

"Then stop trying."

For the next couple of hours everyone is too on edge to even think about getting some sleep. They either try to keep themselves entertained by playing Monopoly, eating potato chips and drinking lemonade, or they flip channels between CNN, Headline News, and the local Fox station.

"Mommy, I'm scared." Reese's eyes well up with tears; she's too distraught to play with Brax. Whenever she hears the wind whip at their windows, or rain pellets smashing against the glass, Reese jumps, then squeezes her hands together.

"Everything's going to be all right, precious," Anya assures her. "We'll be safe as long as we're inside."

Around one in the morning, the entire house turns pitch-black.

Brax starts screaming, "Daddy! Mommy! Daddy!"

"I can't see! Where's Brax?" Dani yelps. Neil fumbles around in the dark until he finds a large flashlight. It takes several minutes for him to locate the kids and turn on the other flashlights.

"Light candles. Hurry," Vette tersely yells and springs into action.

Scottie is with Dani on the sofa. She's cradling Brax in her arms and rocking him back and forth.

This feels good, yet odd. We feel like a family. Yet my little man belongs to my brother. He belongs to me, too, though. Scottie wants to brush his fingers across Brax's head, but even in the barely lit den, Scottie can sense the tension from Neil.

Neil says, "I'll be right back. Gotta fix this light issue."

Outside the wind screams and howls. Brax raises his head from Dani's lap. His large eyes completely fill with tears.

"C'mon, baby, it's okay." Dani shines a minilight on her son and tries to reassure him, but he whimpers and pushes a thumb in his mouth.

Distressed, Scottie reaches over and pulls Brax from Dani's arms.

"Hey . . ."

"No, Dani, it's cool. He's with me now."

Scottie stands and paces across the den, tightly holding the boy in his grip, gently talking to Brax until his little tears subside. Once the boy is totally calm, Scottie pats him on the head and sets him on his lap.

"You're too good," Dani whispers to Scottie.

Neil reenters the den. "Anya, I'm looking for the generator owner's manual." She grabs a flashlight and points it at a wooden end table. "Open the drawer, Neil. It's in there collecting dust like all our manuals." Neil locates the manual. "It'll take no time now," he remarks as he rushes from the den.

A frantic knock at the front door causes Scottie to hand Brax over to Dani. He rises to his feet. "Someone at the door?"

"I got it." Anya rushes to the front door and yells, "Who is it?"

"It's me. Open the damn door."

Anya swings open the door and flashes the light so that it shines in the unexpected visitor's face. LaNecia stumbles in shaking an umbrella that got ripped and bent by the fierceness of the winds. Her shirt and shorts are soaking wet and her shriveled hair lies flat on her head.

"Girl, what are you doing out in this storm? Are you crazy? You could've gotten hurt," Anya says.

"Karetha went out of town and left me by myself. I was scared, but I have no cell service right now and couldn't call. I had nowhere else to go."

Right then electricity from the generator kicks in. The refrigerator and A/C begin humming. Bright lights from lamps and ceiling fixtures pop back on.

LaNecia's soaked white shirt exposes her boobs like she's auditioning at a wet T-shirt contest.

"Cover her up, please," Dani hisses, as she enters the foyer. Scottie takes one long look at LaNecia, then turns his head.

"C'mon, LaNecia." Anya takes her umbrella. "I'll find you some dry clothes. You can probably fit in some of Vette's old things that she left over here."

While Anya takes care of LaNecia's clothes situation, the rest of the gang lingers around the television and do anything they can to try and forget about Ike. Dani locates two sleeping bags and sets up pallets in the den for Reese and Brax.

"I don't know what I'd do if it weren't for you, Scottie," Dani says to him while they're stretched comfortably on the sofa with their backs resting against several throw pillows. "I've never felt so taken care of before. During my past relationships . . ." She chuckles. "The nurturing side of most of these guys sucked, sucked, sucked. Seems like the only goal the men had was to charm me enough to get in my panties, or get a quick payday loan, but they weren't there for me when I really needed them. I learned that just because a man looks good doesn't mean he's good for me. . . . He's gotta be good *to* me."

"I'll be good to ya, good to ya, good to ya," Scottie sings.

LaNecia steps into the den, where Dani and Scottie are lounging. She's now wearing a red long-sleeved shirt and some oversize blue jeans. She takes one look at the cozy couple and instantly reacts. "I'm about to throw up."

"Don't do it in here," Dani says. "Go to the bathroom down the hall."

"You think you're smart, don't you?"

"Not at all," Dani says, unconcerned. "Scottie's a grown-ass man. He picks and chooses what he wants to do and who he wants to spend time with. It doesn't take a rocket scientist to figure that out."

"Well, if you'd give the man some space, maybe he'd have time to . . ."

Scottie glances at Dani. "Can I have a moment with my cousin?"

"Thank you," LaNecia barks at Dani. "No matter what, he and I will always be family. Nothing can change that."

"I'm not trying to change that."

"What did you say? Speak up so I can hear you."

Scottie laughs. "Cousin, you sure are on fire tonight. I think there's more action happening inside the house than outside. C'mon LaNecia. Let me give you some face time so you can stop acting out."

It's now around one-thirty in the morning. Scottie begins walking up the stairs to the second floor. LaNecia follows him. He opens the door to his room and closes it behind her.

Scottie searches LaNecia's deeply troubled eyes. "This night is unreal. I know things must be hard on you. Ka deserted you, huh?"

"Well, at the last minute she decided to leave and drive to College Station. Her older sister is a graduate student at Texas A&M and made her go up there. I didn't know it would be so bad with her gone, but all I did was think about how alone I felt being in our apartment by myself. What if something happened? Nobody who loved me would even realize I was by myself." She gasps, places her hands on her face, and starts weeping. "I hate being alone."

Scottie instantly pulls LaNecia into his arms. He never liked to hear his cousin cry. Even when they were messing around, long before she got pregnant, she'd have these crying spells. She'd worry about lack of money, or she'd worry that her life wasn't going anywhere. Tonight Scottie feels like he's involuntarily carried back to their past: a place he wants to forget these days.

"I–I can't help it, Scottie," she sniffs. "I want someone around who I can depend on when I need help. It hurts to think that I don't have a single guy friend I can call who I know would be there for me through thick and thin. It seems like guys leave when a woman gets in trouble." She raises her head and pours out her heart. "I had hoped you'd be different Scottie. You told me you loved me all last year. Remember that?"

Flustered, Scottie nods but can't maintain solid eye contact. He just squeezes her tighter, inhaling the scent of her flowery perfume, clumsily kissing her on the top of her hair like she's a forlorn little girl.

"You hear me? All I want is love. Why can't you love me? Love is a good thing. . . ."

"Shhh. . . ."

"No, I have a right to say how I feel. My emotions have been all bottled up inside of me for so long, Scottie. If I don't let them out, I know I'm going to die. I just know it." She releases a loud sob and bends over, clutching her stomach in her hands.

Now Scottie feels uncomfortable and guilty. It feels awkward to try and hug LaNecia with her head smashed against his belly. Her wet hair makes tiny water marks on his shirt. He picks her up and gently sets her on top of his bed. She turns on her side facing away from Scottie. Her shoulders jerk as she sobs hysterically. Her sobs wrack her entire body. Scottie debates if he should leave her alone and let her have some space. But he eases down on the bed next to LaNecia and tenderly pats her back.

"Don't cry, LaNecia. I–I'm sorry for hurting you. I *do* love you. . . ."

"No, you don't," she wails, shaking her head on the pillow and staining it with her tears and streaked eyeliner.

"Baby girl, it's a different kind of love."

"No, it's a nothing love. A fake love. A love that hurts me. True love d–doesn't hurt, Scottie. You make these promises and keep breaking them."

"I know. It's wrong." Surprisingly, Scottie feels his throat swell up with soreness as if he's contracted the flu. But he knows he's not sick with a bad cold.

I'm sorry we've come to this. If I would have known how my actions would have hurt her, I never would've gotten involved. She's a cool kid. I love her in a special family-like way. But the love she has for me breaks my heart. And I don't know how to deal with the pain.

LaNecia continues sobbing with her face buried against the pillow. When Scottie touches her shoulder and tries to turn her over, LaNecia's body stiffens. She scoots over until she's lying in the middle of the bed. Defeated, Scottie sits like a statue; he stares into space and listens to her speak unintelligibly until she falls asleep.

Dammit, this is too much. I can't take this. I wish she'd get a grip. I wish she didn't love me so much.

7

ANYA

Take the Good with the Bad

The weekend that the storm hit affected more than just the city of Houston. Sure, when we woke up and went outside that morning, we were shocked yet relieved that we only lost two oak trees that toppled over the garage and damaged the roof. Okay, no biggie. That's fixable. But the mess going on inside our home? Now that's questionable.

I get up around eight in the morning. My back feels stiff like I need my bones popped or else I won't be right for the rest of the day. But when I turn over in bed to ask my partner if he will do the honors and lift my feet up off the ground like we normally do, Mr. Meadows isn't lying next to his wife.

Shoot. I sit up so abruptly my back hurts even more. And on top of that, I am worried because I have a doctor's appointment today. Of all days. Ike or no Ike, it's time for me to find out what the hell is going on in my body. I'm still getting these two-week-long bloody menstrual cycles, and enough is enough.

I grab my cell phone, which is in bed.

I punch in some digits.

"Hello?" Neil's voice sounds thick with sleepiness.

"Where are you, Neil? And I know you fell asleep next to me last night. When'd you leave? Where'd you sleep last night?"

"Anya, don't start."

"I won't if you won't."

"Anya, I'm not thinking about that woman."

He knows I can get paranoid with Dani in the house even though Scottie seems to adore her.

"Could've fooled me. You were staring at her so much last night I don't think you remembered I existed. I'm not about to go through that mess we went through. . . ."

"Baby, c'mon. You're the woman I picked. You got my ring, my last name. . . ."

"All that may be true, but you still let her get to you. I think you should leave Scottie and Dani alone. This is his time to do something good with his life."

"And why should Dani be part of that? She shouldn't be dating my baby brother."

"Aha! So you finally admit the truth. Now we're getting somewhere." All a woman wants is a man who has the guts enough to admit the truth.

"You don't know what you're talking about, Anya."

"I know you're obsessed with what she's doing with your brother. Let it go, Neil."

Hearing him sigh heavily makes me want to scream. It's hard enough trying to keep this man's attention. I don't want his attention to be split between my needs and Scottie's doings. But as long as Scottie is doing Dani, Neil's gonna be tripping.

"I'm just saying, you got other things to think about. Like me, for instance. Don't you know I'm scared to death to go to the doctor today?"

"How you gonna get around all the debris that's lying on every major street, every single neighborhood. Call the office because it might be closed."

"I hope not."

"Anya, you'll be okay."

"Listen to how unconcerned you sound. You're way more into how Dani looks at Scottie than the fact I'm bleeding like a freaking stinking pig."

Neil starts laughing. That's good, but it still makes me mad. Even though we've been married a decade, it amazes me how my husband can get me so upset that I've contemplated skipping out on the relationship. Oh, I've entertained that divorce thing many times. But you learn to take the bad with the good. I guess Dani's being in our house because of Scottie's being sweet on her is "the bad."

"Anya, calm down. You're a strong woman. You'll get through this."

"But will you get through your dilemma? That's all I'm asking."

I still don't know where Neil is. Obviously, he's somewhere in the house. But where is Dani? It still feels weird to have her sleeping in my house, knowing that years ago she used to sleep with my husband. It makes me sick to my stomach. But still, Dani is the better woman for Scottie to be with. Gotta be much better than him being with LaNecia.

"Do you know where LaNecia is?" I ask.

"Last time I checked, she was headed upstairs behind Scottie."

"That's a shame," I mumble. "I hope they didn't screw each other. Not in my house. No-the-hell-way."

"Hmm, I guess I'll go check out things down here."

Neil hangs up without saying 'bye to me. I throw my

cell phone on the floor. I sit up in bed and stretch my arms. It's time to see what's going on in my house.

Taking a deep breath, I find myself outside Scottie's bedroom. I knock once and turn the knob. I see LaNecia spread out on her back. Her face looks peaceful and I'm happy that she had somewhere to go, that she is safe. I check Vette's room and spot Dani lying in bed next to her. I run downstairs and bump into Neil, who is entering the kitchen from the back door.

"A few trees went down. Gotta make some phone calls." He rushes past me toward the library.

"You looking for insurance papers? You should've thought about that before stuffing the room with all that junk. I'll be surprised if you can reach the file cabinet."

I check the den. Scottie's big form takes up the entire love seat. He's in the middle of a loud snoring fest, but I don't care.

"Hey, hey, hey, get up."

He groans and opens his eyes. "Anya, what's up? Is there a problem?" He sighs. "Sorry, I didn't mean to talk to you like that. Are you okay? The kids okay?"

"Yeah, they're fast asleep upstairs, thank God. But I was surprised to see LaNecia in your bed. I thought Dani would be in there with you. What's up with that?"

I motion at Scottie to move his legs so I can sit down. "You're young. Still got a long way to go. Maybe you can learn something. . . ."

"Look, not trying to be rude, but I hate when . . ."

"Ouch, I hope you're not about to call me old."

"Anya, you look pretty damned good for your age."

"My age? I don't want to hear that. Statements like that make a woman feel old. I hate to see what happens when I turn forty."

"You'll be fine."

"That's easy for you to say, Scottie. You're barely in your twenties."

"But I've been through a lot when I was younger, long before you met Neil. I'm sure Neil has told you."

"Not really. He doesn't talk a whole lot about what went on when you guys were growing up."

"I'm not surprised. I think he blames me for some of his shit."

"Really," I say and lean closer. "What happened? Be specific."

"Moms told me that Neil came out of her womb with a serious look on his face."

I laugh. "Go on."

"She told me she named him Neil because she liked the meaning, which is 'passionate' or 'warrior.' She hoped naming him that would make him a strong man, like a fighter."

"In a sense I guess it worked. I mean, he works hard, and I'm glad he finished his education, and he's been hanging in there at the Texas Medical Center for years. He's an excellent provider. We've never had our electricity cut off. . . ."

"Except for this morning."

"Funny, Scottie. That was Ike's doing, not Neil's. He's a proud man, and he makes sure we have everything we need. I couldn't ask for a better husband."

"Then what happened with . . ."

I squirm in my seat. "I don't want to get into all that."

"But you asked me open questions, so why can't I ask you?"

"You know, to be so young, you sure have a stubborn, cocky side."

"I'm sure I get that from ole Everett George Foster, my daddy. Moms gave me her last name, though. I kind of think of myself as both, a Meadows and a Foster. Anyway, my pops was a good-looking whippersnapper kind of guy when they first met, so she says. But, of course, I had my moments with Daddy, too. I remember he was wild. He sold drugs. He got into trouble. But he'd fight for my moms, and I think that's what she loved about him. He was protective. I get that from Daddy."

"I'm so glad you got to know him before he died."

"Yeah, it's a trip that neither Neil nor I have a living father. I really need my daddy, too. Especially now, with so much going on in my life." He quietly studies me before continuing. "That's why I'm, like, crazy happy that you've taken me in, Anya, for real. My uncle James has been there. And you have, too."

"Oh, it's nothing. I'm just doing the right thing. I don't want you to get discouraged with life. I've lived long enough to know that things can turn out okay when we make good decisions. Not that I'm *that* old."

Scottie winks. "I'm telling you, if you weren't married to my brother, I'm sure you'd be pulling men left and right. Especially the young bucks."

"You think so?"

"I know so. Younger men are attracted to older women."

"Is that why you're into Dani?"

"Hey, I'm just trying to get to know her. No harm in doing that, is there?"

"LaNecia's not having it."

"Yeah, I'm aware of how she feels."

"*Are* you?"

"She's told me a million times."

"Have you listened a million times? Or only one time? Or zero?"

"I'm trying to live my life. . . . Sometimes LaNecia makes it hard to do that. She needs something else to occupy her time."

"Like a good-looking man, huh?"

"Well . . ."

"You don't have to admit it to me, but from what I've observed, you Meadows boys are drawn to the forbidden."

"Why you say that?"

"Neil liked Dani. You like Dani. You like LaNecia."

"Now, wait a minute," he protests, sitting up. "All this stuff may be temporary. You don't have to build a fucking case against me. And I am *not* Neil. We don't even have the same father."

"But you have the same blood, similar tendencies."

"Look, I don't mean any disrespect, Anya, but my brother and I are different."

"How, Scottie? You're raising your voice, which doesn't totally bother me, but you get upset when things don't go your way. Neil's just like that. It's not unusual for siblings to share certain characteristics."

"But we don't."

"You've shared the same woman; at least in my mind you have."

Scottie flashes me an angry look. I stand up and gape back at him. It's not hard to see why Dani would be attracted to Scottie. Parts of Neil live in him. I doubt she's ever gotten over my husband. Sure, she's put some space between herself and Neil the past couple of years. But when a woman has loved a man, even the slightest thing draws her back to him. Maybe her slightest thing is Scottie.

"Anya, I don't know what you're trying to say. But for right now, I want to be free to explore what can happen with me and Dani. I haven't totally figured out how to make it work. She's becoming more open with me, but there are some parts of her I need to work on."

"You have your work cut out with this one. I am trying to wrap my head around the fact that she slept under my roof last night, right down the hall from my husband, and not too far from a girl you used to sleep with. All that sounds too close for comfort."

"Um, maybe she's marking her territory. How's that sound?"

"As far as I'm concerned, her so-called territory shouldn't be inside *my* territory." I chuckle at the craziness of it all.

"Anyway, I gotta get dressed. I guess I'll be a nice host and throw together some breakfast for everyone. Then I must remember to call my doctor's office and pray they're open today. Believe it or not, there are other things going on besides Scottie and *all* his women."

I whip up a couple of dozen pancakes and fried bacon. It doesn't take long for the smell of pig to cause Brax to make his way to the kitchen.

"Good morning, little baby," I tell him. He looks so cute in his pajamas with the feet attached.

"I'm not a baby!"

"How old are you, then?"

"Tree." He holds up three fingers, so one out of two isn't bad.

"It's three," I say aloud while I flip over a pancake.

"The-ree."

"Go get your mommy. No, tell Reese to go get her, okay, Brax?"

He races from the room, and I shake my head and snicker.

Dani prances into the kitchen a few minutes later rubbing a body towel through her hair.

"You looking for me?"

"Not really. Your son is hungry."

"What else is new? I'll prepare his plate and take it upstairs."

"Oh yeah," I say. "What's happening upstairs?"

"Well, if you must know, Scottie and I were in the middle of a conversation. Plus he was watching cartoons."

"Ha." I laugh. "That's what happens when you choose to go younger."

"What did you say?" Dani looks perplexed, and she comes and stands next to me. I'm still in front of the stove pouring pancake mix on the griddle.

"Does everything I say to you warrant some type of argument, Dani?"

"I'm not arguing. Just trying to make sure I heard you right." She picks up a slice of bacon, bites off a piece and starts chewing. "You know what? You're right. I'm trying to learn from my elders. . . ."

"What?"

"Oops, sorry. I'm trying to learn from you, Anya Meadows, and know that I can just calmly talk about things. There's no need for me to fight anyone. Even you."

"And not LaNecia? Hmm, you've been downstairs a full five minutes. Aren't you concerned about what's going on upstairs?"

"Well, last I know Scottie made her get out of bed and go take a bath. And unless Scottie decided to join her, I'm not too worried about it."

"You oughta be. Remember you used to scheme and stuff with um, men. You'd think that a woman like you would be scared that she's getting paid back."

"That's a laugh, Anya. Because if it weren't for you . . ." Dani gives me a sly look and walks away. I feel like picking up the griddle and throwing it at her. She hasn't forgotten that Neil hooking up with her was my idea. Ughh. That makes me so mad. All I wanted to do was save my marriage. But things got more messed up than I ever imagined. Do I have to be reminded of what I did?

If you're always reminding someone else of their faults, what makes you think someone else won't remind you of yours?

This still, small voice tries to talk to me, but I don't want to listen right now.

"Hey, everyone, the food is ready." I yell as loud as I can and pray that they all come down soon. I am so ready to get out of the house. We've been holed up here for two days, and I need to see more than the inside, the backyard, and my front porch.

We all eat breakfast together without incident except for Dani, who whines that she can't eat pancakes because it'll make her glucose level higher. Instead of going upstairs to eat like she suggested before, Dani actually comes downstairs and makes herself buttered toast and eats half a banana. When I'm done eating, I ask Vette to wash the dishes and she agrees.

I run upstairs and notice that LaNecia is right behind me. She follows me into my room.

"Hey, what's up?"

"Nothing," she says, but I know better.

I think for a minute. "I am about to go to see my doctor and I want you to ride with me."

"Jeez, do I have to?"

"Yes, you do. We need to talk. Plus I can use the company."

She says okay. We drive over to Memorial Hermann Southwest and sit in the waiting room. The hospital seems busy with extra activity, probably from people who suffered injuries during the storm. After one hour, the nurse calls my name. She checks my weight and blood pressure and asks me a few questions. I'm left alone for another ten minutes, and then Dr. Patterson, an elderly, distinguished gentleman who could double for Sidney Poitier, finally comes into the examination room.

He asks about my bleeding and tells me we should do x-rays right away. I am directed to the x-ray room, where I fill out more paperwork, and I go lie down in a very dimly lit room next to a few intimidating-looking machines.

"We're doing an ultrasound today," says the attendant, who instructs me to get undressed. I try to think positive thoughts while I lie on my back. I shudder when the attendant squirts this clear-looking gel on my belly. The ultrasound begins, and she studies the images she can see on a monitor.

When we're done, I'm asked to wait again in the room where LaNecia's been sitting.

"Why it takes so damned long?"

"Look around. I'm glad they didn't cancel me. Plus we can talk while we wait."

"Talk about what?"

"How on Earth did you end up going in the refrigerator and choosing to eat that yogurt that someone else already started eating?"

"Huh?" LaNecia says.

"Stay with me now. From what I hear, Scottie was eating that Dannon yogurt, but somehow you were trying to get some, too?"

"Oh right." She blushes and observes the waiting room. It's packed with women and kids. She winks at me. "Um, Anya, it's not like I was trying to eat his yogurt on purpose. It just kind of ended up in my hand. Yogurt is crazy like that; you know what I'm saying?"

A woman sitting next to us takes one look at LaNecia and scoots over a few inches.

"Dumb bitch," LaNecia says under her breath. "What the hell, I don't give a damn what people think. See, it's like this. I don't care what anyone says, the man is still feeling me."

"Are you positively absolutely sure?"

"Cross my heart and I'm probably gonna die, Anya. Why you think I'm after him so tough? It's because something is still there."

"Does Dannon know it?" I wink at her.

"Apparently not. Dannon's too busy trying to think it's the only brand of yogurt on the shelf. But most guys like a variety of flavors. Today it might be strawberry, tomorrow it could be pineapple. But you can't tell that to some folks."

"Too much yogurt can make you sick, you know what I'm saying?"

"Bottom line, Scottie's going to have to pick one flavor," LaNecia says with determination in her voice. "And stick to it. Don't mix 'em together. None of that."

I hear my name called, and I promise LaNecia that I will try to keep it as brief as possible.

Dr. Patterson asks me to have a seat in a tiny consultation room that only has a desk and a couple of chairs.

"What's wrong with me?" I ask, getting to the point.

"Mrs. Meadows. There's good news and bad news. There are quite a few large fibroids in your uterus about the size of a cantaloupe."

I stiffen. "And?"

"Your options are to either ignore them because they aren't fatal, but you'd probably get tired of dealing with these lengthy menstrual periods."

"You're right about that."

"You can treat them with medicine and shrink them, but they could return. Another option is to have surgery, and get a complete hysterectomy, which is the only guarantee of complete removal and no more bleeding. You wouldn't be able to have any more children. And you'd immediately go into menopause. Let's see, you're only thirty-nine. You'll turn forty . . ."

"In December. Goodness, this isn't anything I've ever expected."

"Well, there's always a reason when our bodies don't function properly. I recommend that you think about it and let me know your decision. Surgeries are scheduled on Tuesdays. You'll have to come in to a consultation a week or a few days beforehand."

I'm listening yet not listening to my physician. Why, of all things, does this have to happen? A pang of sorrow burdens my heart. I am saddened that I only gave Neil one child, our wonderful daughter, Reese. I had a miscarriage years ago. That baby would have been the son that Neil desperately wanted. Then Neil got Dani pregnant with the son that is now his world. It sucks. I know I have to think about things, and share this shocking news with Neil.

Dr. Patterson gives me some literature and wishes me well.

On the way home, we're rolling along in my SUV. Most of the major streets are blocked with debris that got tossed around from the storm. Tree branches and leaves are strewn all over, forcing us to drive around the clutter. So many signs are completely ripped off of shopping center marquees. And the Popeyes sign now says "opeyes."

LaNecia keeps shifting in her seat, mesmerized by the devastation seen through the window.

"So," she asks me. "What did the doctor say?"

"Um, stress. I'm dealing with a lot of stress, family stuff. So if I eat right and exercise and take it easy, that bleeding situation will come to a halt."

"Hmm, I'm glad to hear it wasn't that serious."

"Nope," I say in a high-pitched cheery voice. "Not serious at all. Hey, I'm more concerned about you, though, LaNecia, because I know for a fact you didn't register for school. And now that the storm has hit, HCC is temporarily closed. I was on the Net the other day; if you missed the August dead-line, you could have registered for the second start. It's only a twelve-week term. You need to be checking into that."

"Oh, Anya, my mind isn't on school."

"Well, it oughta be. C'mon, it'll be good for you."

"Why are you doing this?"

"Doing what?"

"Why are you so concerned about my world when you just got the shittiest news you could ever hear?"

"W–what are you talking about?"

"I may be young, but I'm far from dumb. We waited so long that at one point, I couldn't hold it any longer and I needed to find the ladies room back there in that doctor's office. And when I walked down the hallway, I passed by a closed door and heard you talking. So obviously I'm going to be curious, listen and try to hear what's going on. I mostly wanted to see if y'all's session had ended so we could leave. But that's not what I heard. You gotta have an operation. That's serious. What if you die?"

I shoot LaNecia one of my "Are you crazy?" looks. "First of all, young lady, you have no business listening to my conversation with my doctor. My health is my own private business."

"And whether or not I go to school is *my* business. This is my life and I'm tired of people trying to tell me how to run it. I'm twenty years old. I'm grown. Living in my own apartment with a job. I don't need anyone trying to convince me I need to be in school. Time-out for school."

"Well, excuse *me.* I was only trying to help."

"I appreciate your help. . . ."

"If you really did, you'd take my advice and do more with your life than just run after a man who clearly doesn't want you."

LaNecia gasps. She grabs her purse with one hand and the passenger door handle with the other. "Let me out."

"No. Wait. I'm sorry."

"Too late for that, now pull over and unlock the doors or I'll jump out—and I *will* jump out. Remember, I'm crazy LaNecia."

"You may be crazy, but I'm not and I will not unlock the doors. I told you I'm sorry, so accept my apology and stop talking nonsense."

LaNecia chomps down on her teeth so hard I hear them click.

What's up with this family? Nobody listens. Nobody learns. Everyone has to go to the school of hard knocks to get some sense in their head.

"I'm not kidding, Anya. I don't want to be in this car with you right now."

"Well, where are you going, huh? Have you taken a look outside? The city of Houston is in a state of emergency. I don't see any buses running. We're at least fifteen miles from my house. . . ."

"I don't care."

"Then you *are* crazy!"

"Just because I don't like to be talked to any kind of way doesn't mean I'm crazy."

"And just because I say something you don't like doesn't mean you have to do something so extreme. Let me make it home. Then you can get in your own car and do whatever you want. Deal?"

She leers at me and rattles the doorknob.

"If you break it, you're paying for it."

LaNecia sighs loud, like she wishes I'd shut up. But she releases the door handle and stops making silly threats.

It takes us an extra twenty minutes to get to my neighborhood, and when we pull up in front of the house, I am more than relieved.

"Thank God, we're home. We're alive. We made it through the storm last night," I say to LaNecia, trying to ease her anger with me. "Sometimes we should look at what's most important and let go of petty things."

"Yeah," LaNecia says. "I agree. That's why I'm accepting your apology." She is talking to me but steadily watching Scottie, Dani, and Brax, who have all just emerged from the house. They pile into Scottie's Escalade and drive off.

"The truth is, I need you, Ms. Anya. And I can't be battling with you. I have something to prove. And if I have to, I will use you to make my point."

"And what point is that, LaNecia?"

"That I am worth loving even if Scottie can't show me that love."

8

LaNecia

I'm Sick of You Leaving Me

It's early afternoon in mid-September one day after the storm hit. LaNecia is standing in the front entrance of her apartment with the door wide open. One hand is lodged on her hip; her other hand grips the cell phone. She's yelling into the receiver.

"This is serious. I'm not playing. My entire building lost power, plus my windows blew out and shit is everywhere."

"Dang, cousin. Does it look like anything is missing?" LaNecia loves that Scottie seems concerned for a change. He knows she lives on the first floor of an apartment located in a lower-income neighborhood. She's afraid looters may have come stolen what little possessions she had.

"That's the thing, Scottie. I'm too scared to walk around and see what else has happened. I'm telling you I barely set one foot in the apartment and I can see from here that the living room bay window is now just a shattered memory, no pun intended."

"Okay, um, let me get Dani situated first and I'll make my way over to your spot. Hold tight."

Damn. Ugmo bitch spoils everything. But at least he's going to leave her to come see about me. LaNecia thinks for a moment and calls Scottie again.

"Um, when you come over, don't bring anyone else. I'm embarrassed my place looks so jacked up."

He says okay and she hangs up the phone, happy that he's coming over, but distressed that Ike may cost her some money.

If I would've gotten renter's insurance like people told me to, maybe I'd have money to get a new television. She shakes her head at all the mess. Soaked carpet, window fragments, and some tree leaves and mud are stuck on the HD television.

LaNecia sits in her car and waits for Scottie.

After he arrives, they examine the entire apartment. There's enough natural light streaming from outside to make a quick inspection of the outer rooms, which include the living room, the dining room, the kitchen, and both LaNecia's and Karetha's bedrooms.

"All this ain't too bad," Scottie says after assessing the damage. "Only the living room got messed up. A tree fell against your bedroom window, but it's not like you can't sleep in there."

"Ha!" she says looking aghast. "Ain't no way I'm staying here by myself, Scottie. How about if I stay with you?"

"You're asking the wrong person, baby girl."

"But . . ."

"Hey, I'm sure Anya and Neil won't mind having you there till your apartment maintenance man fixes that window. When is Karetha coming back?"

"Hell, I can't get the bitch on the phone. Cell phone circuits are still messed up. Some calls go through, others don't. If she's tried to call me, I'm sure she's wondering what's happening back home."

"Look, try not to stress. Karetha will be fine in College

Station. And if you want, you can hang out with me for the rest of the evening. If the lights aren't back on by tonight, you may as well stay over with us."

Her face brightens. "Are you sure it's okay, Scottie? I don't want to mess up your evening in case you had other plans."

"Somehow I don't believe that you don't wanna mess anything up, but since this is an emergency, all my plans are canceled. I'm going to do something nice, which is making sure you're okay. How's that sound?"

"Sounds like a great plan, Scottie. Ooo, can you take me to a movie, for real this time? Just the two of us?"

"You're always scheming, huh?"

"I just want to have fun for a change. Life has sucked since you've been gone." She gazes at him happily. "Remember how we'd go roller-skating on South Dairy Ashford? And we'd hit up Sonic and order fries and burgers and just sit in the car and talk?" She studies him. "Didn't we used to have fun together?"

"Yeah. Sure. Anyway, you gonna grab some overnight clothes so we can bounce outta here?"

"Um, right. Come with me to the room. It shouldn't take long."

Excited, LaNecia races to her walk-in closet and flings open the door. The closet is pitch-black. She automatically hits the light switch on the wall.

"Dang, I forgot we have no power. Hold up a sec." She runs to the kitchen and rummages through a utility drawer for her Maglite. Then she pulls out a tiny stepladder that's next to the refrigerator and grabs it by the handle. Once she returns to the closet, she points the light at the top shelf of the high-ceiling closet.

She unfolds the ladder and climbs a couple of steps until she manages to touch the small piece of luggage.

"Need some help?" Scottie is so close she can feel his hot breath on her neck. "No, I got this, I think," she replies in a soft voice and hands him the Maglite. He points the light at an angle that brightens up the closet. LaNecia lifts both her arms toward the shelf. Scottie bumps into her back trying to reach over her. The feel of Scottie's flesh against hers makes her shiver, then moan.

LaNecia turns around until she's completely facing her cousin. Her mouth is now inches away from Scottie's gorgeous plump lips. They lock eyes for a moment. LaNecia then moves out of the way and lets Scottie grab her overnight luggage. Sweating profusely, she steps off the ladder, rushes to the bathroom, and turns on the water faucet. She splashes water on her face and dabs it with a towel.

Scottie sets the flashlight on the bathroom counter. "You gonna be all right?" he asks, then stares. She is standing in the bathroom dressed in her black lace bra and see-through panties.

"I–um," she says and falls into Scottie's arms. "I'd feel better if you gave me a kiss, Scottie, I need this so bad. I need you."

"No, no, cousin."

"Please stop calling me cousin."

"That's what you are."

"I don't have to be."

"Baby girl, you can't help but be my cousin. Now pack your bag, please, and let's go. I don't want to deal with this extra stuff." He pulls himself out of her arms.

But she throws her arms around his waist and squeezes him so tightly he lets out a gasp. "Mmm, mmm, mmm. That's all I've been wanting." With Scottie locked inside her grip, she puckers her lips and kisses him on the cheek. His body stiffens.

"I know it's been a long, long time and you have to get used to how I am again."

"Hmm."

"Tell me something, Scottie. When you were up in Michigan, did you fuck around with other girls?"

"Huh?"

"Don't 'huh' me. Once you got settled in, did you hit the clubs, meet some girl that reminded you of me and have sex with her?"

"Why would you ask me fool-ass shit like that?"

"Because I want to. I know you love to have sex, so I figured that you were up there doing it with somebody."

"How about you?" he asks in a husky voice. "Did you fuck any guys after I left?"

"Oh no, you don't," she says with a laugh. "You don't have the right to be jealous and ask who I was fucking. You left *me*, remember?" She turns around and storms from the bathroom and heads back to her room. She finds a new shirt and some tight blue jeans and gets dressed. Scottie, who followed her from the bathroom, is now waiting in the doorway of her bedroom aiming the Maglite as he watches her pull her arms through the sleeves of a hot-pink blouse. She makes sure to stick her chest out while she talks.

"If I sucked a Negro's dick, I'm sure you'd understand. But I won't kiss and tell."

"Oh, but you expect me to?"

"Look, Scottie. I know you. The way we used to fuck every other day, ain't no way you can go up north and not find a girl who you can smash on the regular."

"Yeah, whatever, man."

"One thing for sure, you probably didn't love her. It was just sex."

"You're crazy, LaNecia. But that's what I love about you."

"See," she smirks and slips her feet inside four-inch pumps. "You just admitted it. You love me and you know you love me, but you're too scared to let Ugmo know how you feel."

"Ain't nothing ugly about Dani."

"Hmm, with a little bit of plastic surgery, she'd be lucky to upgrade to a three."

"Dayum, cousin, that's cold."

"Cold sch-mold. I don't want to talk about her. Where's the old bitch at anyway?"

"She's home, remember?"

"Not really. I'm not trying to keep up with her. I'm worried about my own self." LaNecia starts tossing a few sexy bras and panties and a couple of shirts and shorts in her overnight bag.

"Scottie, baby, can you give me a payday loan?"

"Here, LaNecia." He reaches for his wallet and hands her three twenties.

"Don't tell anyone I gave you that. I wouldn't want anyone to know how nice of a man I can be."

"I won't. I swear."

"You'd better not."

For the rest of the afternoon LaNecia walks around with a poker face. After they arrive at Neil's and explain her situation, Anya insists that LaNecia stay with them until her electricity is restored. She, LaNecia, and Scottie are standing around the kitchen sipping on ice tea and eating microwave popcorn.

"Girl, we got this curfew thing going on, so no one has

an excuse to be outside after nine unless they're coming home from work or school."

"Yeah, speaking of work, I've been missing a few days. And when I called to see when's the next time I'll be on the schedule, they say 'Don't call us, we'll call you.' Can you believe that?"

"I sure can. In these tough economic times you better smile and act like you love your job even if you can imagine setting a bomb and blowing up the place," Anya tells her. "I'm sure they'll be calling you back to work soon. Just be careful, okay?"

"I ain't worried, Ms. Anya," she replies and throws a few pieces of popcorn in her mouth.

"She ain't worried. Ha!" Scottie laughs and heads toward the den.

LaNecia snatches her glass of tea and plops down next to Scottie, who's now sitting on the love seat looking at TV.

"Do you mind?" he asks.

"What are you talking about?"

"We're the only two in the den. There's a big empty sofa over there."

"What's that got to do with me?"

"Oh, you really think you're funny, LaNecia."

"Do I see a smile? Is Scottie Meadows actually smiling?" *Damn, I'm good. I knew I could get to him. All I gotta do is be myself, work my magic, and things will be just like they were last year. Can't nobody tell me I'm not good at what I do.*

"Shhh, I'm trying to look at the sports highlights. I do not want to be bothered."

"Yes, sir." She forces herself not to grin too wide. She sits back on the love seat, content just to be sitting near him, close enough to smell his deodorant.

Even though Scottie may complain and make "zinger"

remarks to her, LaNecia knows good and well he enjoys the attention she lavishes on him. She feels he puts up a front around Dani.

But Ugmo's not here, is she? Good for me.

They get comfy and watch football highlights for another half hour. Then he asks her if she wants to play two-man spades.

"You damn straight I do. I know you need to brush up your skills, so let's do it."

LaNecia and Scottie are sitting in the dining room playing spades when the doorbell rings.

Dani strides into the room and stands in front of Scottie. She leans over and puckers her lips. Scottie hesitates for a second, then gives her a kiss. She opens her mouth and they kiss for a couple of minutes.

"Sorry I was late. I tried calling you, but you didn't answer," she says, wiping her mouth. "You ready to go?"

Pissed, LaNecia glares at Scottie.

"Yeah, I gotta go upstairs and get my phone. Be right back."

LaNecia dashes up the stairs right behind Scottie. After he enters his bedroom, she slams the door behind her and locks it.

"What the hell is going on?"

"LaNecia, please. I had a previous engagement with her."

"See, this is exactly what I'm talking about. You can't keep a promise to save your life."

"Look, I said you'd be able to hang out over here and you are. I—I am just gonna go find a bite to eat with her and then I'll be back."

"That's foul. Scottie you told me that all your other plans were canceled. So to me that should include Ugmo, too."

LaNecia's eyes are burning with jealousy. "I don't know what you see in her. It confuses me. She's so much older than you. What do y'all have to talk about? Geritol?"

"Baby girl, you just don't understand."

"Oh, I do understand. I think you're in denial. That's what I think."

He walks up to her and sweeps her braids away from her forehead. "Your nose looks so cute when you're mad. I actually like it when you get mad at me."

"Negro, please," she snaps, but she still allows him to smooth back her hair. "Can't you tell her no for once? For me?"

"That wouldn't be cool."

"Scottie, she's so much more of an adult than me. She'd be all right. It's not like she's your woman, right?"

"Well . . ."

"So she's just a good friend. I'm family, Scottie. Family comes first."

"But, um."

With a gleam in her eyes, LaNecia places her hands on Scottie's chest, kissing him on the cheeks, and pushes him until he's sitting on his bed. He stares in her eyes as she gently shoves his chest until he's lying down.

She gyrates her hips and licks her lips. She reaches down and begins slowly unbuttoning her hot-pink blouse. Scottie's eyes are locked on her, and she's thrilled. She has him exactly where she wants him. *I'm the type of woman who's willing to go above and beyond to get the job done. I gotta do whatever it takes to get this man's mind off that heifer who acts like she's the Queen of England.*

LaNecia has unzipped her blue jeans. She hooks her fingers in the belt loops and slowly pulls down her pants, inch by inch.

"You like this?" she whispers. She feels her panties getting soaked and can't wait to take them off. She can imagine Scottie sticking a couple of his fingers deep in her vagina. That used to drive her crazy.

"You know it's been a while since I've been fucked good," she purrs. She takes a sniff and detects the aroma of sex on her underwear.

"You smell that?" she asks. She starts pulling down her pink lace underwear, making sure that Scottie's imagination is completely engaged. She crawls in bed next to him and lies sideways.

Men are visual. They love to fantasize. That's what he told me when we first started hooking up. He used to enjoy my little stripteases. His dick would be so long and hard it felt like a microphone, and all I wanted to do was put it in my mouth and start screaming.

LaNecia reaches for Scottie's right hand and rests it against her vagina.

He moans.

"You're so fucking wet."

"You did that, baby. That's all you," she whispers. Scottie removes his fingers. LaNecia grabs his hand and forces it to touch her again. Her eyes roll back in her head. She begins to pant heavily and pumps against his hip like she's having sex.

"You want me to ride you?"

"Yes," he whispers, his mouth wide open as he lies flat out on his back. His eyes pop open. "No."

She feels his body stiffen, and not in the way that turns her on. He removes his hand from her vagina. Small dots of white cream stick to his fingers.

She grabs his fingers, shoves them in her mouth and starts sucking.

"You know what, you little freak? We can continue this conversation later. Company awaits."

LaNecia frowns and removes his fingers from her mouth.

"Scottie, don't do this. How can you leave me like this? I'm sick of you leaving me."

"But I always come back, don't I?"

"Yeah, but . . ."

"I know it's bad timing, but I swear I'll be back," he says, changing his voice to sound like the Terminator.

"What time?"

"In an hour."

"You better not be lying to me."

"Face it, cousin. Nothing I do will change how you are."

"Ouch. That hurts."

"Sometimes hurt is a good thing. Now I gotta be going. I mean it." He scoots out of the bed and heads out of the room.

She springs off the bed and yells over her shoulder, "You may wanna wash your hands before you go downstairs."

LaNecia can't bear to watch Scottie leave out of the front door with Dani by his side. It's now around seven o'clock. She makes a feeble attempt to eat the dinner that Anya prepared, steamed vegetables and tilapia with homemade bread and coleslaw. Although the food looks and smells delicious, she slumps in her chair at the dining room table, making loud scraping sounds with her fork as she pushes her broccoli, carrots, and cauliflower around her plate.

Vette tells her, "We're getting out of here in a minute. I'm going stir-crazy, and I can see you need to get out, too. We'll steal Neil's ride and see what kind of trouble we can get into."

"Girl, is it that obvious?"

"Women know women even when we try to front. Let's roll."

Vette finds Neil in the backyard raking a small pile of leaves. She sweetly asks Neil if she may borrow his Ford Explorer.

"Why not secure a down payment and get your own car?"

"Thanks Neil," Vette says as she grabs his keys, which are sitting on the picnic table.

"I won't be long. LaNecia and I are going to see if we can find bags of ice."

"Yeah, right."

Vette laughs out loud and rushes into the house gleefully holding Neil's keys up in the air. She grabs LaNecia's arm and pulls her from the dinner table and out the door.

Soon they are speeding down South Braeswood, a picturesque boulevard with dozens of oversize brick ranches, perfectly manicured lawns, and pricey homes that have enormous curb appeal.

"Now what's up? I saw how you looked so devastated earlier when Dani pranced into the den like she's the lady of the house."

"Ain't that a bitch? If I were Anya, I would have to beat that lady down. Why doesn't she get on that homewrecker like any sane woman should?"

"My sister-in-law handles matters in her own way. But all the Meadows are dysfunctional, so what do you expect?"

"I expect a wife to put a wannabe in her place, that's what. Ugmo voluntarily went into the refrigerator like she's throwing down on bills or something." She pauses. "You think she and Neil are still messing around?"

"That would be outright nasty. No way she's doing two

brothers at the same time. But who are you to talk, kissing cousin?"

"Girl, please. I don't see why he and I can't be running buddies like we used to be."

"Y'all were way more than that. I get sick just thinking of it. You two remind me of Angelina Jolie and her brother, who she kissed one time on the red carpet. You ain't seen or heard from that guy since."

"He couldn't take the heat, I guess."

"And what kind of heat are you trying to put on my brother, huh? Tell the truth."

"I already told you, Vette."

"You told me a lie, that's what you told me."

"Dang, look at that!" LaNecia ignores Vette's question and points to a long row of CenterPoint Energy white utility trucks that are lined up on the right side of the boulevard.

"Looks like the electrical power rescue teams are out in force," Vette says.

"Hmm, that's what I'm talking about. When people are in a crisis, someone is out there ready to respond ASAP. It seems like the only time Scottie pays attention to me is when I stir up high drama. Why are men like that?"

"Most guys seem very self-absorbed trying to take care of their own needs first. They aren't thinking about a woman unless she is giving him pussy, or money if he's one of those broke-ass scrubs."

"Hmm, you may be right. I need to know what moti-vates Scot . . . I mean, men. I need to get inside a man's head and see what makes him tick."

"The best way to understand a man is to ask another man, preferably a man who isn't trying to sleep with you. Sex screws up everything."

"You're too funny, but I guess you're right. Shit, I had sex for the first time when I was just fifteen. I actually regret that experience."

"Why, 'cause it turned you into a freak?"

"Shut up, dude. Seriously, I wanted my first time to be special. But this Negro named Clarence was a senior and I was a freshman going into my sophomore year. We'd go to the movies or the mall. And he'd ask me to come by his house when his mom and little sisters were gone. Like a dummy, I did."

"Oh, then what happened?"

"Of course, he led me on the typical lame-ass tour of this teeny-weenie town house that they were renting. And we go upstairs. He showed me his room, then his mother's room, which had a king-size bed with lots of pillows."

"Oh, you wanted to get in that bed, huh?"

"Well, Clarence was like, 'Let's play a game. Husband and wife.' I said okay. And he got in bed, took off his clothes and ordered me to take off mine. I was like, 'What if your momma comes home?' He was like, 'I'm the man of the house and I know what's best, so do what I tell you. Do you trust me? Do you love me?' Girl, I was so confused, but flattered that he wanted to act like he was my husband. So I got naked, got in bed, and we got busy."

"Did it hurt?"

"Hell yeah. I was squirming and squeaking, sounding like a freaking chicken mixed with alley cats. But Clarence kept going till he got a little nut. Then he got up, put on his clothes, and washed his hands, just like that."

"That sounds messed up."

"Yeah, it was awful. That experience taught me never to let a man be in control." LaNecia suddenly feels a tingle of depression settling inside her heart. She remembers how strange it felt for her when Clarence didn't want to take her to the movies anymore. He made up excuses, saying he was busy with his studies and football practice. But LaNecia didn't believe him. She kept trying to call him and get him to take her out again, this time to a decent restaurant plus a movie. But he never responded to her requests.

"Well, like I said before," Vette says, "most guys are hard to figure out. Yet Anya says that guys are pretty simple. She had to learn that the hard way."

"What else did she say?"

"That if you want to secure a man, feed him with good food, always be willing to give him the bomb sex whenever he wants it, and, yes, sometimes you gotta give up the cash. Now, if they make their own money, you're straight. They will be giving you the dollars. But if they're young and don't have much money, they may want a little help."

"That sucks. I mean, I know I can fuck. I can cook. But I don't have much money." She frowns. "I'm going to try and get another job. My whole future is at stake."

Vette shakes her head. "I know you got something crazy going on inside your head, cousin, but you be careful what you wish for. You gotta really think if Scottie is worth you losing yourself with all the little scheming you're doing."

9

ANYA

Middle-Aged Beauty

It's *early* October, *two-and-a-half* months away from the big 4-0. My older girlfriends warn me about what to expect. They say once I reach middle age, I will look at life differently. Well, that new perspective has kicked in, and I haven't even reached forty yet.

It's a beautiful Saturday afternoon, and the temperature is so hot you'd think it was the middle of July. I felt like getting out of the house today, and now Vette and I are at the Memorial City Mall, hanging out near the food court. She's hungry for a chicken pasta salad from Le Petit Bistro. I have no appetite, and I'm sitting across from a double-decker Venetian-style carousel waiting on Vette to get her order.

Children of all ages run around the perimeter of the massive merry-go-round. Other kids are content to sit on top of the high-gloss painted horses as they bob up and down and travel in that perfect circle to circus music.

My eyes follow one little boy who looks seven. His head is chock-full of blond hair. His piercing blue eyes light up every time he laughs. His little hands are gripping his striped pole for dear life. I stare at the ride as it comes to a stop. Next thing I know, I'm getting in line and climbing on top of an off-white horse with a long mane.

I know people are smiling and pointing at me, but I don't care.

The ride begins, and I lurch forward. "Oh, this is fun, brings back so many fond memories," I say out loud to a pudgy Hispanic kid, who stares at me like I'm an alien.

I close my eyes and get lost in childish wonder. When the ride comes to a stop, and my feet hit the ground, I have to grip a pole to keep from falling.

"Anya, you must be out of your mind."

"Shhh, girl, don't say my name."

"You don't want anyone to know that it's the great Anya Meadows who's looking like a fool with her big butt on a kiddie ride?"

"Hush, child. Nothing wrong with having clean, innocent fun."

"Sure." Vette deadpans. "If you're ten and under. Don't worry. Your secret is safe with me." We start walking toward the clothing stores. "Where you wanna go next, Toys 'R' Us? Or to the children's play castle over by Sears?"

"Very funny. I don't know where I wanna go. Let's just walk."

We pass by Forever 21, the Gap, and Gap Kids.

I self-consciously look at how I'm dressed: a four-year-old Texas Medical Center oversize T-shirt that Neil got from his job, some wrinkled blue jeans, and a pair of Sketchers that should have been thrown away in the trash long ago.

"Wow," I say as we pass by several window displays. "I could use a wardrobe makeover. It seems like the styles are getting jazzier and trendier."

"The teen clothes look better than the adults', and they cost just as much."

"Who you telling? By the way, I need to go to Kids Footlocker and buy Reese a new pair of kicks. Her feet are growing every month, and I can't ignore her complaining anymore about how much they hurt."

"Okay, let's buy the little princess new gym shoes," Vette agrees. "Hey, have you told Neil about the operation? Did you set a date?"

"No and no. I'm still trying to make a decision."

"What? Why haven't you at least told him? . . ."

"Because I just haven't. And don't you say a word, Vette."

"I won't it's just . . ."

"This hysterectomy thing is a very serious issue. I just don't want Neil to look at me differently."

"Girl, he loves you and you know it."

"Ha, I'm not so sure sometimes. We've been together so long that sometimes I wonder if his love is on autopilot."

"What's the matter?" Vette asks, looking concerned. She can read my face like it's an open book.

"Vette, so much is going on. I'm not too good at handling lots of stress. My birthday, the surgery, Dani being around the house with Scottie . . ."

"Wait? I thought you were happy that she found someone else."

"I am, but I don't like how Neil is acting about the whole matter. In my opinion, he shouldn't care what Dani does. He's too protective. I don't like it."

"That's Neil. I don't think he's aware of how transparent he can be sometimes."

"But that's what I like about him and what I hate about him. It's hard for him to lie to me because I've known him long enough to see straight through him . . . most of the time. But when I can see the truth, I don't always like what I see."

"I don't envy you at all. That's why I'm still single."

"You're so young you don't need to be making that kind of serious commitment yet. If you aren't totally prepared to be a wife, there's hell to pay. And that's another thing," I say pausing as we walk in front of Motherhood Maternity. "I'll admit I've been a fool. As a married woman I have made some stupid mistakes. The main one was letting Neil go find a mistress. Yet I place a lot of blame on Dani. It's like I am not willing to take my share of accountability for what happened."

"It's hard for a woman to admit she's messed up."

"And it's harder for a woman to have to live with that mistake every day for the rest of her life. That's why I've been so tempted to just walk away," I say and take a seat on a couple of brown Massage Center seats that give us an unobstructed view of the Motherhood Maternity store.

"You want to leave Neil?"

"In my heart, no, but when I'm having a tough day I want to say *Screw it* and find someone else. That way I can start all over, leave the mistakes behind, and make sure I do not repeat them in a new relationship. But I'm no spring chicken. You'll never find me in the pages of a magazine with the caption 'Young Movers and Shakers.'"

"Woman, please. You aren't that ancient."

"I am, too. See this." I turn over both my hands and spread them before me. "Dozens of ugly wrinkles everywhere. I feel ashamed of my hands sometimes. And see how my eyes are sinking into my head just a little? I've never considered plastic surgery before...."

"And you shouldn't now, Anya, you're so attractive and strong."

"Yeah, but is it enough? Is my almost middle-aged

beauty going to keep Neil from upgrading to a younger version of me, from trading me in for a new set of wheels?"

"Well, you aren't the only one getting older. My brother may find himself being traded in for a sportier model himself. So there!"

"Thank you!" I laugh and wipe a few tears from my eyes. I don't want Vette to know they're genuine tears, so I act like they're silly tears. There's no way this twenty-something young lady can understand how it feels to be me.

I glance at the mannequins wearing maternity dresses and place my hand on my belly. I feel heartbroken when I realize that if I have the hysterectomy, my body will never produce life again. So why am I here on this Earth? In ten short years, my daughter will be dating, applying for college, leaving the house, and making her own way through life. Then what will I do? Will Neil and I still have anything significant to talk about? Will the sex be exciting? In an effort to change the subject, I hop up and say to Vette, "Let's go check out the maternity clothes."

"Oh, Lord, I'm scared someone I know may catch me in here and assume things about me," Vette yelps as she trails me into the store.

"Vette, please. You are *not* famous. No one is going to recognize you, Ms. Britney Fears."

"Aw, you're wrong for that."

I browse several racks of turtlenecks and stop at a row of colorful fall dresses. "Beautiful. These styles don't even seem like maternity clothes with the faux wrap. The clothes are so much better than when I was carrying Reese. Child, I couldn't wait to go into labor, have my baby, and throw 'em in the garbage."

"Hmm, I can only imagine how that feels."

I turn down another aisle. A bright-eyed, clear-faced woman with a very round belly is oohing and ahhing over some cute and sexy nightgowns.

"You think my husband will like this?" She addresses me, holding up a pink sleeveless nursing gown with a V neck.

I want to say, "What difference will it make at this point with the condition you're in," but I tell her, "That's a very pretty outfit. You'd look good in that."

"I think you're right. Thanks so much," she says. Her eyes rest on my stomach.

"So what type of clothes are you looking for, and most important, when's *your* due date?"

I blankly stare at her, but she keeps running her mouth. "I'm due around February fourteenth. That would be *awesome,* wouldn't it? A child conceived in love being born on the most romantic day of the year."

"Um, yeah," I say and take a few steps away from her. "Vette, come on, let's go. Now!"

"What's the matter?" she asks trying to keep up with me as I head directly across the hall to Kids Footlocker.

"Nothing."

"What's wrong?"

"Nothing's wrong."

"C'mon, Anya, tell me. You're certainly acting like something's wrong."

"Okay, now something *is* wrong because you *keep* bothering me. Getting on my last nerve."

A few days later on a Friday afternoon, Dani comes by the house to pick up her son. I'm in the kitchen preparing one of Neil's favorite meals. Vette agreed to take Reese for a visit with Sola. LaNecia's power finally got turned back on, so she returned home.

"Mmm, that sure smells good. What are you making, Anya?" Miss Thing, of course, follows her nose the second she gets in the house, trying to see what I'm up to.

"I'm chopping raw onions and bell pepper. You want some?"

"No, thank you." Dani wrinkles her nose. "I smell meat. Is that a T-bone?"

"No girl, that's porterhouse. Only the best for my man."

"Oh, I see."

"When are you going to cook for *your* man?"

"Scottie isn't my man."

"Quit playing around, Dani. You two are thick as thieves. Every time I see him, you're not far behind. So what's up?"

Dani walks to the refrigerator and swings open the door. "Wow, is that banana pudding? My mama would make this all the time when we were kids. Is it okay if I have just a tiny spoonful?"

"Don't you have diabetes?"

"Um, hello, one tiny spoonful isn't going to kill me."

"Okay, then, how about half a bowl?"

"Anya Meadows. That isn't funny!"

I laugh and wave my hand. "Dani, I don't care what you eat. It's your life, your body."

"Where's my baby?"

"I'm assuming you're referring to Braxton."

"Of course. Who else would I call by that name? Definitely not Neil."

I don't say anything. Scottie comes into the kitchen and says hello to us. He kisses Dani on the forehead, but she ignores him. I continue chopping veggies and look in the refrigerator for some prechopped garlic.

Neil bounces into the kitchen. "Something sure enough smells good up in here."

Dani hugs Scottie around the waist. "It's probably Scottie. He just showered, I think." She presses her nose on his neck. "Mmm, you smell so delicious, sweetie."

"Do I, babe? What you wanna do tonight? Neil told me to get the fuck out his house so he can fuck his wife."

"Man, you tripping. If you keep talking mess like that you won't have a house to come to."

"Whew, calm down, Neil," Dani says. Neil immediately takes a few deep breaths.

"Well, I don't want to intrude on you and your wife's date night." She laughs, then stops. "I can't believe you're making us leave. There's room enough in this house for all of us."

"No," I say adamantly, ignoring her sarcasm. "No, no, no. Go on, get your kid, and y'all can hang out at your place."

"This place is way more exciting than mine," she says. "Dinner is already prepared. You probably have some DVDs already stacked up and waiting in the den."

"Don't pay her any mind, Neil," I say and whack an onion with a long butcher knife. "Dani's just being Dani. Dinner will be done in about thirty minutes, so if you wanna go and, um, get ready, now's a good time."

"Eww, I think she's talking about him getting ready for some . . ."

Neil steps up to Dani and covers her mouth with his hand. I look at Neil like he's lost his mind. He removes his hand from her mouth and disappears from the kitchen.

"Men are such little boys," Dani remarks and laughs. "Ready, Scottie? I'm getting Brax. We're leaving. Now!"

* * *

I am leaning over the dining room table, which is draped by a white silk tablecloth. Two vanilla-scented candles set in silver-plated holders burn on each end of the rectangular table. Neil is sitting on the opposite end staring into space. I have just served him his meal of well-done steak, mashed potatoes with gravy, green beans smothered in onions, side garden salad, and some hot buttered rolls.

"You're too good to me, Anya," Neil says as he slides some potatoes on his fork and places it inside his mouth. "Mmmm, these are so delicious. The best ever. What have I done to deserve this, my love?"

"I know when it's time to spice things up, that's all. The last time we did something this exciting was back in July during our anniversary, and it just felt like that time again."

"I gotcha. Well, keep doing what you're doing. . . ." The rest of his words can't be understood. He's too busy stuffing his mouth.

I guess I can't complain. My hubby is at home with me where I can see him. Other women's husbands are on the other end of a telephone line, spitting out words that may or may not be the truth.

I'm working late, babe.

I'm hanging out with the boys, that's all.

I'm not doing anything wrong, so stop tripping. You know I love you.

I just got in the car and I'm on my way home now. Gotta get some gas first, though.

Very few men will have the balls to say what's really going on.

My chick on the side and I just got through having butt-naked sex. You just missed it.

I'm in love with another woman. She's kind, supportive, and gorgeous. She and I are having dinner right now, then we're going to sneak away and hang out at her spot.

I'm on my way to meet a beautiful woman in a bar. We're going to have a few drinks, share a few laughs, then who knows what will happen after that.

Oh, hell no. Ninety percent of men, married or in committed relationships, will never have the courage to tell the truth about what they're really doing. We hope and pray to God that he is where he says he is. Because we can't really see what's going on for ourselves, we have no other choice but to trust.

And that's why moments like right now are so important. He's here, in our home, with me.

"Neil," I say for the third time. "The food couldn't be that good."

"Huh?"

"I've been calling your name for the longest. You have this faraway look in your eyes."

"Oh, um, it's nothing. Work stuff."

"Oh yeah?" I say with a raised eyebrow. "What's happening at work?"

"Budget cuts. A couple of white-collar folks got pink slips."

"Your job is not in jeopardy, right? That would be weird since you're the moneyman."

"You never know. Anyone who has a job can lose a job, I don't care what your title or duties are. Anyway, I am not going to stress about it."

"And you shouldn't. Try to enjoy the moment. Our moment." I raise a glass of wine.

Neil picks up his glass of white wine and tilts it toward me. We share a laugh. He takes a sip and begins eating again.

Sometimes I wonder if my cooking is really that appetizing or if he's using eating as an excuse to not hold a serious conversation with me.

"What are you in the mood to look at?"

"It doesn't matter. Whatever you choose is fine."

"I was looking for a more committed answer than that."

"Anya, you know I'm not that picky when it comes to movies."

"That's 'cause you usually fall asleep halfway through the film. I swear, if you conk out this time, do not wake up and start badgering me about what happened. I cannot stand when people do that."

Neil actually starts laughing heartily. It's good to hear him sound happy.

I take another celebratory sip of wine from my glass.

Neil clears the table and loads the dishwasher while I set up the Blu-ray DVD player.

I am wearing a red silk nightgown with spaghetti straps. I've slipped my feet inside some white velour Smart-Dogs indoor-outdoor slippers that feel divine on my skin.

Neil is lying on the couch with his hands clasped behind his head. I pick up the remote, aim it at the player, and sit down on the floor in front of the sofa next to Neil.

"Am I blocking your view?"

"A little. Your head is as wide as Peter's on *Family Guy.*"

"No way." I chuckle. "Let me know if I'm in your way."

"Just kidding, *Peter.* It's cool." Seconds later I hear loud, obnoxious snoring sounds.

"Ahem, stop playing around, Neil. The opening credits

just started. I've wanted to see *American Gangster* for the longest."

"Yeah, me, too."

We watch in silence for a good thirty minutes. After a while, Neil began touching my neck, his fingers softly kneading my skin.

"That feels really good. Thanks, Neil."

"That's not the only thing I can make feel good."

"W—what you say?"

"You heard me." He whispers at my neck. "Get up."

I lift myself up until I'm on my knees looking down at my husband, who's lying flat on his back.

"Kiss me," he commands.

I lean over and press my lips against his. He runs his fingers through my hair and pushes my head closer to his. I thrust my tongue deeper inside Neil's mouth, which is hot and wet.

I remove my underwear and climb on top. His eyes enlarge. He slides off his boxers, and I slide him inside of me and hop up and down enjoying the friction that makes me want to scream.

Neil's eyes are glassy.

"You're enjoying this?"

"Yeah," he says, breathing hard.

"I love you."

"Mmm," he moans and grunts as he grabs my hips and pushes himself violently into me.

Hmmm, I love his aggressiveness. He likes when I take charge.

I keep pumping while Neil stares into space.

"Oh, you came already?"

"Uh, yeah. Sorry."

"You look like something heavy is on your mind."

"Um, work stuff."

The next morning I wake up before Neil and get out of bed around nine, which for me is late for a Saturday. I take a quick shower and wash off remnants of the lovemaking Neil and I shared last night. We went one round and a half. For some reason, in the middle of the night, Neil tugged at my panties and got himself a quickie. I was halfway asleep and definitely wasn't feeling it, but as long as he got his I didn't care.

I am in the kitchen trying to decide if I want to be bothered with making waffles or should I do a quick-and-easy bacon and scrambled eggs with toast breakfast.

Neil rushes into the kitchen and glances at the wall clock.

"Scottie made it back yet?"

"No, why? You need him for something?"

"Damn. When I do need him, he's never around."

"He has a life, Neil. Not like he's a little kid you have to babysit . . ."

"I know that!"

"Don't you dare raise your tone at me, Neil. What's wrong with you?"

"Nothing!"

"Don't lie to me. I know when you're lying."

"Then since you know when I'm not telling the truth, and you have such insight into what I'm thinking at all times, why ask me what's wrong?"

"I want to hear it come from your mouth."

"You're tripping as usual."

"Don't put the blame for your rotten mood on me, Neil.

Shoot, I'm in here thinking about you, trying to prepare something good for you to eat."

"Love is more than about what you can put in my stomach, Anya!"

I throw an uncracked egg at the wall and scream.

Neil runs to me and places his hand over my mouth. "Woman, shut up. You better be glad we have the house to ourselves."

I yank my head back, but Neil maintains a solid grip. "No, you listen to me. Calm down, Anya. You've been acting so freaking moody lately, it's unreal. Are you gonna be okay? Can I trust you to not get loud?"

He gently releases his hand and holds my shoulders. "Whatever you're going through, it's going to be all right. Okay, Anya?"

"Have a seat. I have something to tell you."

We sit at the breakfast bar on black leather stools.

"Babe, I have been holding back, and it's hard to tell you what I need to tell you, but . . ."

"Just say it, please."

"What do you see when you look at me? When you stare in my eyes, when you see this?" I point to my stomach, arms, and thighs.

"Anya, is this a trick question? Do you want me to say I see an overweight slob?"

"Well, I wouldn't believe that, because it's not true."

"Exactly. You don't weigh what you used to weigh, but it doesn't matter because I still love you. Now, you could stand to do some sit-ups. . . ."

"I know, but even if I did, it wouldn't do any good. My doctor told me I need to have surgery. I'm scared. I hate anesthesia."

"What? Why?"

I explain to him about the ultrasound and the fibroids and how sick I am of stinky menstrual periods.

"You're just now telling me? Were you going to have the surgery without letting me know, too?"

"Of course not. I'm sorry for taking so long in telling you, but I just wish I weren't in this position. I've heard about other women who had surgery and they didn't make it through. And Kanye West's mother passed after surgical complications. I'm afraid to die, Neil."

"Anya, are you serious? You're not going to die!"

"I will one day. I am not ready for this." I stand up and pace the kitchen. Neil is right behind me.

"You gotta have faith and think positive and know that everything will turn out fine. You will be better than ever, and you'll never have to buy expensive maxipads again. Isn't that something to look forward to?"

"I guess," I say wistfully, thinking how stupid he actually sounds. "More important than that is will you still be attracted to me?"

"Now, Anya, you know me better than that. I'm not that shallow."

"What about . . ."

"What about?"

"Dani!" There! I said it.

"What does she have to do with this?"

"Everything!"

"You're being silly. So you're telling me that if you don't have the surgery it will make you feel better and more on the same level as Dani? Ha!" he says and walks away so I can't see his face. "She's not thinking about me anyway. Scottie's the man who has her attention."

"Do you have to sound so depressed when you say that?"

"I'm not depressed. Just facing the truth."

"Neil, look at me."

"No, I'm good."

"But I'm not, so turn your face around so I can see your eyes."

He turns around and averts his eyes like he wishes he could be anywhere else instead of standing before me.

"You still love her?"

"No!"

"You're a terrible liar."

"Again, since you know the answer to the question, why ask? Not that you truly know. You just *think* you know."

"Hmm, I don't want to talk about any of this anymore. It hurts. It does. I don't know what to think or what to do."

"Anya, in spite of you feeling all these insecurities," he says, "I'm positive you'll figure out what to do and come out stronger."

"Yep," I say with sadness. "If I do have the surgery, it'll definitely have to happen early next year. December is almost here, and I am determined to see my fortieth birthday."

10

DANI

Love Is Sometimes Selfish

It's the fourth weekend in October, almost three months since I've met Neil's brother, one week before Halloween. Scottie decided he wants to show me off, so we're on our way to a costume party that one of his friends is hosting.

I feel it's only appropriate that Scottie meets my close girlfriend Summer Holiday. She's heard about him, and now's her chance to see him face-to-face. A week ago, I called Summer and asked her to meet us at the get-together. This moment is huge. I've never taken this long to introduce Summer to the man in my life. But now that Scottie and I have been going strong for months, it seems like the right thing to do.

"Why you so jumpy?" Scottie asks me while I'm seated next to him in his car.

"Do I look petrified?" I ask him as he's driving north on I-45. "I just have so many mixed emotions. How do I look?"

"Like I told you when you were getting dressed, I ain't feeling the cop outfit, but I gotta admit, your legs look hot, hot, hot, baby."

"Of course, you'd say that." My costume consists of a

long-sleeved navy blue jumpsuit with shorts that come mid-way down my thighs. Silver plastic handcuffs are fastened to a wide black belt that fits tightly around my waist. My hair, which is combed straight, is covered by a police hat with a wide black plastic rim. And I am wearing thigh-high black leather boots.

"Please, Mrs. Officer. Don't arrest me," Scottie sings.

"I'm not a Mrs."

"Not yet."

"Oh, hush."

I settle in my seat. The temperature is amazing, almost eighty degrees on this pleasant Saturday evening.

"I hope Brax is okay," I murmur. "He was pitching a fit when he saw us sneaking out of the house. Earlier, when I was getting dressed, he ran to his room looking for his plastic pumpkin and his Transformers outfit. I had to tell him over and over it's not Halloween yet. That boy took one look at me and didn't believe a word I said."

"Aw, that's my little man." Scottie laughs, then flashes me a serious look. "My momma loves him to death. I wish my father could have seen him."

"You don't talk much about your dad."

"I know. I was fourteen when Daddy died. I guess that's why Neil acts how he does with me. But a brother is not a dad. Neil can never take his place."

"Of course he can't. I'm sure Neil knows that."

"I dunno. Sometimes he treats me like I'm still little Prescott. I hate that."

"I know, Scottie. But I'm positive he has your best interests at heart."

"If that's true, then you and I wouldn't be together in this car right now headed to a wild party."

"Maybe you're right." I bite my bottom lip. "Just because Neil has your best interests at heart doesn't mean he has mine."

"Hey." I raise my voice and carefully look in the outside mirror. "Watch your speed."

"Aw, shit." Scottie slows down from going almost eighty in a sixty-five zone. A police car pulls up on the side of us and drives at the same pace as Scottie. He looks straight ahead. After several minutes, the patrol car increases its speed and within seconds is way ahead of us.

"Bastards. All of 'em."

"You're good, baby. Just try to drive the limit, okay?"

Scottie doesn't speak another word to me for the rest of the trip. We exit the freeway in The Woodlands and coast along until we come to an intersection that leads to a private road. We stop in front of a white frame house complete with dozens of towering trees and a horseshoe driveway. A series of orange lanterns sits on the ground next to several wooden posts.

"Hey," I tell him once he turns off the ignition. "Let me call and see where Summer is in case she needs better directions."

I get her on the phone and realize she's about five minutes away. "If you don't mind, I want to wait in the car. Summer and I can go in together."

"No problem. 'Bye!"

The minute Scottie leaves, my cell phone rings.

"What's up, you dope?"

"Is that any way to answer the phone? I was wondering about Brax."

"Then you should call your mother and ask," I tell Neil. "Sorry for being such a bitch. You know your son. He was complaining and begging me to let him put on his Hallow-een costume. I kept telling him the holiday is in one week. He looked at me and said, 'Hal-ween is tonight, Mommy.'"

"The boy is smart. You can't lie to him, Dani."

"So are you really calling to see how Brax is doing, or are you calling for another reason?" I can't resist messing with this man.

"Dani, I just haven't seen him all day, since it's your weekend." His voice is warm, even sexy.

"Neil, you could have kept Brax tonight if you wanted."

"I couldn't. Anya wanted me to take her to see a play at Theatre Under the Stars."

"Aw, good for you. Y'all need to get out for a change."

"Dani!"

"Neil." I laugh hysterically. "You don't know how to treat a woman, I swear."

I hear him make disapproving noises. I know I've got-ten under his skin.

"I don't know how to treat a woman, but I do know how to treat my wife."

"Oh, here he goes again with the wife thing."

"That's something you know nothing about."

"Well, if your brother has his way, that's going to change."

"Don't be stupid, Dani. My brother is infatuated with you, but . . . he can't marry you."

"And why the hell not?" I say indignantly. "You think I'm going to spend the rest of my days being some man's lifelong fantasy? I'm not good enough to be a Mrs.?"

"I didn't say that." He pauses. "You could have been mine."

"Okay, I've gotta go, Neil. My girlfriend just parked next

to me, and you're talking unbelievably shitty right now. I don't appreciate you saying things like that. You know good and well you turned me down. I *couldn't* be your wife because you were too scared to get divorced. So there!" I hang up on him and open the passenger door of the car to greet my girl.

She emerges from her Corvette wearing a black Spandex halter and matching leggings and a red miniskirt. A decorative red rose is clasped to the side of her brownish red shoulder-length hair. A black-and-red choker is fastened around her thin neck. She told me she was coming dressed as a Spanish dancer.

Summer refers to herself as a "mutt" because she is known for saying "Like a cake made from scratch, I'm mixed up with some of everything." Her mom is Asian, African American, and German. Her dad is Hispanic and Irish. She told me when she fills out job applications it takes her fifteen minutes to decide what race she wants to be that day. She used to live in my apartment complex but last year relocated to a more luxurious apartment closer to downtown. We've kept in touch and I consider her the closest girlfriend I've ever had.

When we first met and were getting to know each other, I spilled the beans and told her the lowdown about me and my baby daddy. Summer, kind and sympathetic, agreed to step in and act as the peacemaker when it comes to our child. Brax loves her to death, and she feels the same about him. I consider her Brax's godmother even though she's only twenty-four.

"Hey mamacita!" I squeal.

"Okay, where's this godlike man you've been chilling with, girl? I bet I can point him out based on the photos you've texted me. Sorry I've been so busy with Andre that I'm just now able to hook up with you."

We knock on the door one time and enter the one-story ranch. The ceiling is covered with a black plastic spiderweb net. Orange and black helium-filled balloons bob along the ceiling. The sounds of thunder and lightning play in the background through surround-sound speakers. Dozens of people are packed in the dimly lit living room holding drinks, talking, and dancing.

"Damn, it's so dark in here I can't even see the white people, let alone the black ones," Summer jokes.

"Girl, hush." I am in front of her and reach behind me to grab her hand. "Let's keep going. I hear people in the back-yard, too."

We pass by a bearded magician who's doing card tricks.

"Pick a card," he says, "any card."

We giggle and run toward a lighted room.

"Hallelujah, we're out of the dark. I've never been so glad to see a kitchen in my life."

"That sounds funny coming from a chick who doesn't like to cook." Summer laughs. "How are you going to keep Scottie's attention if you don't cook?"

"I cook in the bedroom."

"You've never told me about that."

"Some recipes must remain secrets."

"He must be putting it on ya, then. I heard that."

We scoop up a tray of cheese popcorn and pick out two small cups of orange punch.

"Ready to go outside?" I ask.

Scottie calmly walks into the kitchen. I grin at his half-buttoned purple silk shirt, white elephant pants with two pockets stitched in the front, and white platform shoes with matching shoelaces. He takes one look at me, yells, and rushes toward me. He picks me up around my waist and swings me around. Orange drink leaps out of my cup and spills on the floor.

"Scottie, dammit, put me down. You act like you haven't seen me today."

"Sorry, babe. Don't worry, it can be wiped up."

He walks over to a paper towel dispenser and tears off a sheet.

"Here." He hands it to me.

"No, you made me spill, so you can wipe it up for me!"

Scottie bends down and vigorously wipes up the orange drink.

"Hey now, mama. So far, so good, Miss Danielle Frazier. I think you've scored a decent man," Summer gushes.

"Oh, stop. Check him out for more than two seconds before forming your opinion."

Scottie rises to his feet and extends his free hand. "Scottie Meadows. It's about time she let us meet, huh? She has a lot of nerve keeping her best friend from her man."

"Well, Dani just wanted to make sure that you're a keeper, and she wouldn't let us meet until that part was secure."

"Is that right?" he says and grabs me around my waist, hugging and kissing me on the lips. "Am I a keeper, babe?"

I turn the other cheek so he can kiss it, too. He starts nibbling on my ear, and I tilt my head and moan like a kitten getting stroked by its owner.

"Ahem, can't y'all do that after the party?" Summer teases. "I'm feeling left out."

"Scottie, let me go. Down, boy!"

He releases me and puts his arm around my shoulder and gestures at Summer.

"So, what do you think? Honestly. How do we look together?"

"You do look like you're together. Physically, it can't get any better. But how you click mentally, emotionally, and spiritually is something I wouldn't know."

"Well, physical is a good start." He grins like he's proud and then asks, "You ever been married?"

"Um, no, that's probably number eight on the to-do list."

"It's number three on mine," he says.

"Hey, you guys," I butt in, "can we please go have a seat or something before we dive into this really deep conversation?"

Scottie tells me okay, then leads the way down a gravel-covered path to an area of the backyard that has a raised oak deck with ten lawn chairs situated around a table filled with sodas, candy, and miniature hot dogs.

Summer and I take a seat while Scottie observes the other guests.

"As you were saying?" Summer asks as she eyes Scottie. "Dani, this is fucking unbelievable. A man with a plan. Do you know how rare that is?"

"Having a plan is nothing. Executing it is what's important."

"Well, I not only have goals, I have the vision and determination to see all this stuff happen in my life. Don't forget I've practically been on my own since I was a teen," Scottie says.

"I never knew all this."

"After my father passed away, I set out to make my own path. Neil couldn't keep up with me."

"Ahhh, the infamous older brother who loved your woman before you even knew she existed. How's that working out?"

"Summer!" I shriek. "Not now."

Scottie turns away from us and holds a conversation with a guy dressed in a red Thriller jacket.

"Why not? This is something you'll have to deal with. It's obvious your boo is crazy about you. I notice how he keeps staring at you, smiling, and he looks like he wants to touch your arm, your hand, your face every second. He knows who he wants and isn't ashamed. But the fact that his brother's child could one day be his stepson is an absolute bitch. It is quite fascinating in my opinion."

"Summer, wipe the grin off your face," I say, feeling embarrassed. Everything she's saying is true. But I'm just not ready to face the seriousness of our complicated situation. I have tried so very hard to keep a tight lid on my emotions when it comes to how I feel about Scottie. Do I like Scottie for himself, or is it because I could never have his brother the way I wanted to have him?

Scottie finally takes a seat next to us.

"Don't think you're the first one to have to deal with this," Summer replies. "Have you heard the true Hollywood story about how Woody Allen married Mia Farrow's young adopted daughter? I saw it on one of those entertainment shows recently. Anyway, it was such a huge scandal. But Woody and the girl didn't care. They went on with their lives, and I think they're still married to this day."

"Soon-Yi," I softly say to myself. "Yes, I saw that same show. This ugly ass weirdo is twice her age. He sneaked behind his partner's back and was having sex with her, and she was a twenty-one-year-old woman at the time. He's white. She's Korean. And Mia Farrow never spoke to that girl again, but, still, it's crazy how someone who Mia used to love and care for hurt her with that level of betrayal."

"I agree," Summer tells me as she sips her punch. "But let's step into the real world. People like us probably couldn't get away with some sick-ass stuff like they did."

I shift in my seat, feeling uneasy. Although I've told Summer how great Scottie is to me, I still haven't let her in on who LaNecia is and how he and his cousin were involved. Some things are too hard to talk about, even with your best friend.

Summer continues, "It's like the scandal hits, people gasp, and everyone goes on with their happy little dysfunctional lives. Hollywood is not real. Neil isn't Mia. You aren't betraying your relative."

"Scottie would be, though," I quickly reply. "What if Neil never speaks to Scottie again? Or me? Or what if he doesn't want to be bothered with Brax ever again because of a decision that we've made? I may not act like I care, but in reality, yes, it bothers me sometimes."

"Hey, hey, hey. I would love to be included in this conversation, especially since I seem to be the topic," Scottie says. "I don't want you to be stressed out over us. Over anything. I got you, boo!"

And that's what I love about Scottie Meadows. He's a calming presence in my hectic life. I've been independent for so long that it feels wonderful to know that someone else is there willing to take over the reins.

"Love is sometimes selfish." Summer shrugs. "Think about it. What if almost every girl is in love with the most popular guy in high school? He's attractive, charming, friendly, and popular. But he only has eyes for one main girl. And he chooses to take her to the prom. And the other girls feel hurt, angry, and jealous. Now, I'm talking about a situation where no one is anyone else's brother, or adopted daughter, or ex-anything. Yet people are getting hurt left and right. The guy who was so beloved by many women has now made twice as many enemies because now the women who had a crush on him are hurt, and whoever else they've told is also mad as hell at the guy because he hurt the women who were in love with him."

"Extreme analogy, but guess what? You're right. There will be pain inside of love. Shit, when I gave birth to Brax, it hurt like hell. A million times worse than cramps. But I loved him the second I laid eyes on him. Men are such bastards."

Scottie blinks. "Where'd that come from?" Before I can answer, he looks away and tilts his head.

"Ah, hell. Sounds like someone is playing some Run DMC. It's all over." He hops to his feet and starts dancing.

We spend another two hours at the party. Whenever one of Scottie's friends arrives, he introduces me as "my gal." I blush and try to engage his buddies in conversation for several minutes. Other times Summer and I steal away to a private area, giggling and laughing at people's outrageous costumes.

By the time we leave, Scottie is singing at the top of his lungs.

"Hey, you want me to drive?" I ask with concern. "You seem like you're a little too happy."

"Yeah, you do that. You take the wheel."

Summer and I hug, and I promise to give her a call to let her know we've gotten home safely. I take I-45 to the 610 West Loop. We're flying down the freeway and soon enter the city of Bellaire, a suburb with lofty homes and wealthy residents that's located in the middle of Houston's southwest side. This spoiled city is eighty-nine percent white, and barely one percent African American.

"We're in Bellaire? Slow your ass down; you know how these cops can be."

"I already know, Scottie," I tease.

"Do I sound like I'm playing? Either slow down or get your ass out the car and I'll drive."

"Why the fuck are you talking to me so rudely?" A crazed look covers his face. I swallow deeply and begin shaking.

He doesn't say another word to me until we pull up in front of Neil's home. Earlier we discussed how we'd stop by the house so he could pick up some fresh clothes.

"If you like, I can just leave you here and go back to my spot by myself. Wouldn't bother me one bit."

"No, Dani, please don't be mad. I'm sorry."

"You better be more than sorry, Scottie. I didn't deserve to be treated that way back there. I don't get it. We had such a good time tonight," I reply, choking back tears.

"Babe, I was wrong, I know, but I gotta tell you something." He exhales. "I don't like going through Bellaire, ever!"

"Yeah, I know the white cops like to ticket black drivers, but so what. . . ."

"The white cops *killed* my black daddy."

"W–what?"

"Some stupid drug dealer robbed a white woman at gunpoint. This was when I was barely a teenager. And my daddy happened to be in the great city of Bellaire," he says sarcastically. "His Chrysler New Yorker broke down. Daddy loved that car. Back then that boxy-looking sedan was *bad*. So here he goes racing down the street searching for a phone booth. His car was stuck in the middle of Bissonnet, and he was worried about it getting hit. So he's sprinting like a track star, minding his own business. The cops drive by and notice this big, bulky black man running through this mostly white suburb. They slow down, pull next to him, and yell out the window. Well, Daddy hasn't done anything wrong, so he doesn't think they're talking to him. They kept yelling, and he gets mad and runs faster. And those no-good bastards shot him like a dog in the street."

Scottie's veins pulsate on the side of his head as he stares into space.

"If you a black man, you can't run down any street in America. They'll think you've done something crime related every single time. But my daddy didn't do anything. He didn't do a fucking thing. They rushed him to the hospital. Someone called my mom and told us to hurry and come see him. But he took his last breath right when we pulled into the hospital parking lot."

Scottie slumps down in his seat with his head against his chest, sobbing. "I never got to tell my daddy good-bye, Dani. Last time I saw him was that morning before I went to school. He dropped me off at the bus stop and told me he loved me, and that he'd see me later."

Scottie silently cries for a few moments and I don't know what to say at first, so I just let him get it out.

When his tears subside, I tell him, "Scottie, I'm so very sorry. I shouldn't have hollered at you earlier, but I had no idea."

"It's not your fault. I—I just don't like Bellaire and I hate cops even more." He sniffs and wipes his nose on his sleeve.

"One more thing I gotta tell you. I did a brief jail stint when I lived in Michigan."

"Oh no."

"But it was because I refused to testify against a friend of mine. They tried to teach me a lesson, break me down, thought I'd do anything to get out that cell."

"I can't imagine what that must have felt like."

"I hated it." He laughs bitterly. "To this day I can't stand confined spaces." He peers at me. "So now you know more about bad-boy Scottie. I hope you understand. I hope you let me spend the night with you, too."

"Of course, Scottie. I wouldn't have it any other way. Thanks for sharing that with me. The more I learn about you, the more I feel I know you."

When he opens the car door so he can go into Neil's house to get some clothes, he eyes me curiously. "Don't think for a second I'm letting my Mariah sit outside in the car, in this hood, by herself. Come on."

He spends the night over at my place. The next day, he makes breakfast and we laugh, and talk, and watch movies all morning.

Vette brings Brax over in the afternoon, and all of us spend time reading *Thomas the Tank Engine* and *It's the Great Pumpkin, Charlie Brown*.

But by early evening, I yawn. "All this lying around is fun, but I gotta work off all the food I've been pigging out on. Anyone wanna join me working out?"

My apartment complex has a tiny workout room with two treadmills, two exercise bikes, and two elliptical machines. Most of the time the room is empty, which is fine with me because I usually listen to my iPod while I go through my routines.

I grab my wallet in case I get thirsty and want to buy something to drink from the vending machine. I also pick up my keys and my music and stand at the door waiting.

Vette shakes her head. "No thanks. Me and Brax are deep into Charlie Brown."

"Don't be so lazy, Vette. I'll get Brax dressed, and you can come, too."

"Trust me, Dani. I am perfectly fine being here, doing my lazy-afternoon thing with my nephew."

"Suit yourself." I turn to Scottie with an expectant look.

Scottie tells me, "You go on. I'll be there in a minute."

"Why can't you come now?" I smirk, just to give him a hard time.

"Gotta use the men's room. Is that okay with you?"

"See ya in a bit."

Thankfully, all the machines are available when I arrive. There are two rows of equipment, and my eyes settle on a machine on the front row that's next to a plain yellow wall. The front and back walls are covered by floor-to-ceiling mirrors. I glance at my reflection and place my wallet and keys on the empty machine next to me, put on my headphones, and stand on a treadmill eager to do an hour workout.

I immediately get lost inside the playlist, which starts out with "Spotlight" from Jennifer Hudson's debut CD.

I punch a few buttons and the tread belt moves underneath my feet.

One, two, three, four. I count and march to the beat. *One, two, three, four.*

I'm staring straight ahead, counting, daydreaming, and listening to music. Two minutes into the workout, the hair freezes on my neck.

Scottie's behind me. I pause the machine, then turn around to acknowledge him. But this eerily skinny man who's sporting a bad haircut and a wrinkled T-shirt and stretch pants is staring at me with his hand pointed toward me. I gasp, turn my head toward my wallet. He looks, too, then crazily smiles at me. I nervously look in the mirror, my body tense with anticipation.

He steps onto the machine with my wallet. I feel his eyes on me the whole time.

I hear Jennifer singing, "Hoo hoo, hoo hoo."

Then Scottie bursts in the room. "Hey!"

The skinny guy looks agitated. "You talking to me?"

"What do you think you're doing?"

"None of your business. I–I'm leaving."

Scottie walks up to the guy and pushes him so hard he stumbles. "You're crazy, man. I haven't done anything."

"I saw you the whole time." Scottie snatches my wallet from the other machine. "If I ever see you around my gal again, I'll give you a beating you'll never forget."

The guy scurries backward until he reaches the door, then runs out of the room.

"You all right?"

"Scottie, he gave me the weirdest feeling. I can't be in here anymore by myself. What would have happened if you hadn't come?"

"I'm telling you, Mariah, you gonna have to sign up at the big, expensive gym. I don't like this small-ass workout room, and I go crazy when it even looks like a guy is trying to mess with you."

"I didn't ask you to go Incredible Hulk on anyone."

"I know. But I will. I will turn into any Superhero. On anyone."

"But, why?" I ask in a shaky voice.

"I know you've heard of ride or die. I'm your ride-or-die guy. I'm riding this relationship till the wheels fall off."

11

LaNecia

Trying to Play the Game

Yep, I am more serious than a heart attack." LaNecia raises her fingers to the sky, then crosses her hand over her heart.

Neil is seated at a small table across from LaNecia at Pappadeaux restaurant. She just got off work and earlier contacted Neil and asked if he could come see her since they work in the medical center area. She had some interesting news for him.

"So you're saying that Scottie is messing around on Dani with another woman?"

"That's exactly what I'm saying."

"How do you know?"

"Look at this." LaNecia logs in to her MySpace account and shows him her cell phone.

"Scottie has been on my friend list for a long time. And I've noticed that every time I click on his page, strange women appear on his friend list. Gorgeous women who live in the Houston area." She purses her lips. "How does he meet these chicks? And if he's so faithful to her, why he talking to women online?"

"But how do you know that?"

"I just *do*. So I think you should tell her what's going on. Because so far she is blinded by him and can't see his true nature."

"I dunno, LaNecia."

"What don't you know? The evidence is right in front of your face. He's cold busted."

"But why do you care so much that she knows?"

"I don't want her to get hurt like I did."

"LaNecia, please. You can't stand Dani."

"Look, nerd. I mean, listen to me, Neil. I don't know what else to tell you. Scottie is a sneaky little something."

"Well, I may have a little talk with him. Regardless if you've discovered he has a ton of new female MySpace friends, he and her need to slow it down. I don't like her spending the night in his room in my house like they're broke teenagers. She has a place. Go over there."

She leans over the table. "That lady still likes you, Neil. She does. I see how she's always smiling at you when Scottie leaves the room."

"That's because she thinks it's funny that she's ended up with my brother."

"Well, she may be laughing now, but I know the bitch will be crying hard later on. Scottie is the type who draws you in with his personality, good looks, and charm. Then once he knows he totally has your heart, something happens and he'll break it in two. The way he did me, I never saw it coming, I swear." She winces as she recalls painful memories.

"LaNecia, you may mean well, but I don't think you have enough proof. I doubt that Dani will break up with him over some MySpace junk."

"Then I guess I'll have to get more proof."

Two days later, Neil calls LaNecia during his lunch break. She is also on her job but ducks inside the ladies room to take his call. She stands in front of the mirror, toying with her braids and holding the phone to her ear.

"Hey, what's up cousin?"

"Have you heard from Scottie?" he asks.

"No, why?"

"I'd stay away from him at this point. When I told him that you brought up the women he's friending on MySpace, he sounded upset and wondered why you were still prying in his business. He claims those females are work colleagues that he's met in the construction industry. That's all."

"I don't believe it. Men will say anything to save their asses. You know how y'all do. You claim 'she's just a friend' until the girlfriend catches you in bed with the so-called friend. You just can't believe him."

"I'm just relaying to you what he said."

LaNecia hangs up and thinks hard about what she can do to prove that Scottie isn't as perfect as Dani might believe. She's miffed at him because he broke his promise about getting back with her after she unsuccessfully tried to seduce him a whole month ago.

Since that trick didn't work, maybe a different plan will.

She logs on to MySpace on her phone and types in Scottie's e-mail address. She types in "yssup," a password she knows he used in the past and feels relieved it's the correct password.

"This is crazy fun." She clicks a couple of links and checks his friend requests. She sees that he's asked to friend three different women last week. "They sure don't look like construction industry workers to me."

She glances at his profile and turns blind with rage

when she reads that his latest update reads, "I'm singing in ecstasy with my new lady."

She changes his status from "In a relationship" to "single." And she recalls all his new friend requests and deletes his five latest female friends.

LaNecia logs off and sends Neil a text that she's coming over for dinner "but don't tell anybody."

Later that evening, she arrives at Neil's front door. Instead of ringing the doorbell, she stands on the front porch and texts Neil she's waiting outside.

"He's in his room," Neil tells LaNecia as he widely opens the door for her. "You better make it quick because my baby's mama is about to come over."

"I'm not afraid of her." LaNecia runs to the second floor two steps at a time.

She quietly settles in front of Scottie's closed door and leans in. The only sounds she hears are pelts of water splashing in the bathroom down the hall.

The lyrics "You are everything, and everything is you, Ohhhh" wail throughout the hallway.

She walks a few doors down and wants to laugh out loud when she discovers the bathroom door is unlocked. She steps inside, turns down the toilet seat, and sits on top of it.

Her clothes start to feel damp right away. LaNecia strips until she's only wearing thong underwear, then slowly walks toward the shower. Scottie continues singing behind a black plastic curtain decorated with tan umbrellas.

She stands at the end of the shower, then slightly draws the curtain aside and peeks inside. Scottie squirts a handful of green apple shampoo on top of his hair and starts massaging his scalp.

Perfect.

She takes a deep breath and steps inside the shower behind Scottie. She stares at his bare bottom then hugs his waist. His wet soapy skin feels good in her hands. She lays her head against his back and squeezes.

"Mariah?"

"Ummm," LaNecia groans, savoring how it feels to hold Scottie in her arms once again. She presses her nipples against his back and starts rubbing her hands up and down his slippery belly.

"Hey, babe," he says, but his voice is filled with uncertainty.

"Ummm," LaNecia says again and mashes her lips on his back and lightly kisses his skin.

"Hold on a sec, I want to see you. I gotta rinse off my hair and dry my face."

"Mmmmmm," she moans helplessly and caresses his shoulders.

"That feels good. Hold on, babe."

Scottie tries to turn around and face her, but she forces her feet to stay in place. He struggles again until he overpowers her and finally opens his eyes.

"W–what the hell you doing? Get outta here," he hisses, lowering his hands over his penis.

"C'mon, baby, I'll give you some right here, right now, like we used to do."

Scottie hurriedly steps out of the shower. He snatches a huge body towel off the rack and twists it around his hips.

LaNecia counts to three then shyly steps out of the shower.

"Do you have another towel?" she meekly asks.

"No!" he snaps. "Here, use mine, hurry up, then get out of here. My gal will be here any minute. What if she . . . ? I don't want anybody to see you in here with me. Especially my gal."

"So you honestly care what she thinks?"

"Yes, I do."

"What did you mean when you told me you loved me? Tell me. You owe that to me."

"Cousin, please."

She prays he sees the earnestness in her eyes, her body. Long ago, she was told men are weak, that every woman possesses the power to bring down any man. From U.S. presidents, politicians, and popular preachers, woman can use her sultry voice to utter the right words, her thick and luscious lips to engage his imagination, her sexy curves, or ample cleavage.

If I'm so powerful, why can't I get what I want?

LaNecia stares at Scottie and sees pain and confusion in his eyes. She wonders what it all means. *Is he feeling regretful because he knows he's hurting me?*

She finishes patting herself dry, tosses the damp towel at him, stares at her clothes that are scattered on the floor, and decides to get dressed.

"You know what I think? You are playing games, Scottie."

"There's something I want and crave so much, and you can't give it to me."

"But *she* can?"

"I'm trying to do with Dani what I couldn't do with you. I *couldn't* do it with you."

"And you're changing your true nature to try and capture this, this . . ." She sputters, unable to come up with an appropriate word to summarize her feelings.

"No, see, that's where you're wrong. By being with her, I am learning that I can be the man I was destined to be."

"What type of man is that?"

"Honest, faithful, trustworthy."

"Ha, yeah right. Does she know about all those women on your MySpace?"

"Yes, she does. And by the way, I know you've hacked into my account. I've changed my password so you can't snoop around anymore."

LaNecia bares her teeth and quickly recovers. "I don't care. I was just messing around."

"You overstepped your lines, cousin."

A loud knock on the bathroom door interrupts them. Scottie holds his hands together as if he's praying. He looks at LaNecia and whispers, "Please."

She folds her arms over her chest and waits.

"Scottie, are you in there?"

After a while, the knocking ends. Several other minutes pass before Scottie releases the breath he was desperately holding.

"Cousin, I hope you understand."

"Well, I don't, but what difference does it make? Anyway, I need some cash," she lies. "Can you help me out? I got another job but don't start until next week. Then I won't be paid for another couple of weeks. . . ." She knows he can't give her time, but he'll part with money, probably out of guilt.

"Sure, I'll help you."

"Thanks."

"No, wait. I can't."

"*What?*"

"I have a goal, and I need to save every dollar I can. Been saving ever since I got the construction gig."

"You can't even lend me . . . ?"

"No, cousin, no."

"I think someone would be very shocked to know that you didn't answer her when she was at the door."

"Um, thanks for not saying anything."

"Scottie, the fact that you hid from her tells me you aren't honest, faithful, or trustworthy."

LaNecia gives him a hateful look, then slams the bathroom door behind her.

Minutes later, LaNecia pumps herself up to give herself the strength she needs to stick around for dinner. She rushes downstairs straight for the kitchen, where she knows she'll find Anya.

"Hi, there." She waves at Anya, who's using two pot holders to carry a glass container of sweet potato casserole to the breakfast bar.

"Need any help?" LaNecia asks.

"Huh? You're asking to help me with dinner? I think I've got it covered. If you want to do something, you can slice that pork roast. You know where the knives are."

"Sure, I gotta do something, anything." LaNecia opens the knife drawer, picks out the one with the sharpest blade, and presses the knife against the rack of meat and starts cutting.

"Whoa, watch it, girl. You sound like you chopping off someone's head."

"Oh, I guess my attitude is showing. I don't want to chop off his head. I mean, I am not trying to chop off anybody's *anything*. I just want to understand men."

"Let me guess, you aren't getting what you want and now you're pissed off . . . again."

"Well, I don't see how you've lasted so long with Neil. Doesn't he get on your nerves?"

"Girl, all the time!"

"But he still stays with you. Y'all still love each other."

"We have to work at it, LaNecia. Any relationship worth having requires tons of work."

"That's what I thought. But what if the other partner isn't willing to work at it, to try to make things better?"

"You know what, I just think you're way too young to be so concerned about perfecting a relationship with a man. You ought to concentrate on yourself."

"Please, Anya. No lectures."

"I can't help it. If young people would only do half of what adults tell them . . ."

"I *am* an adult!"

"Based on what? A number? The fact you drive a car that someone else paid for? The fact that you don't live under your parents' roof?"

"Well, yeah," she says indignantly.

"Young people these days are living in a dream world." Anya laughs and shakes her head. "Dang, when I say stuff like this, it just proves I'm old, huh? But as much as I wish I were younger and could have the knowledge and strength that are inside me right now, I wouldn't want to be twenty-one again for anything in the world. That's when people think they know everything, when in reality they don't know anything. You think older people are stupid. But the opposite is true."

"Why you ragging on me?"

"Don't ever say you're grown and you can do what you want to do, because, guess what? You really can't! I'm twice your age and I can't do what I please, so what makes you think you can?"

" 'Cause I know how to play the game. I just gotta be willing to play. It's just like playing Monopoly. At first you're kidding around. But after a while, when the stakes are high, you know you can't be merciful anymore. You gotta snatch up those properties, bankrupt a Negro, if you want to go all the way and win the fucking game."

"But some things that seem like just a game aren't." LaNecia notices the biting stare that Anya gives her. She feels like telling her to be quiet. There are times when LaNecia is willing to listen, but today isn't one of them. She feels too frustrated by Scottie's wishy-washy attitude to totally consider what any person over thirty-five advises her to do.

"Well, jeez, no need to get loud, Anya."

"Huh? Oh, LaNecia, you're right. I apologize. I–I there's just a lot going on right now."

"Tell me about it."

"Well, for one, we're having a ton of people over next month for the holidays. . . ."

"I didn't mean tell me literally."

"Oh!"

"I gotta go. Going to say my good-byes, then I'm outta here."

"You're not staying for dinner?"

"Change of plans. 'Bye, Anya."

"Before you go, ask yourself one question. When it comes to you trying to play the game against the other woman, what qualities do you have that are far superior to what she's bringing to the table? If you don't rank higher than her in just about every category, you can forget about Boardwalk. Don't even think about Park Place. You won't even be in the game, let alone win it."

LaNecia nods her head thoughtfully and tells Anya she'll get with her some other time.

She walks into the den and immediately spots Dani sitting on the sofa with Scottie nestled on the floor, seated between her legs. He's freshly dressed and relaxing after his shower. Dani's fingers tenderly rub Scottie's shoulders. His eyes are closed, and he looks peaceful.

"Ahem." LaNecia clears her throat. "Hey everyone, I don't mean to interrupt. But I think I left my bra upstairs from a few minutes ago when we were showering. . . ."

"Cousin, don't front. Ain't no bras upstairs."

Dani jumps in. "He's right. I can see right through your shirt and it's obvious you're wearing a bra. Not that you need one."

"Um, excuse me. Talk what you know. Because he sure got an eyeful when we were upstairs. Or didn't you know that?"

"He told me how you just invited yourself in when you knew good and well he was in the shower. He told me what you said, everything you said."

LaNecia stares at Scottie. *How can you tell her what we did?*

"I know my man. And for the record, I do trust him. He is faithful. He is honest."

"But . . ."

"Another thing, I told Scottie he needs to remember to lock the bathroom door whenever he's in this house. You never know who or what is going to just wander in."

"This is my family's house, you hear me? I am welcome in every single room in this place, you got it?"

"Well," Dani says, "next time you even *think* Scottie is in a room, don't even try to go in."

"Is that right? He's in *this* room and I came in *here.* That doesn't even make any sense. You can't keep me away from my own family, old lady. I don't care what you say."

"Cousin . . ." Scottie butts in.

"I'm Necia. I'm baby doll. I'm the best piece of ass. . . ." LaNecia stops herself before finishing with "you've ever had," words he used to tell her after they had sex. She absolutely doesn't want to break down even though she feels she's coming close to it. She stares at Dani with hatred and realizes she's been playing the game all wrong. *I always end up doing what she wants me to do. I gotta make this old lady do what I want her to do.*

LaNecia barely says good-bye before she runs out of the house and to her car.

She flips opens her cell phone, logs on to the Internet, and is relieved and happy that Scottie hasn't changed his e-mail password. She quickly requests the new password that Scottie recently changed for his MySpace account.

No way this game is over. The dice haven't even started to roll yet.

12

DANI

Olive Juice

It's Saturday night. I've just given Brax his bath and read him a story he loves called *The Berenstain Bears Count Their Blessings.*

We're seated on a taupe polyester recliner that I got on sale from JCPenney. It's my favorite place to snuggle with my son, especially on a rainy evening like tonight.

"Sister Bear is happy for the things that her parents have given her. See, Brax?" I point at the colorful illustrations while he sits on my lap with his head comfortably pressed against my chest.

"She's hap-py," he shouts.

This little girl bear feels happy but I wish to feel like her.

I continue engaging Brax. "We should be grateful and happy for what we have."

"Hap-py! Hap-py! Hap-py!"

Inside my heart seems to sink lower than my knees. But outside is what counts because outside is what Brax sees.

"Mommy not hap-py. Mommy sad. Mommy cry baby."

"What did you say?" Earlier I was in bed wiping my eyes with some tissues. When Brax wandered into my room, I pressed the tissue to my nose and coughed. He said, "Excuse me," and then ran out of the room.

But now he keeps looking from his book to my face. "Kiss Mommy!"

"Of course," I yelp, and I let him kiss me on the cheeks.

"Okay son, it's nine o'clock. Way past your bedtime," I say, trying to sound cheery so he won't think I'm too upset at him for not going to bed when I told him to an hour ago.

"No, Mommy."

"Don't say no to me. You go to bed right now or I'll call your daddy."

I feel like a creep pulling Neil into this. But I don't have any other options. After all, Neil is Brax's daddy, right? It's not like he has any other daddy.

Once I get Brax tucked into his bed and attempt to sing him a lullaby, he protests for a few minutes until his eyelids droop and he starts snoring. I give him a peck on the forehead and close the door to his room. I go back to the living room and throw his book on the floor. I pull my knees up on the recliner so I can get comfy, and I check up on Neil. Anya and Vette mentioned they might attend a children's play at Solomon's Temple even though Reese's role is somewhat minor.

"Hmm, what's the matter?"

"Neil! Is that any way to greet the sexiest woman in Houston?" I murmur into the phone. "What are you up to?"

"Nothing."

"I'm glad you're home."

"Why's that, Dani? What are you even doing calling me if it doesn't have to do with Brax?"

"Hey, I resent that." I pout. "I think we should be able to have a conversation that doesn't totally center on our son."

"Whatever, Dani."

I feel a slight pinch in my chest. Normally Neil is elated

to hear my voice. I can tell when Anya's not home because his voice grows tender, softer, and sexier by the minute. But right now he sounds like his regular stiff self.

"Won't my brother feel resentful that you're sitting in his face and calling me?"

"He's not here."

"Where is he?"

"Um, he said he had to do something important." Problem is, I feel uneasy about what that exactly means. Scottie's been acting secretive lately, and it bothers me.

"He's doing something without you? I thought Saturday was your weekly date night." Neil sounds sarcastic, which makes me feel better. That's the Neil that I know.

"Well, um, it is, but I guess he had something critical to take care of."

"You better hope the old Scottie isn't on the prowl."

"What do you mean by that?" Feeling scared, I sit up in my chair and twist my hair into a circle.

"Back in the day, this man would see three different women in one day. He'd meet one chick for breakfast at IHOP. Then he'd join another chick for coffee that afternoon. And by night, he'd be laid up with some girl after they went to a midnight movie."

"Neil, don't tell me. I don't want to hear all that," I say, feeling sick to my stomach.

"I'm doing what you wanted. And if you ask me, that's something he should have already told you."

"He does tell me a lot of things, but tonight he was unusually evasive."

"Figures. Oh well. Not like I didn't warn you. Not like my cousin didn't try and tell you."

"Wow," I murmur. "Why does this always happen to me?"

"Don't tell me you got socked in the eye by so-called love?"

"No, no, I wasn't in love. But your brother is a lot of fun to hang around with. He was connecting with me in a strong way. We just enjoyed dinner with your mom a few nights ago. Nothing real fancy. We met her at a Pappadeaux...."

"Where LaNecia worked?"

"No way. We were on Westheimer near Kirkwood."

"How'd it turn out?"

"Interesting, to say the least. It was weirdly polite at first. Then it became a kind of open forum. Your mom asked some pretty direct questions about Scottie and his plans, his job, and how our relationship was affecting you."

"Did she? My mom's looking out for her favorite."

"Don't flatter yourself. She cares for Scottie very deeply. I can see that." I pause and choose my words carefully. "She told me that she finds it hard to believe that I can sincerely have feelings for Scottie after what you and I have been through. She was hoping that Scottie and I had dated for a few weeks, and then it had turned 'into nothing like the rest of 'em.' That's what she actually said to me. Can you believe that?"

"That's a mother for you. She doesn't play."

"Yeah well, we managed to get through all that, and by the time the evening ended, we were laughing and talking about Brax. So that was good. Still, I dunno. I thought he wanted me to bond with your mom on a whole different level. Now he's nowhere to be found."

"You sound like you don't trust him."

For a second I wonder if I have a right to tell Neil such personal things that have happened between Scottie and me. But who else can I tell? I've already called Summer three times tonight describing what's going on, and I've worn out my welcome on that conversation. Neil is the only other person who I feel I can talk to. I do believe that he'd kick Scottie's ass if he ever hurt or betrayed me in the slightest way.

"Until your brother does something outright disrespectful in a way that I know he's dissing me on purpose, I can't find any fault in him. He's tried to capture my heart."

"Has he succeeded?"

"Only time will tell."

At one in the morning I am dead asleep having a dream about people getting shot and killed when my cell rings. Groggy, I pick it up and say, "Hello."

"Open the door."

"Scottie? What's going on? Where you been?"

"I'll explain in a minute. Open up."

I hang up the phone and stumble out of bed, down the hall, and swing open the front door, which squeals like it's angry.

Scottie gives me a sheepish look, then brushes past me and starts pacing across my living room. He looks a combination of frustrated and worried.

"You need to start explaining yourself," I say and fold my arms under my chest. I gape at him and wait for his excuse.

"Well, you see, it's like this. I was going to do one thing but ended up doing another. And then it seemed like things weren't going to work out, but I had to do something. No way was I going to let the night end without doing *something*."

"I've never seen you act this way before."

"I've never felt this way before. It's confusing and hard and . . ."

"Are you trying to tell me something?"

"Yes, Mariah, yes."

"I really wish you'd call me by my name. Because as long as you call me Mariah, I feel like you're living in a fantasy. Like you're afraid to face who and what I really am."

"Yeah, yeah, yeah, I hear what you're saying. And I think you're right."

"Scottie, please. Do you want anything to drink?" I sniff the air and know the answer without him having to say anything.

"How many beers did you already drink?"

"More like shots and beers!"

"You went to a bar?"

"It was a nightclub."

"Without me?"

"I had to work for a minute and then I had to do some other things. . . ."

"Did the other things have to do with a woman?"

He gives me a solemn look. "Of course, Dani."

I throw my hands in the air and start pacing opposite him. "I see. I should've known better. You can't fit a square into a triangle. It wouldn't have worked. Too many odds."

"Dani!"

"No, it's cool. I'm okay with it. I'm glad you had the guts to come and tell me to my face. I've always hated cowards." I laugh, then stop. "At least you're different from the guy I dated last year. His name was Marc Fletcher. White guy! Can you believe that? When he realized he started feeling me too much, he sent me a freaking text message. He claimed how he cared about me, but he was too scared of his strong feel-ings, as he put it. He never told me he loved me. Five months of dating. Exclusive dating, mind you, and he couldn't get his mouth to form those words. But he had no trouble saying he wanted to date other women just to see if his feelings for me were real." I stop walking and look angrily in Scottie's direc-tion. "Since the bastard never called or texted me back, I guess his feelings weren't real, huh?"

I storm toward my bedroom without waiting for Scottie to reply. I stand at the foot of my bed and crawl in. I imag-ine myself being a three-year-old, like Brax, getting into bed with someone who's promised to love and protect him. I pretend like I'm crawling and making steps toward a person who will hold me in his arms, surround me with pure love, and promise that he'll never leave, he'll never hurt me, he'll never choose anyone else over me.

When I reach the top of my bed and all I find are four fluffy pillows, I can't take it anymore. I let out all the fear and anxiety I've been holding in since the last weekend in July and maybe even before.

When you've blown it in relationships too many times to count, there comes a point when you have to face the hard truth that some people just aren't meant to succeed in love. For whatever reason, God is mad at me. He doesn't want any man to stick around longer than a few nice fuck sessions, and he certainly doesn't want any decent man to put a ring on it.

I sit up, tilt my head toward the ceiling, close my eyes, and let out a piercing wail. I scream for all the times a man has told me he loves me, just to up and marry the next woman he dates after he's dumped me. I scream for every lonely night I've spent on New Year's Eve, looking at stupid music video countdowns, noticing other people smile and party with their partners, watching them kiss and hug the one they love, the one who's there with them at the end of the year, and the one who's with them at the start of another year. Scottie bursts through the door and cups his hand on my mouth. I twist and turn, and sink my teeth into his hand. He winces but still holds me. My screams weaken with every second. I stare at him, trying to breathe through the small open crevices that his fingers allow.

"What's wrong? Why are you acting like this?"

"Just go, please," I say hoarsely when he releases me. "It hurts. I can't hurt anymore."

"Me? Hurt you?"

I turn over so I won't have to face him and look into his eyes.

"Dani, talk to your man. Tell me what's going on. If you don't tell me, I won't know how to fix it."

"You should have thought about that before you did what you did."

"What did I do?" he asks, his voice filled with bewilderment.

"Break up with me!"

"W–what? Are you crazy? I'm madly in love with you."

"Right. The last man who was in love with me, took such a long-ass break that I'm still waiting to see if it'll come to an end."

"Hold on. You're with me now, not with this guy, not with Neil, not with any man but me, you get it?" Scottie kicks off his shoes and slides under the covers.

"Dani!"

"What?"

"Olive juice."

"Oh, Scottie."

"What's that? Is that a smile?"

"A smile I'm not sure you deserve." I can't help but let him see me grin. Every time he says "olive juice," which is what he said to me the first time he admitted he loves me, I can do nothing else but smile.

"I want to believe you, but your behavior tonight . . . it isn't something I'm used to. You broke our date night for the first time ever. You went to a club without me. It makes me feel uneasy, Scottie."

"It's all for a good reason. It's part of a surprise that I've planned. It'll be revealed in due time. You just have to trust me."

"T-r-u-s-t. Such a little word."

"L-o-v-e. An even smaller word. But they're both important. I'm learning things about them this year that I didn't know before."

Even though I don't understand what's he talking about, and I don't want to believe him, I do. I'm scared. But I must trust him. Trust is like the rope I need in order to hang on.

One of the biggest obstacles to diving headfirst into a relationship is getting over the trust barrier. And one thing my mother told me when I reached my twenties is, "If you can see it, it's not faith."

When I asked her what that meant, she said, "As hard as it may be, in order to love a man, you must learn to trust him, something I wasn't any good at when I was with your father. If you trust him, instead of worrying about every little thing in the relationship, things tend to work out. If he's doing something he shouldn't be doing, it'll come out in the wash," she said. "And if he proves himself to be trustworthy, you'll feel strong, the way a woman ought to feel when she loves a man."

And tonight, when Scottie asks me to trust, I take a mental leap of faith. I decide not to strip away my peace by trying to figure out his mysterious ways.

Besides, like mama says, if he's doing anything inappropriate, what I don't know now will be known one day.

The next day is Sunday, my favorite day of all because it's the most relaxing day of the week. Scottie sets up camp in the living room, watches football, and eats microwave popcorn oozing with butter and sprinkled with nacho cheddar topping. Brax stays occupied playing with fire engines and his animal farm until he's pooped and ready to take his nap. The Texans game has just started. Scottie's sitting on the love seat; his big ole feet are propped on a handcrafted wooden trunk that doubles as a coffee table.

Holding a cold beer in one hand, and a can of sugar-free ginger ale in the other, I stand next to Scottie. "Scoot over."

"C'mon, babe. What's up? You want to watch the game or you in the mood for something else?"

"Game." I sit down and place my leg on his thigh.

"Don't start nothing you can't finish, Dani."

"Oh, I can finish it all right."

I place my hand on his jersey sleeping shorts and carefully ease my fingers inside until I'm gripping his lengthy cock.

"Hey, watch it. I thought you wanted to watch the game."

"Shhh, be quiet. I'm multitasking."

"That's not what I'd call it. Hey. Ooo. Stop that unless you ready to get fucked."

I hold his cock in my hand, rubbing the shaft.

"You aren't thinking about the Texans right now, Scottie. Shame on you. I thought you were their number one fan."

He pounces on me. Instantly we're tangled together, my lips reaching for his lips. He stares me in my eyes, kissing me deeply and with so much passion my eyes roll in the back of my head. He runs one hand through my hair and maneuvers his body so that I'm sitting on the side of his lap.

"Mmmm," he moans. "C'mon. Let's go."

"Hold on a sec." I lift my arms and strip off my short-sleeved sweater. My breasts are exposed, and Scottie nuzzles my nipples with his lips. He gently bites on my breasts. I arch my neck and let him suck on me.

"Fuck, you do this to me every time. I never get to see the whole game."

He lifts me up in his arms and carries me to my bedroom. He tosses me on the bed, and within seconds he's totally naked. The sound of an afternoon rain shower heightens the atmosphere and soothes me.

"Give me some of that DSL," he says and pushes my head toward his cock. "I love your dick-sucking lips."

"I know you do."

I lie next to him and scoot down so I can swiftly take him in my mouth. I suck then lick his erect penis and hold it between my hands. Scottie rubs my hair and jerks around every few seconds. When I'm done with him, I lie on my back and spread my legs. He starts kissing my inner thighs and makes a trail on both sides until he makes small quick pecks around my vagina, like he's teasing me.

"Mmmm, go ahead, big daddy. Put your mouth on it. Suck me like I'm a frozen fruit bar."

"Mmmm," Scottie growls and presses his big tongue on my dripping twat. I love it.

I relax and let Scottie do his thing; he laps and nibbles on my twat, working his tongue on my recently shaven labia. He makes me feel so good I want to savor this feeling all night. He continues to suck my clit, staying on it until he knows he's touched my spot. I let him build me up until I start rolling my head back and forth on the pillow. I pant and moan and release the sexual energy that is bound inside of me.

"Hmm," he says, carefully examining me after eating me out. "Your twat looks like sliced pork roast, smells like tilapia, and tastes like salt."

"Sounds like I don't have to cook tonight."

"Hey, I'm ready for dessert."

He grabs a condom package from inside a drawer, rips it apart, and lets me slide it over his throbbing cock.

I climb on top of Scottie and straddle him between my thighs. We slowly stroke each other. When I thrust into him, we howl and whimper like we're singing a sexual duet.

"Does that make you feel good?" I kiss his lips and keep him from answering. He cups his hands around my butt cheeks and squeezes. I love the way Scottie's body feels when he's inside of me. Every inch of him feels like he belongs totally to me. The sexual connection we have erases any doubts I sometimes entertain when it comes to us.

Are we a really good couple or am I just fooling myself? Are the changes he says he's making only temporary? And why, by the way, did he choose to get with LaNecia last year when he could have avoided that situation altogether?

We rarely fight, but a week ago we got into it. We were over at Neil's. It was after work and time for me to pick up

Brax, but my son was asleep when I arrived. I decided to visit Scottie until Brax woke up.

I happened to need change for a fifty. I asked Scottie if he could help me out.

We were in his room chilling out on the bed. I was watching TV. Scottie was listening to his iPod.

Scottie gestured at me to get his wallet, which was sitting on the chest of drawers. I casually got out of bed, retrieved his wallet, and tried to hand it to him. But he waved his hand like it was okay for me to get change myself.

I unfolded his wallet, and the first thing I see is a small photo of him and LaNecia hugged up together. A tight knot immediately formed in my stomach. One part of me said, *This is an old picture. She's the past. He's not that into her anymore.*

Another part of me asked, *What kind of sicko messes around with his younger cousin and keeps photos of her in his wallet?*

I was so upset I didn't care about getting change anymore.

I tossed his billfold on the floor, climbed back in bed, and turned over on my stomach.

When fifteen seconds passed and the man still didn't figure out I was pissed, I sat up in bed, reached over and snatched the earbud from his ear. "Why the hell you mess around with LaNecia in the first place?"

He turned down his music and said, "You don't want to know this."

"I do, too. That situation is starting to freak me out. Summer was telling me some stuff. . . ."

"About me? She don't know me."

"True, but she brought up some valid points."

"She's just hating on us, Mariah."

"She's my girl. She knows me. She knows I'm so into you I can't see straight."

"Oh, so her job is to straighten out your twisted vision?"

"Love is blind. And maybe I need to start looking at some things I haven't wanted to see. So again, answer me. Why?"

"I, um."

"Didn't you know that wasn't cool? Did you think about the harm you could do to the girl? To yourself?"

"I don't want to talk about it."

"This is too important to ignore. It hurts me to know you were involved in something so dark and forbidden."

"You aren't one to talk."

I couldn't believe he went there with me.

"I have my faults, but at least there's a reason why I did what I did with your brother. I still don't know yours. And until you tell me something, I think I don't want to talk to you."

"Look, Dani. All I know is I care about you. The future is what's important. I know we were wrong for what we did. LaNecia is a big tease. She threw it at me. I didn't think. Plus we share great-grandparents, so hooking up with her didn't seem as bad. I blocked out the fact that we're blood. I–I just wanted to give her a try. Back then she was . . . dangerous and alluring, and I was stupid and immature. And I felt bad afterward."

"But your bad feeling didn't stop you from having sex with her again . . . and again."

"You're right. But that's basically what happened. Now you know. I'm sorry about it all and I would never, ever do anything like that again. You believe me?"

I didn't know what to believe. God knows, I felt a mixture of sadness, curiosity, anger, and confusion. But at that time I chose to believe the thing that I felt would help me and him get through this. Everyone screws up in life and deserves second chances. If Scottie could admit he made a mistake and tried hard to correct it, then I wasn't going to hold his sins against him. I felt compelled to help him live a better way. He helped me to do the same. We were connected like that.

And today, one week later, I am still acknowledging that connection. Especially the fantastic sexual chemistry that I love.

Good sex makes up for a few arguments every single time.

So here we are.

In the aftermath of a fabulous and delicious round of some of the most sensual, satisfying, yet perplexing and complicated sexual encounters I've ever experienced.

"Ahhh," Scottie moans as he lies flat on his back. Streams of sweat cover his forehead and chest.

"Hmm, you stink. You need to find your way to a shower. Now!"

"If I stink, that means I did a good job."

"You did more than good. You were wonderful."

"Am I the best you've ever had?"

"Not answering that."

"C'mon Dani. I need to know."

"You do not. We've already had this discussion. I don't want to tell too much about my past relationships."

"You asked me why I did what I did with LaNecia, so why can't I ask?"

"It's just not good for us. We should always do things

that promote our relationship. Isn't that what we agreed on?"

"Yeah, but . . ."

"But it's hard to do, isn't it Scottie?" I talk to him with gentleness. I want him to know I understand. Sometimes I adore his dedication, but it scares me if I think he's trying too hard.

My mama always told me if you have to work excessively hard at being with a man, than it wasn't meant to be.

"Babe, I don't have to know all the details. I just want to know where I fit in."

"How's this: On a scale from one to ten. You're an eleven. You're one of the few elevens I've ever had."

Scottie grins at me widely, swoops me in his arms, and cradles me like I'm a child. I love how this feels. And in spite of our challenges, I don't want this feeling to ever end.

13

ANYA

Thankful

I can't believe it's that time of year again."
It's five o'clock in the morning, during the wee hours of another Thanksgiving Day. The Earth is so quiet and peace-
fully still, it sounds as if God has gone to sleep.

I'm at home, alone in my oversize garden tub. My legs,
arms, breasts, and everything else on my body are totally
immersed in soothing hot water filled with healing salts
and jasmine-scented bubble bath. My hair is in rollers and
wrapped in a silk scarf. My head is resting against a white
foam bath pillow that perfectly supports my back. I'm reading a book of poetry and intermittently talking out loud.

"Dear Lord, thank you so much for another year. It hasn't
been a perfect year, but things could've been worse. And
I just want you to know that I feel grateful this morning. I
sure do."

As the years go by, it's easier to make assessments about
life, and think about where I've been, and decide where I
want to go. But one thing that never seems to change is how
elated I feel to be a woman. Although we don't live in the
best and safest neighborhood in town, we're not in foreclosure, and I am sentimentally attached to my home. And

even though I wish I'd given birth to more children for Neil, at least I'm Mom to a fine and mostly obedient daughter who I adore; and I'm no fool. Neil and I may have our issues, but I have a husband who's still employed, and he wonderfully manages our household. Nope, how can I feel sorry for my thirty-nine-year-old self? A lot of women would trade places with Anya Meadows. They sure would.

I close my eyes and enjoy my rare moment of quietness, which is a gift that a woman needs so her spirit can rest; then she's ready to listen and can be in tune with what she needs to do.

Minutes later, when I hear a loud rap on my door and I know it's not Neil, because he always sleeps in on Thanksgiving, I am beyond annoyed.

"Who is it?" Several people spent the night, so it could be anybody. "I'm busy."

"Scottie. May I come in?"

"What the . . . Scottie, I'm trying to take a bath, if you don't mind."

"I'm not trying to disrespect you, Anya, but it's important. Can you draw the curtain? I want to talk to you."

"I cannot believe this." I sigh. I slide the shower curtain so that I'm hiding behind it and I tell Scottie, "Come in."

I hear him open and close the door. Even though he cannot see me, I feel like he knows what I look like without clothes.

I drag the washcloth over my breasts. "What's going on?"

"Anya, I know this is going to sound crazy, but I need your advice."

"Yes, it sounds crazy!"

"Anyway, h–how did you know Neil was the one?"

"All I know is Neil didn't seem as immature as most of the other guys I dated. He was reliable, and he seemed ready for commitment. And I felt he loved me in a way that I needed. Those traits were enough to let me know Neil had what it took."

Scottie doesn't say anything. I mentally pray that God hasn't left the room and that he'll answer my prayer to make my brother-in-law go away. Far, *far* away.

"Did your family like him? Or did you care if they did?"

"Humph. My mama just told me no matter who I was with, I better not take my eyeballs off him because all men are the same. She was too busy chasing behind my daddy to be completely involved in my relationships. But I do remember when it was time to celebrate our fifth wedding anniversary and Neil paid for a week's vacation to Hawaii, my mama acted like she didn't want to take care of Reesy while we were gone."

"Why not?"

"When one woman has a hard time snagging what comes easily for another woman, she's gonna have trouble dealing with it. She'll ask herself what makes that woman better or any different than her. Neil was such a good husband. . . ."

"Was?"

I raise my voice. "Neil *is* mostly a good husband when he's focused. But I tell you, Scottie, when that lady you're chasing after was messing around with Neil, my mama couldn't wait to laugh in my face. She acted happy that my husband was unfaithful."

"How could your own mother act like that?"

"She said it was the first time she viewed me as *human*," I say, almost in a whisper. "If feeling angry and bitter and crying every night about my relationship is her definition of being human, then I guess I am."

Let's face it. There are so many unhappy people on this planet. If one woman is doing significantly better than another, sure, the lady will pretend to be happy for her. She'll say the right things with her mouth, but in her heart, and especially in her eyes, bitterness and envy take residence. The woman actually cannot wait for something bad and tragic to happen. That's the only way some people can feel good about themselves.

"So your moms was hating on her daughter because of some bullshit?"

"Pretty much. But I learned over the years to ignore those kinds of things. It's my life. The only life I will ever have. So I had to ignore the pain."

"You ignored it because the marriage is what you wanted, regardless of what anyone else thought or said?"

"Every couple goes through that. You can't please a hundred percent of the people one hundred percent of the time no matter what you choose to do." I sink farther into the bathwater. The bubbles are quickly dissipating. I wish he'd hurry.

"Have you asked all your questions?"

"Not quite. But thanks, Anya. You've helped me much more than you ever know." The smile in his voice is so bright I can envision his eyes. His feelings are clear. I've learned once a man has made up his mind about something, there's no turning him back.

"Sounds like you're in love."

"That's my baby."

"Hmmm."

"Can you see yourself loving Dani even though you don't like what happened in the past?"

"That's a tough one," I admit. "I don't hate the girl. I just wish I could reverse time. But wishing for that to happen is a waste. It is what it is."

"Do you trust her?"

"That is something for you to answer, Scottie. If you're going to be in a true, strong, and committed relationship with Dani, it's all about how you feel, not me. Now, if you don't mind, my bathwater is getting so cold I can rinse my vegetables in it."

"Sick."

"Whatever, Scottie. Let me enjoy my morning. I have a lot of cooking ahead of me and folks coming over, so . . ."

"I hear ya. We'll talk later, Anya!"

An hour later, my kitchen resembles a Ford Motor Company assembly line.

We've gathered in my usual spot. Spices, metal pans, glass bowls, casserole dishes, and utensils border every inch of counter space.

"Reesy, you can start cracking the eggs in that bowl over there. Be careful. Do it like I taught you."

"Okay, Mommy. I'll crack the eggs first in this bowl and make sure that no chickies are in the egg yolk. Yuck," she says making a face.

"That's a good girl." Vette instructs Reesy to hold her arms up so she can wrap a bright red apron around her thin waist. Reesy grabs her white cotton chef's hat and pulls it over her braids. "How do I look?"

"You look good, baby. Now get to work." Neil smiles down at his daughter, then takes her photo with his digital camera.

"Daddy!"

"Hush, girl. This is just a picture. In a minute I'm changing the setting so I can videotape y'all. That'll be good for a few laughs."

"Whatever, Neil. Anyway, Dani, don't just stand there like you've never been in a kitchen before," I say. She's at the farthest edge of the kitchen, staring at the mini flat screen that Neil bought for me and installed in the kitchen last Christmas.

"Hold on," she says looking distracted. The television is turned to the local news. Anchors are gabbing about the Thanksgiving Day parade, which is just beginning.

"I haven't been down there in ages," Dani murmurs. "Thank God the weather's nice. Maybe I can take a break and go downtown real quick. Brax would absolutely get a huge kick out of going to the parade . . . unless you need me here."

"Dani, how can you take a break when you haven't even done anything yet?" I smile, halfway teasing. "Unless toasting bread slices and putting butter on them counts for anything."

"Ouch, okay, never mind. We will skip the parade this year . . . like every year," she says. "I can only imagine what Ma and my sisters will be doing in a few hours. Cooking or going to a parade near Long Beach. Humph, knowing them, they're probably still under the covers. Good for them."

"What do you need me to do, Mrs. Meadows?" she asks tearing herself away from the television.

Just then I hear noise at the front door, which I intentionally left open earlier. Loud clicks from a few pairs of shoes sound on the hallway floor. Then LaNecia and Karetha appear in the kitchen.

"We're here," LaNecia says in a singsong voice.

"Awww, shit," Dani says. She picks up a knife and starts

chopping the green pepper and onions while trying to watch the commercial breaks from the parade.

"It is so pretty outside. It's going to be a great day." LaNecia beams.

Vette says to her, "Why are you in such a Katie Couric mood, Miss Cheerful?"

"It's a good day, girl. I ain't trying to be having a scowl on my face all the time, now am I? Plus my girl Ka is here with me, and I always feel a thousand percent better when she's around."

"Hey, everybody, what's popping? Let me wash my hands and help out."

"Ka is good people. I like that," I say. "I do. Join us. The more the merrier."

Dani murmurs, "The more, the messier. So be it."

We ladies manage to work together, each of us with our assigned kitchen duties. Ka and LaNecia oversee making homemade potato salad. LaNecia tosses ten potatoes with the skins covering them inside a twelve-quart Crock-Pot set on the rear burner of my electric stove.

Scottie walks into the kitchen, scanning the happenings with his hands on his hips.

"What's this supposed to be?" he asks Vette, who's stirring the ingredients of corn-bread stuffing.

"Boy, don't even try it. Get out the kitchen. Nothing in here for you."

"Yes, there is," he says, but his eyes remain on the stuffing.

"Greedy ass, you gotta wait till everything's done," LaNecia says out loud, cackling. "I can hear your stomach growling all the way over here."

"Whatever, cousin."

The grin drops from LaNecia's face and a grimace replaces it. "What I tell you about calling me . . ."

"Hey," Dani butts in. "Be thankful. He could call you worse."

"And I could call you worse, but I won't."

"Oh, come on now," Vette complains. "We were doing real well till the troublemaker showed up. Scottie, go on and get outta here."

"Shoot, don't worry. I gotta go on an errand anyway. I'm just saying," he says, and goes to stare at the boiling potatoes. "I'm a big, hungry man. You need to think about throwing more potatoes in the pot. I love me some 'tato salad."

"Where are you going?" Dani asks.

"To hell if I don't pray. Do you trust me, Dani?"

"Sure, of course."

"Then I'll see you in an hour. Just don't go anywhere. I want to break bread with you today."

Dani's eyes are stuck on the television. The news anchors animatedly talk as live footage of travelers are being interviewed while standing in line at Hobby Airport.

"Busiest travel day of the year. Humph. Not me. The airlines have gone nuts charging up the ass just to carry a funky bag of luggage. Crazy."

"Yep, Dani. That's why I'm glad to be celebrating the holiday at home. With family. The way things should be," I tell her. "You must miss your mother."

"I do. But that's how it goes when folks are spread out around the country. Best we can do is be on the same long-distance cellular plan and talk all we can. I tried calling Ma last night but got no answer. I'll try again in a couple of hours."

"My mother-in-law is coming over, so that'll be good.

She's gonna be watching us," I tell her and LaNecia. "All of us, so we must act like we got some good sense . . . at least while she's here we gotta act the part."

"And as soon as she leaves," LaNecia says, air-boxing with her hands, "it's on like popcorn." She high-fives Karetha.

"No popcorn today, young lady. Only good food, good conversation, and good times," I firmly tell her.

Two hours later, all of us are seated at the dining room table. A red tablecloth covers my oblong oak dining set. Neil just said grace and is scooping up greens and rice casserole for his mom.

"Where's Scott-Scott?" Sola asks, looking around the table. She's seated next to Neil, but the chair next to her is empty. "I thought this chair is for him?"

"I don't know where he is, Mother," I gently say. "He left a while ago. On an errand or something."

"He's always up to something," Neil states.

"Don't talk about your brother while he's not here, Neil. You know better than that."

Sola's words quiet the chitter chatter. I am impressed by how she takes control of the atmosphere. She's a thin-boned woman who hails from Louisiana. Her fine, dark hair is combed into a neat bun that's secured with a butterfly hair ornament. She's wearing a light wool sweater and dark slacks that for any one of us would look out of place, but Sola appears regal and classy.

"I want to say I'm glad to be able to have dinner with you today. I was sick for a minute, but God blessed me to regain my strength, and being here with the family is a true blessing."

A commotion at the front door causes everyone to turn their heads in unison toward the hallway.

Scottie, looking sheepish, steps into the dining room.

"Well, hello there, Scott-Scott." Sola beams at her son and stands up.

"Hey, gorgeous." He smiles back and gives her a kiss and a hug. "I'm sorry I'm late."

"No, you're not," Neil snaps and keeps eating.

"Brother, calm down. It was for a very good reason. I have a surprise. A huge surprise. Um, Dani, look over this way. There's something I want you to see."

Dani's eyes enlarge when she sees two young women standing in the hallway.

"Brenda!" she screams and leaps from her chair. "Chana? What are you two doing here?" She runs into the older woman's arms and hugs her so tight that the woman has a hard time laughing.

"Calm down, Sis."

"Hey, everyone, forgive me for acting like a fool, but this here is my oldest sister, Brenda. I can't believe you're here. How?" Brenda, a thirtyish-looking woman with curvy hips and a thick physique, points at Scottie.

"Scottie!" Dani laughs and throws her arms around his neck and plants kisses on his cheek.

"That's the surprise I was working on. One of the reasons I was saving my dollars so I could make this happen. I kept hearing you talk about your family. I sneaked and got their number from your phone and set up flying in Brenda and Chana."

"Excuse my rudeness. This other chick is Chana. She's two years older than me, and Brenda is four years older."

"Oh, wow, y'all look so much alike," Vette says. She gets out of her seat to shake the sisters' hands and goes to pull out additional chairs so they can join the table.

"This is such a surprise. I still can't believe it. I just don't know what to say."

"Ha-ha." Vette laughs. "This girl is in shock and, believe me, that's a rare thing to see."

Scottie takes a seat next to his mom and looks around the table, then at the food. "Hey, is anybody gonna serve a brother? I'm hungry as hell."

Dani excuses herself and grabs some extra dinner plates for Scottie and her sisters.

"Brenda, girl, it's been so long. How's Ma? I wish she could have been here. I tried to call her, but she hasn't answered. Have you talked to her?"

"Girl, calm down," Brenda answers. "You all have no idea. When Dani is around her family, she gets real excited."

"And, girl," Chana speaks up, "we've been excited to get all the dirt from your boyfriend. On the way from the airport, he's been telling us all your business."

"He'd better not." Dani pouts. "Oh, baby, you're so good to me." She covers her hands with her face and closes her eyes. Everyone at the table hushes. It's kind of a cool moment. I don't exactly care for the girl, but no matter how awful a person is, she is still someone's sister or daughter. She deserves to have her family around regardless of my issues with her.

"No, really. I'm just so happy. I . . ."

"And which of these dishes did you contribute?" Brenda asks.

"Shut up, Bren. You're pushing it now."

"Oh, you gonna do something about it? Huh? Remember how I'd beat up your little skinny behind when we were kids. Remember that?"

"Damn straight I remember. Because of you, I had to learn how to fight."

Brenda throws back her head and laughs. "Yep, 'cause before then, only thing my sister could do to save herself was to scream for Ma. I'd be pulling on her hair, pushing her on the bed, and what would Dani the baby girl do, Chana?"

"Ma! Help! Ma! Help!" Chana and Brenda burst out laughing. Brenda frowns at Dani, then points at the dining room doorway.

Dani looks up and lets out a piercing scream. "Ma!"

14

DANI

Scottie's Ultimate Surprise

I know I see what I'm seeing, yet I can't believe what I'm seeing. I take one look at my precious mommy and can't help myself.

Instead of getting up and saying hello, helping her to her seat, all that, I merely sit in my chair and release the tears that have played with my emotions ever since I saw my sisters come into the house this afternoon.

"Girl, you weren't raised right," Chana smirks. She takes over, leading our mother into a seat right next to me. My heart is bursting with love, joy, sadness, so many things.

Snot slides down my nose. Brax runs and gets me some tissues and tries to wipe my nostrils.

"Thanks, baby," I say and pull him into my lap. "See Grandma?" I laugh and shake my head. It's all I can do from kissing my mother's cheeks till they sink in. After I get over the amazement and happiness of Scottie's ultimate surprise, we all calm down and try to finish eating the best Thanksgiving dinner ever.

All we Frazier women talk nonstop. They fill me in on what's happening in California.

"Governor Terminator is totally fucking up California.

Everybody's in foreclosure, folks' cars getting repo'd. Even the movie stars are getting laid off TV shows, soaps. You name it."

"Why don't you move here?" I ask my sisters and glance at Ma. "Houston isn't suffering like the rest of the country."

"I love my good weather," my mother protests. "You can't beat California sunshine."

"Especially if you're homeless with no car, huh, Ma?" I tease.

We continue to dish about Long Beach until Vette is the first to push herself back from the table and declare, "I'm through."

Once she does that, Neil follows suit. Before long, most everyone makes a trail into the den or the kitchen. The sounds of cheering during a televised NFL game can be heard from where I'm sitting. Ma sighs contently and rubs her belly.

"That was some tasty food," Ma replies. "And that man Scottie, now he's a good one. I was skeptical at first with him being so much younger than you."

"Ma! Only five years."

"The most important thing is how he treats you. I can tell you like being around him. That's a good thing. God knows I hated how you were involved with what's-his-face."

"Ooo, Ma. Neil. You know his name. I see you said hello to him after a while," I gently scold. "Neil's your grandson's father."

"Yeah, well, that's not my schnookum's fault."

"Ma. Be good. How long will you be here?"

"As long as the good Lord sees fit."

"Don't even try it. What's the date on the ticket for your return flight?"

"Don't worry about it. You need to be filling my plate with some of that homemade apple pie I've been staring at. It *is* homemade, isn't it, and not one of those frozen pies that you like to defrost or anything?"

"Ma, I'm going to get you." I laugh. "I love you, Ma. I do. This is one of the happiest surprises."

We're interrupted when Anya returns to the dining room, followed by LaNecia. Anya is holding the digital camera in her hand. The red light is on, and she's pointing the darned thing at me.

"See, LaNecia, go on; don't be scared," Anya says. "La-Necia here wants to be a filmmaker. I've asked her to go around and videotape us enjoying the holiday. She was supposed to enroll in school so she could learn how to do this professionally, but we're not going to talk about that right now."

"Aw, Anya, that's wrong. It's cool, though. I'll videotape a few people."

"Remember, I asked if you'd like to start making videos a while ago."

Scottie walks past us and stands next to the apple pie.

"This isn't exactly the type of video I had in mind, but I guess it'll have to do for now." She snickers, then aims the camera at Scottie's back and starts filming. He doesn't notice because he has a huge knife in his hand and it appears like he's on the hunt for some dessert. He calls over his shoulder, "Anybody want some of this so I won't have to eat it all by myself?"

"I do. I do," LaNecia shouts. "Cut me a piece, sweetie."

LaNecia continues walking slowly behind Scottie pointing the lens at his butt.

Ma frowns and gives me a questioning look.

I whisper, "I'll tell you about it later."

Later that evening, many of us are sitting around the den. Anya decides it's a good time to start pulling out her stupid Christmas decorations. That's my cue to get the hell out of the room. I keep yawning anyway and I am anxious to go home to my own apartment, kick off my shoes, and curl up on the sofa and watch a classic movie.

I notice that Scottie is MIA. I excuse myself from the room and start walking around the first floor. He can't be found in the kitchen, dining room, or library. I run upstairs and don't bother knocking on his bedroom door. I hold my breath but exhale immediately. He's not in his room, and the bed is neatly made up.

I am about to go back downstairs when I hear voices coming from the room where Vette and I slept during the hurricane, the spare room she hangs out in whenever she spends the night.

"So girl, um, what's up with you and him? Y'all gonna meet up tonight or what?"

I recognize Karetha's voice, and I lean in so that my ear's touching the door.

"Got to. It's getting ridiculous. Please, I need to do this. It's been much too long since I've been fucked good."

"Mmm, I heard that. I'll bet you'll be screaming home-boy's name like crazy by the time midnight comes."

"I sure hope so. His dick is so thick and long. . . ."

"Ugh. I do not want to hear this. . . ."

"Well, you're going to hear it, Ka. I love how he lets me get on top and bounce up and down. It feels so good. Hmm, what time is it?"

My heart beats so loud I'm sure they can hear me snooping outside the door. What the hell does Scottie think he's doing scheming to meet with LaNecia after he's done this dog and pony show bringing my family to Houston for the holiday? He's not about to embarrass me. I step away from the door, but they start talking again and I run back over to listen.

"You love him?"

"I dunno," LaNecia says. "Love is weird, complicated, tricky, and most of all, it can be the biggest liar."

"You have never lied," Karetha says.

"Ha! Yes, I have." The two disgusting tramps hoot and holler like something is funny. But nothing is funny. I feel like crying, falling to the carpet and lying in a fetal position. This is why it's hard for me to feel happy. It seems like a trick, but not a magical trick like my mama was talking about earlier. This feels like one of those cruel tricks that start out seemingly promising, but the next thing you know a curtain gets pulled back and all your worst enemies are on the other side of it laughing at you.

I feel furious.

I try my best to quietly and calmly walk back downstairs without letting my emotions give me away. I go in the den and sit by Brenda. A Tyler Perry movie is playing on the TBS channel and she's engrossed in what the character Madea is doing. But seconds after I take a seat, I feel my sister's eyes boring into me.

She whispers, "What's up, Yell?" *Yell* is a childhood nickname. She's the only person who calls me that.

"Nothing." I shrug.

"Don't bullshit me. I know you, Yell. Your hands are shaking. What happened? Tell me."

"Shhh, come with me outside."

I begin walking until I reach the front door, which is

still open. I can see straight through the full-glass storm door.

When I look outside, Scottie's standing next to LaNecia. Her arms are folded across her chest. He is leaning toward her and grabs her arms, like he's about to shake her. I can tell she's saying something back to him. Piercing anger covers her face. Then she looks calmer. He takes his hands off her. They continue talking. But what are they talking about? Are they making final arrangements about how and where they're going to meet later on? I can't believe how Scottie had all of us fooled. My mom, my sisters, Summer Holiday. And especially me. Is this what happens when I try my best to trust someone?

With a thick lump closing up my throat, I turn around and gesture at Brenda. She remains close behind me as I run upstairs. I start to go into Scottie's room, but it would feel like entering a brutal crime scene. So I walk into the bathroom, tell her to come on in, and shut the door.

"Girl, what the fuck is your problem? You look like you about to lose your mind."

"LaNecia is about to drive me nuts."

"Yeah, she's so annoying. Like overkill with all the talking, laughing, and gesturing with her hands."

"She's so full of shit." I begin to explain that she's Scottie's cousin, but she is attracted to him and refuses to leave him alone.

"Oh, hell no, this is where you're wrong. This is your man's problem, not that young bitch. Put the blame on him, never on the other female."

"But he says he's done with her."

"Then why is he outside having private conversations with her instead of being in the house with you like he oughta be? I have a mind to go out there and cuss his black ass out."

"No, Brenda, please don't do anything, don't say anything. Damn, I hate this."

"You got yourself into some shit this time. Damn, Yell. Why you always end up with the wrong kind of man, huh?"

She's making me feel bad, and I want to curse her out because it's not like she's anybody's wife or girlfriend, so why is she getting on my case? But I decide to chill and deal with Brenda later.

I tell her about the conversation I overheard between LaNecia and Karetha.

"They got some fucked-up ghetto names, man, oh man. Maybe you're better off, Sis. Let that ho have him. That's some twisted shit. You don't want to be involved with a man who'll fuck anybody, anywhere."

"Please Brenda, you're making things worse."

"*I'm* making things worse? How? I haven't cheated on your ass. I'm just talking about it. That's worse? You need to decide how you gonna handle your business or else I'm 'bout to do it for you."

"No, no, don't say anything. I don't want Ma to know."

"Ooo, you better be glad I'm up here right now. I could go and kick that mutha's teeth out his damn mouth. And he got a pretty set of teeth, too. I'll have that punk looking like Leon Spinks after a boxing match."

"Brenda, shhh. I hate that I told you."

"I'm glad you told me, because I do not like hearing about any man mistreating my baby sis. He's got to be outta his mind. Sick fuck!"

My cell phone starts ringing.

"Who is it?" Brenda asks. I show her the phone.

"Oh, let me answer the bitch. I got something for his ass."

"No, Brenda. I'll let it go into voice mail. Maybe Scottie will leave a message."

Seconds later, my phone rings again.

"Let me get that." Brenda snatches my phone from my hand.

"Hello," she says loudly. "Yeah, she's right here. How may I help you?" I look at my sister like she's insane. "Yeah, all right. Later."

She hands back my phone. "He said for you to come downstairs in about ten minutes. He has some special type of dessert that he wants everyone to sample."

"What?"

"Don't kill the messenger, Sis."

"That's not who I want to kill."

We emerge from the restroom after ten minutes of arguing about why Scottie is taking time to make some stupid dessert. I am so mad at him I really want to say *Fuck him and his pastries*. But Brenda convinces me to come downstairs. We hear a lot of noise coming from the dining room and decide to see what's going on.

As soon as we enter the room, it gets a teensy bit quieter. Ma, Neil, and Anya are sitting at the table. Chana's seated next to Vette. LaNecia and Karetha are standing against the wall whispering to each other. I feel very awkward. All I want to do is corner Scottie and ask him what's up between him and his cousin.

Scottie pokes his head inside the doorway and barks orders. "Dani, Brenda, have a seat right there."

I slump in my chair. Ma smiles gently at me and whispers, "I've had the best time, daughter. This is the most fun I've experienced in a long while."

"I'm glad you feel that way," I murmur.

Finally, Scottie emerges from the kitchen holding a turkey-shaped cake pan between two red pot holders.

"Hey, that's so cute," Vette chirps. "I never knew my brother to be a baker."

"There are a lot of things I'm trying to do that are different," he replies.

"So I've heard," I say, unable to help myself.

"Before y'all think I've turned gay, I just wanted to do something real special for the holiday," Scottie says, looking around the table. He comes and stands next to me and sets the cake pan on the table. "First of all, I can't go any further without saying that for obvious reasons I have a lot to be thankful for. I've gone through a lot in my twenty-five years. Lost my dad. Got into some trouble with the law. Made some decisions that my family didn't like," he says, looking down at his feet then back at us. "But I take complete responsibility for the choices I've made. My goal is to be happy that God has spared my life, given me another chance, and blessed me to do better than what I've done in the past."

I sit there listening to him and fuming on the inside. I don't care to hear his phony-ass speech. If I could throw up I would, but I don't even feel like wasting a good turkey dinner on this dude.

Scottie continues talking. "One of the best things about today is because of a young lady who's in this room right now."

I stiffen. *Uh-oh. Here it goes. He's about to embarrass me. What have I ever done to him?*

"And because of how I feel about her, I want her to do the honors of having the first piece of this Thanksgiving cake."

"Cute," I say and glare at him. "Funny how this cake looks just like you."

"Dani, babe, open the cake pan and let me slice a piece for you." Perspiration covers Scottie's forehead. He laughs nervously, gawking at me like he really wants me to taste the dessert he's made.

"Go on. Take a look at the cake, Dani."

Annoyed, I place my hand on top of the cake pan, then lift it.

"Oh my goodness," I shriek. Instead of a cake, there's a sparkling diamond and gold ring sitting inside a ring box. "What's this?"

Scottie looks from me to my mother. "Mrs. Frazier, I love your daughter very much. . . ." I hear gasps in the background. "And nothing would please me more than to get your blessing. 'Cause I wanna marry her and I need to know it's okay with you."

"Scottie, stop it. . . ."

"Neil, please," Anya says, her voice rising. She sounds so seriously angry that Neil shuts up.

Oh my God, I say to myself. *This is unreal. It's crazy.* Brenda beams at me and hugs me in a tight squeeze.

"It's great, isn't it?" she beams.

"You knew?" I ask. "You just pretended to dislike him when you were complaining about him in the restroom?" She nods and blows a kiss at me.

"Yep, I know how much he cares about you, and no other woman," she answers, glancing at LaNecia. "You lucked out this time, Yell. My baby sis is gonna have a hubby."

Ma nods and claps her hands. She turns to Scottie, who's anxiously waiting by her side. "I give you my blessing under one condition. Promise me you'll treat my daughter right."

"I promise."

"If I ever hear that you've hurt her . . ."

"Then give me a call," Sola interrupts smiling graciously at my mom.

I cannot believe Scottie's mom is taking up for me. I mean, the lady has always been fairly pleasant with me, but I would never claim that she's absolutely crazy about me. So her gesture touches my heart in a deep way. And, instantly, the stress and strain of the entire day takes its toll. I laugh, giggle, smile, and cough uncontrollably.

"Damn, the girl is gonna choke to death before she even says yes to getting married," Brenda teases.

Soon everyone in the room is excited. Everyone except LaNecia. From across the room, she glares at me with the most hateful look I've ever seen.

As soon as Scottie hugs my mom and then Sola, he gets down on one knee and takes my hands in his.

"Babe, I know we haven't known each other long, but I know what I want. And what I want is you. Nobody but you. So you wanna do this? You wanna take a chance with your boy and get married?"

"Scottie, don't play. This is unreal."

"It's not fake, baby. It's real. I love you, Danielle Frazier."

"Go on, say yes," Vette says. "You're like family anyway."

"I hear you and I know what you mean. And I am so touched and so moved, Scottie, believe me. I–I care about you so much, it hurts. And you're the best thing that's happened to me in a very long time."

"So is that your long-ass way of saying yes?"

"That's my way of saying 'Um, I gotta get back with you on that.'"

"Eww, I knew that bitch was crazy," LaNecia says and

storms from the dining room. Karetha gazes at me like she can't believe what I just said. She leaves the room, too.

Scottie looks confused. "What did you say? You don't want to marry me?"

"Yes, I do, I do want to marry you, Scottie."

"Then that's a yes."

"No, it's not. It's a 'Wait a second and let me think.'"

"What's there to think about? I love you, Dani."

"I know but . . ."

"But what?"

"Stop yelling at me. You're confusing me. I–I just . . ."

Rushes of frantic voices fall on top of one another. I see mouths moving, but I can't hear anything. My eyes remain transfixed on the ring. Three round shimmering diamonds are clustered in the center of the gold band. Scottie quickly snatches the ring off the cake pan and flees the dining room. The front door opens and slams.

My sister's lips curl into a frown.

"You really fucked up this time, Yell. You see how big those diamonds are? Oops, *were*?"

15

SCOTTIE

I Want to Be Your Husband

Scottie's behind the wheel of his Escalade speeding down Airport Boulevard. Where he's going, he doesn't know or care. When he sees the outline of a neighborhood patrol car, he barely hits his brakes.

Just go on and take me the fuck away. I don't give a damn. I don't care about anything or anybody.

His cell phone rings incessantly. First the screen reads "Mom." Then "Sister." Then "Necia." Then "Mom" again. Then his phone starts making bleep noises. Texts fill his Inbox.

One part of him feels glad that people are trying to get in touch with him. *But none of these is who I want to hear from.*

The Escalade glides along, going west. Scottie reaches the Beltway, turns right, and figures out what he ought to do.

She said she needs to think about it. If you love someone, there's nothing to think about. Oh! Right! The woman doesn't really love me. She's been going through the motions. She's been too polite to tell me she really ain't feeling me like I've been feeling her.

Scottie continues to think about where he went wrong. He knows that he and Dani have been experiencing good times the past several weeks. Their daily routine has consisted of waking up in each other's arms whenever he spent the night with her. But many times she's told him to his face that he wakes up to go to work way too early for her tastes. Five-thirty sometimes. And she has to be at work at eight-thirty, sometimes nine.

"Honey, as much as I get a kick out of reaching out at night and feeling your hot body next to mine, I enjoy sleeping in. So you can't spend the night all the time. Okay?" That's the news she gave him not too long ago. He felt hurt, but he understood. He figured he needs to know as much info about her quirks and preferences as possible. Since he's been planning on making Dani his wife, some things he just needs to know.

1. No matter how much she begs, try not to feed her anything that has more than ten grams of sugar in it. Her blood sugar will go up, and that's no good for her health.
2. If he uses her toilet and lifts the seat up, remember to put it back down. And if he accidentally pees on the toilet, clean the shit up (her words, not his).
3. Please be a good guy and do things like taking out the trash from her apartment without her having to ask. That gesture means he cares about her and is willing to do those manly things that she's always been forced to handle on her own.
4. If they get into a big argument, don't even let his mind consider putting his hands on her. He told her, "Oh, you don't have to worry about that. I can never hit a woman." She laughed and told him, "Yeah right. That's what thousands of men have said. And the judge sentenced them

to capital punishment, and now these men are sitting on death row thinking about their last meal."

5. If you need to borrow money, skip over asking Dani. Dani told Scottie a man should never rely on a woman for money. He should be responsible enough, or have enough hustle to get money on his own without nickel-and-diming his girl. She told him, "If you can't afford me, you shouldn't be with me." So he works as much OT as he can. And he's picked up a few deejay jobs here and there just so he can make the kind of money it's going to take to make Dani a keeper.

6. You are not Braxton's father. You are not Braxton's father. Dani has reminded Scottie of that fact a few times. He would try and discipline Brax, who sometimes insists on his way. When Dani would remind him, he'd insist, "I'm acting like his uncle, not his daddy." Dani took one look at Scottie and said, "Hmm, I'll be the one who decides that."

7. Don't even think about asking to move in. Dani told Scottie that she hates to bring up her past, but one time she met a man who she really started liking. Before she knew it, every time he came over to her place, he'd bring a shirt here, pants, razor kit, gym shoes, and some hand weights. "Whoa, whoa, whoa," she told the guy one day when she noticed he'd stolen the extra key to her apartment as if he had a right to it. "If I ever decide that you and I should live together, it's going to be a mutual decision. Not because you'll argue that all your shit is over at my place anyway."

8. Women. "I am faithful to you." That's all she told him a month ago. She said what she had to say, then walked away. Scottie read between the lines. He knows Dani

has nothing to go on except her trust in him when he swears he's not fucking LaNecia. But Scottie also knows that although she may not say it out loud, maybe it's not only LaNecia she's referring to. LaNecia isn't the only woman with a pretty face, hot body, and a willingness to have sex with Scottie.

Scottie travels along the highway and drives until he comes to the Katy Freeway. Then he starts traveling west on I-10. He drives until he finds himself sitting in his vehicle outside Dani's apartment. He sits and he waits.

Heavy eyelids and a wave of sleepiness fall over him. He's sitting in the driver's seat, leaning his head against the coolness of the hard window, when he hears a knock. He jumps and peers out somberly.

Dani struggles to hold Brax in her arms. Scottie jumps out of the car, takes Brax from Dani, and together they enter her apartment. Scottie carries his nephew to his bedroom; removes his clothes, shoes, and socks; and dresses him in his PJs. He tucks the boy in bed, gives him a kiss on the forehead, and secures a stuffed animal between his little arms, then closes the door.

Dani is in the living room, perched in a far corner of her sofa, hugging an orange-and-brown-striped accent pillow. Scottie, with his hands lodged in his pants pockets, sits near her.

"What you thinking about?" he softly asks.

"Us."

"And?"

"I think you took things the wrong way."

"How else do you expect me to take them?"

"If you want us to be together, you're going to have to be patient and understanding."

"I'm listening."

"Understanding means giving me time to explain myself. Maybe I–I didn't say it very well over there, but you gotta trust that I mean well. I dunno, Scottie. You absolutely caught me off guard. The entire day actually. My family coming in like that. My sister pretending like she disliked you. Then an unexpected public proposal, mind you." She laughs, then turns serious. "It felt like a fucking dream. I wasn't sure if I was gonna wake up, and it would be the day after Thanksgiving, and I'd be waking you up in bed, trying to explain to you this crazy dream I had."

"So you think all of this is a game?" He stands up. "A man needs to be told point-blank. Men can't catch hints, so don't throw them."

"I wasn't throwing any. . . ."

"If you don't want me, tell me. I think that's the best way to handle things."

"See, there you go. You're getting upset for no reason."

"I made a complete fool out of myself. Did you see how happy Neil looked when you were fucking around back there, not sure if you wanted to be with me or not? I swear he almost came on himself. Maybe you ain't over my brother like I hoped you were."

Dani stands and stares at him incredulously. "Okay, now you're wrong. I–I don't care about Neil like that anymore. Life has gone on. Don't you know that?"

"Do *you* know that?"

"Well . . ." She bites her lip. "Maybe you shouldn't propose to a woman who has a child with your brother."

"So that's what this is about? I knew it. You're still fucking in love with Neil."

"Scottie, don't say that."

"Why not? Because it's the truth?"

"It–it's complicated, Scottie. Yes. I'll admit that much. But it's not what you think."

"Then what is it exactly? Explain!"

"Well, in the beginning, it was kind of confusing and somewhat freaky, actually. I'd never ever in my life dated two guys from the same family. It felt weird. Then it felt all right because I developed genuine feelings for you. You are kind, funny, different. We click in a way I wasn't expecting. I let down my guard."

"But I didn't compare to him, huh?"

"Scottie," she begs. "Please. But then I got scared and started worrying. I wondered what I would say if I ran into anyone I knew. What would I say if they asked 'Who's this guy? How'd you meet?' Would they be disgusted when they found out we met at Neil's family reunion? Would they think I'm so desperate for a man that I will do anything to have one? Scottie, I could hardly sleep at night sometimes, I'd be freaking out about things so much, I–," she says in a quieter, calm tone, "I even ran to the drugstore and bought a bar of chocolate."

"You what?"

"Yes." She nods emphatically. "The stress got to me so much I thought the only thing that would soothe it would be either sex or chocolate. You were gone, so sex was out of the question."

"Hmm, well, that's good to hear. I'd rather you turn to a Snickers bar than another man." He laughs bitterly. "Especially if that man turns out to be my brother."

"See, that's my point, Scottie. I am hoping you've thought everything out."

"You think I don't wonder if you and I will have a big-ass fight one night, and you go crawling back to him behind my back?"

She nods, her bottom lip trembling.

"I have thought and thought about all this. Wondering if I should give it up, wondering if I'm being too hard on myself, trying to make myself into a better man." He pauses. "Sometimes I wonder if it's easier just to go back to being a manwhore and screwing the whole thing."

"Is that what you used to be? What you want to be?"

"I want to be your husband, Dani. That's all I want."

Scottie feels so stressed out that his shirt is sticking to his chest, making him feel uncomfortably hot. "May I get a cold drink, please?"

"You don't have to ask. You know where the beer is."

"Ha!" He laughs and walks to the kitchen. Dani follows him. "That's what I'm talking about. I'm free to get a beer if I want, but I can't do this or do that. You have a lot of rules, woman."

"I'm sorry you feel that way, but I just think I'd feel better if I know what I'm getting myself into. I have to know and understand what makes me happy or comfortable."

"And that's the problem. Everything is about accommodating Dani Frazier."

"W—what did you say?"

"Don't get me wrong. I have been busting my ass to please you, Dani. I knew you were high-maintenance the first time I laid eyes on you. But a brother needs some sign of appreciation. Not that I'm bragging, but I didn't get that engagement ring from no bubble gum machine."

He opens the refrigerator, snatches a cold can of beer, pops the top, and takes a swig.

"You're right about one thing. I do have rules. And my number one rule is for you to back off from LaNecia. You told me she's the past. I want to believe you because of my insistence that Neil and I are over, too."

"Mariah . . ."

She clears her throat.

"Excuse me. Dani, I promise you on my father's grave, I am done, forever, with LaNecia. If I really loved her, why did I propose to you?"

Dani gives him a tiny dazed smile.

"Can I, um, you still have the ring?"

"C'mon, Danielle." He takes her by the hand, and they return to her living room sofa. They sit down this time right next to each other. He reaches in his pocket, takes out the jewelry box, and retrieves the diamond and gold ring.

"Wow, it's beautiful. Where'd you get it?"

"Not telling you."

"How much it cost?"

"Ha!"

"May I put it on, please? I just want to see if it fits."

"What?"

"Scottie, I'm Cinderella who's looking for her glass slipper. You're the prince and you have to slide that glass slipper on me to see if it perfectly fits."

Scottie moans and stares deeply into Dani's eyes.

"If the ring fits, sounds like I'm going to be your wife. Besides, I've always wanted to be a Mrs. Meadows."

PART 2

FOR BETTER
OR WORSE

16

DANI

Why Are You Marrying My Brother?

My family's visit lasted through the weekend, and it felt so good to spend time with them. But now the holiday is over. The marriage proposal is a done deal. I ask permission to get off work early on the Friday following Thanksgiving. I need to take care of some business with an issue that involves upgrading my high-speed Internet connection. I'm puttering around at home waiting for a service person to arrive from Comcast.

I begged Neil to pick up Brax early from day care for me and drop him off at my place since I am basically captive in the apartment from noon to five until the cable guy shows up. Earlier, when I first asked, Neil hesitated, then agreed, and now he's here. It's been months since he's been with us in my spot. I feel a little nervous having him here, especially since my engagement, but I decide to play things off.

We've congregated in the living room. Brax is sandwiched between us on the couch. He's giggling and yelping as he tinkers with his daddy's Amazon Kindle. Brax gives Neil a sheepish look. He then lifts up the Kindle and sets it against Neil's jaw, and tries to roll it up and down his cheeks.

"Ha-ha, he's trying to say you need to shave, Neil. My baby's going to be a fashion stylist."

"The heck he is. Braxton's going to do something good with his life. He'll either be an architect, an engineer . . ."

"Or a mack daddy. . . ."

"Dani, stop acting silly. Take it back. Don't put that mess in my son's head."

"He's my son, too."

"Only fifty percent."

I smirk and roll my eyes. "Then fifty percent of him might be an architect. . . . The other fifty of him just might be a clothes designer, or an electrician. You know he's fascinated with turning lights on and off."

"Yeah, he's probably putting on the lights to see if you've made it home at night and are in your bed like you're supposed to be."

"If I wasn't sure if you still cared about me, now I know. Dammit, Neil, when will you accept the fact that I am not your freaking daughter? I had your child, but I'm not one of your kids, and you need to stop trying to run my life."

"You hate that I do that, huh?"

"Very much. About as much as I hate brussels sprouts."

"I'll make sure and fix brussels sprouts for dinner next time you invite yourself over to our house to eat."

"Ha! I don't need to roll up in your crib to eat. I can cook."

"Heating up a frozen microwave dinner isn't cooking, Dani."

"Fuck you, Neil. I'm sick of you dissing me every time I turn around." Hot water springs in my eyes but I quickly wipe my tears. Thank God he's busy kissing Brax on the top of his head. I wouldn't want Neil to see me cry. In the past, I could get away with coming to him and discussing certain problems that bothered me. But now? My problems won't be Neil's problem anymore.

"I'm just saying . . . it's time you learned to do certain things you've gotten away with in the past." He pauses. "Y'all set a date yet?"

"What? Absolutely not. I'm still getting used to the fact that I won't be single for much longer."

"It's never too late to change your mind, ya know."

"Of course you'd say that, Neil." He can't look me in my eyes. I can tell he's thinking, maybe even harboring regrets. And this is the part I hate the most. I am trying my damnedest to move on. Gosh I am. But Neil makes it hard for me whenever he wears his emotions on his sleeve. Sure he may act gruff and unconcerned, but I know this man so well. No new guy can erase that. Especially since I was so deeply in love with Neil that it hurt me to pieces. I used to sniff my sheets and pillowcases every time he left my bed. I wanted to savor his scent, just inhale his presence; it was my way of filling the void he left every time he went back to his wife. I know it's wrong. But it's part of my history, and the pleasures I shared with Neil aren't anything I'm soon to forget, even though I doubt I can ever admit these feelings to my soon-to-be hubby.

"He can barely take care of himself. Have you seen him wash a load of clothes?"

"I know. He mixes whites with dark colors. Crazy. But I handle his laundry now."

"That's a shame. A real man should at least know how to read labels on his clothes before he decides to pop the question."

"I doubt that being an expert at washing clothes makes anyone ready for marriage. You know that, Neil. You're being silly."

"I don't care what you say. My brother has no business getting married."

"Were you one hundred percent ready when you wed what's-her-face?" I smile.

"That's cold, Dani. But I'll be honest. No one is ever really ready to get married."

"Thanks for admitting that, Neil."

"You just gotta go for it. That's especially true for a man. He can date a dozen women who he really cares for, but he won't commit. Then one will come along at the right time, and he'll jump up and marry her. No reasonable explanation whatsoever. And his exes will be pissed wondering why he didn't shape up and ask her when he had the chance."

"Men are weird."

"Then why are you marrying my brother?"

"Scottie's been good to me."

"I was, too."

"It's funny how men have selective retention when it comes to certain topics. You thought you were good to me, but you really weren't one hundred percent good."

"No, but I was close."

"Not close enough, obviously. What time is it? I'm getting a headache talking about this. Bottom line, it doesn't matter how much you pout, like it or not, Mr. Meadows, one day I'll be your sister-in-law." I throw back my head and laugh. Brax looks shocked, then he joins me and starts giggling. I place my fingers under his arms and tickle him. He fights me and rolls back on his daddy's lap, kicking and screaming.

"Does he deserve you, Dani? Did you know one of his favorite computer passwords is 'yssup'? Pussy spelled backward."

"How did you know his password?"

"Because Scottie was stupid enough to go around and brag about something like that. Does that tell you anything? He's good for what he's good for. That's all I'm saying."

"Well, thank you for giving me your blessing in your own strange and totally selfish way, Neil. I'll take what I can get at this point."

Fate is an amazing thing.

I may not have gotten Neil, but I got the next best thing. And now I'm prepared to deal with everything that goes along with the preparation of officially being declared Mrs. Prescott Meadows.

The next week, I go to my job as an executive administrative assistant at a pharmaceutical company in West Houston. I hold out my hand and smile at my coworkers. They gape, scream, hop out of their swivel chairs, and jump up and down with me in a circle.

Then I ask Summer to cancel whatever she has going on and meet me for lunch and shopping. She says okay and I pick her up, and we drive on the north side to Willowbrook Mall. This mall is so substantial, it houses *two* Macy's: One for women, and another one just for men and furniture.

Summer and I park and begin a casual trek through the mall. Christmas is only a few weeks away; the flickering holiday lights, giant wreaths, and stringed decorations give the mall an enchanted and magical atmosphere. As we walk around admiring the scenery, I am nearly bursting inside with news about my engagement, but I decide to hold it in. Summer's been traveling out of state lately, and I am dying to see the expression on her face when I share the good news.

Today she is wearing an off-white cashmere sleeveless sweater and light brown slacks with four-inch pumps. She's clutching the handle of a spiffy-looking Dooney & Bourke leather tote with a croc print, a bag so huge it's nearly half her size.

"Christmas must have come early for you." I tease her, admiring her fancy new outfit and sophisticated bag.

"Oh, girl, my honey Andre got me these things. And yep, you're right, they're an early Christmas present, with more on the way. I feel so lucky." She sighs contentedly. I feel like I should let her enjoy her moment.

But when we pass by a Waldenbooks, I grab Summer by the hand and drag her inside. I head straight for the videos and DVDs section. When I find what I'm searching for, I screech "Yeah" and snatch up a copy of one of my favorite films.

"I's getting married," is the line I steal from *The Color Purple* to break the news to Summer. I wave the DVD at her, then my hand, and flash my engagement ring.

"Oh, fuck! Oh, shit!" she screams. I laugh and hug her, and we rock back and forth on our heels for five minutes. "I can't believe you held it in so long and didn't tell me."

"I wanted to share this moment with you in person, not on the phone."

"Well, thanks. I appreciate that."

"You're in the wedding. I know that much."

"I'd be honored, Dani. I've never been in a wedding before."

"That makes two of us."

We hug again, then browse a couple of jewelry stores to ogle other engagement rings and wedding bands. We simply enjoy ourselves on a chilly but pleasant December afternoon, talking about men and dreaming about the future.

"What about you?" I ask. "How are things with you and Andre?"

Andre and Summer have been dating for about six months. His eyes are wide and deep-set; his skin is golden brown like a delicious honey bun.

"You know what, girl. I hate to say this and knock on all kinds of wood, but our sex life is getting better and better. And that's strange, because at one point, it seemed to dwindle. I even got bored. It was routine and sucked, no pun intended."

"What changed things?"

"I went out with another guy. Nothing serious. He's my homeboy for real, and I don't care for him in a romantic way, but when I decided to be honest with Andre and let him know my plans, girl, he straightened his ass up big-time. He called more, wanted to spend the night with me. And that's when the freaky stuff really got started."

"Oh, do tell."

"Well, we're very much into oral. Our lovemaking is three steps: foreplay, raw fucking, and pillow talk. When we stick to that, and throw in a little bit of surprises here and there, Andre always comes over on time."

"Mmm. Scottie and I have a pretty active sex life, too. It's funny. We usually do it after we've eaten and my baby loves to grub. I like to tease him that he has so much cholesterol in his body, if you suck his dick you'd swear you were eating an omelet."

"Yeah, right, you wish you *could* eat an omelet."

"Oh Scottie's body is delicious. Especially after he's

showered and shaved. His skin is so smooth it feels like velvet. I love our sex life. But I want to be like you and Andre. I want something to happen that gets his attention."

"What do you mean? Obviously something already did. He proposed!"

"Yeah, but Neil told me it's never too late to change my mind. That if I want to break off the engagement for any reason, I should, even if I have to pull an Eddie Murphy and dump Scottie two weeks after the wedding. Can you believe that?"

"He can be a self-centered prick. Sorry, I know that's your baby daddy and all, but jeez. Anyway, like I was saying, I had to do what it takes for my own relationship. And if going out on a casual date is what needed to change things, it was worth it. That's when the guy seriously started to buy me really nice presents."

"Damn, so that did the trick, huh? The threat of another man? Even if it's just a bone-headed friend?" I file that info in the back of my head.

"Girl, these men are so territorial. Andre has his little blue toothbrush standing prominently in the toothbrush holder in my bathroom. He's got his own drawer where we keep condoms, and K-Y Jelly, and . . ."

"Okay, I get the picture."

Summer beams at me.

"Things are about to change for us in a major way. I have big decisions to make."

"Both of you have decisions. Get used to including your man in these things."

"Right. It's funny to dream of what you want and then when you get it . . ."

"You don't know what to do with it. You aren't lying,

girl. Now that I have a good, happy relationship with Andre, it's like I'm looking over my shoulder, under my bed, to see if I'm forgetting anything."

"We women are so programmed to believe that we can't have or deserve happiness that when we find it, we may feel guilty, or undeserving."

"Fuck that, Dani. I am going to enjoy my man for as long as I can. But I still gotta do what I gotta do to keep his ass on his toes."

"Girl, did I ever tell you this? Remember I told you how I heard LaNecia and her friend talking in the bathroom at Neil's house? And I was so pissed because it sounded like I heard her plans for them to hook up with each other and have sex behind my back, all that?"

"Yeah, whatever happened?"

"A couple days after Scottie and I got engaged, I decided I couldn't hold it in any longer, so I brought up the topic to him. I admitted I overheard that conversation."

"And what did he say?"

"First, he told me I shouldn't eavesdrop. Whatever, right?" I laugh. "But he said if I ever want to know something, I should immediately come to him no matter how awkward it makes me feel. Because what really happened is that LaNecia decided to get her horny ass some loving, and not with Scottie. It was with another guy, Summer! I heard wrong."

"Damn, that little girl is a mess. What was she trying to do, make Scottie jealous or something?"

"That's what she hoped would happen, but it backfired. And if that bitch keeps stepping into my territory, it'll be time for me to fire back. I'm the one he put a ring on, and now it's my job to make sure she doesn't do anything to take my ring off."

— 17 —

ANYA

The Day I Turn Forty

Damn," *Vette says to* me. "It's kind of weird that you're going to help pick out supplies for your own party." It's one week before December twentieth, the day I turn forty. My birthday falls on a Saturday this year and I look forward to doing something special. Vette and I have just stepped out of my SUV and are walking into Party City, a discount superstore located off the Southwest Freeway in a busy part of town near Joel Osteen's famous church.

I've decided that a casino night theme will work perfectly. At this point in my life, there's no turning back. Life is like a gamble, and we're going to be rolling some major dice next Saturday.

"Vette, please. I don't mind picking out decorations and party favors. It's fun. Why wouldn't I want to be involved?"

"I know you're not having a surprise party, but still . . . you're taking the fun out of things."

"Don't worry. I plan on having tons of fun. Thank you guys for letting me handle the invitation list. It'll be interesting to see what happens."

Vette pulls out a shopping cart, and we breeze through the aisles until we locate the section that stocks casino party goods.

"I'm so excited," I exclaim. "I hardly know where to begin. Okay, I want the tablecloth with the black background, red dice, cards, and blue dollar signs bordered in green neon." I tell her to throw that in the basket, plus the matching cups, some dice, casino money, a roulette wheel, and gold coins.

"How about these flashing rubber dice that light up? That looks pretty cool."

"Yeah, get that, too. I plan on going all out."

We pore over Party City's vast selection of tableware and then wait in line to pay. We're about third in line with four more customers waiting behind us.

"That clerk is so slow. Why would they only have one person at the register on a Saturday, two weeks before Christmas? That doesn't make any sense."

"Who knows? It won't do any good to complain," I tell Vette. "Normally I cannot stand waiting in line, but you know what? I'm just glad to be alive. Not in jail. Not in the hospital."

"Not yet," Vette reminds me. "When is surgery?"

"Oh, I went ahead and scheduled it for next spring."

"Next spring? Why so long?"

"Now that those lovebirds have set a date, I will go into the hospital after the wedding takes place. That way I know I'll be physically strong enough to attend."

"Oh yeah. February fourteenth. It'll all be over before they know it."

"Listen. When a man and woman get married, the day they say 'I do' is just the beginning."

There are some occasions people never forget. When I wake up in bed on December twentieth, the first thing I do is open my eyes and raise them to the ceiling.

"Oh wow," I say and shove Neil, who's shaped in a lump, lying next to me in bed. "I can still see. No blurry vision. Check. Now, say something to me, Neil. Talk to me."

"Huh?" He rolls over and continues his loud snoring.

"My hearing is fine. Check."

I inhale the air around me. The aroma of fried bacon, scrambled eggs, onions, and bell pepper fill my nose. "Mmm, my sense of smell is still excellent."

"Woman, you're crazy."

"Not crazy. Happy."

I get out of bed and make my way downstairs.

"What? Scottie's cooking breakfast for me?"

"You're my favorite sister-in-law, and you deserve nothing but the best."

That's how the remainder of the day goes; my phone rings off the hook with well wishes. My daughter hugs me and presents me with a card that she made out of fabric swatches, glue, poster board, and fashion magazine cutouts.

Even little Brax closes both his eyes and belts out "Hap-py birdy to youuuu."

And hours later, when my official party gets into full swing and twenty-five people fill my house to eat, gamble, and celebrate with me, nobody can tell me a thing. Scottie's playing groove after groove. Kool & the Gang, The Gap Band, and one of my favorites that I loved to dance to in the 80s—a time when guys told me I was a hot young thing—"Let the Music Play."

I dance and shake my butt till my hair goes from neat and stylish to slick and stringy. Strands get stuck to the side of my face from the sweat rising from my skin. I energetically fan my face and tell my guests, "I've been dancing ever since Scottie's been deejaying. I gotta sit down. I may not be old as dirt, but I still need to catch my breath." Neil's popping his fingers and moving his neck around like he's about to have a seizure. I wave at him as I walk away to take a seat on the couch.

"Go on and sit down, Ms. Anya," says Riley Dobson. "As a matter of fact, save me a seat right next to you. I'm worn out myself, hon."

"C'mon, Riley. It's been a minute since we've had a real good chat anyway."

Even though Riley lives next door and we frequently wave to each other in passing, I rarely make time to bond with her like I ought, so it does feel good to spend time with her for a change.

"Mmm, hmm! I hope I look as good as you when I turn the big 4-o," Riley says, her long chandelier earrings dangling and sounding like wind chimes. "Of course, I hope to have a hubby by then. I sure don't want to grow old by myself much longer. I heard about Dani, too. I'm glad for her. She needs to settle down."

"Tell me about it." I nod. "Who woulda thought she'd be my sister-in-law one day?"

"Ha, God works in mysterious ways, I know that much. 'Cause first of all, when I heard Scottie was back in town, and I saw him at the family reunion, then I saw her checking him out, hon, I smelled trouble on the horizon just like I can detect a cup of Starbucks a mile away."

"So are you saying you can look at them and tell that a divorce is in their future?"

"I won't go as far as to say all that, but Dani is a special kind of woman. She doesn't think like a normal chick."

"What makes you say that?"

"What makes me say that? You know it as well as me."

Then a romantic love song comes on that I haven't heard in years. But I know Whitney Houston's voice the second I hear it. She's singing a pretty, melodic song from *The Preacher's Wife* sound track, "My Heart is Calling."

Neil looks expectantly at me, but I shake my head no. My feet are hurting and I'm still trying to listen to Riley. He grimaces, spots Dani sitting alone in a corner, goes and takes her by the hand, and they start dancing. Even though it's a midtempo song, almost a ballad, he doesn't dare put his arms around her. They're just standing in front of each other; she's leaning in listening to him talk.

"It's like some women are so similar that they get along without much effort. They're cut from the same cloth, think the same way, and share the same values. Then other females . . . Lord have mercy. Nothing you do can make them get along. They just don't mix, don't click, and will never understand each other. They can barely stand to be in the same room together."

"Hmm, you're right," I say to Riley while staring at the way Neil looks into Dani's eyes. His hands aren't on her, but they might as well be. I feel my cheeks warm up, but I have too much pride to act like I care. So I giggle and nod at Riley even though the woman hasn't said anything worth laughing about.

"What does he think he's doing?"

"Huh, what?"

"Your hubby, that's what. Why don't you go up there and interrupt? This is your day, Anya."

"Oh, I'm not worried about that. I mean, I am looking right at him. He'd be a fool to try anything right in front of my face. Neil isn't that crazy."

"But Dani is."

"I–I can't appear insecure, Riley."

"Well, everybody's *looking*, so . . . they're expecting you to do something."

"I'll give it another minute. I know my husband loves me."

"Love doesn't stop men from having affairs does it?"

"Riley, shhh. Let's change the subject."

"Oh, don't get me wrong. I'm not angry. He's not my man. But if he were, he'd be wearing that whole bowl of fruit punch right about now. I'm just saying."

"You're sweet to care, but he and I have been married a long time. You have to pick your fights, and you definitely shouldn't air your dirty laundry in front of other people. I try not to roll like that."

"Why is it that you have to act so demure and mature and all the other fancy words and, on top of that, feel too embarrassed to make a scene, but the woman who *should* be ashamed isn't?"

"It's because of what you said. Dani and I are two different women. And I don't care what you say, I doubt that God meant for every woman to act exactly alike."

By the time I get those words out of my mouth, Dani prances over my way, smiling and waving at Riley. Riley waves back likes she's so excited to see Dani. She grins like the girl is her BFF. I want to throw up, but I manage to hold in my nachos and guacamole.

"Hello, ladies. I was just telling Neil that if I can reach my fortieth birthday and still be married to the same man, I'll give up having sex for an entire week. Wouldn't that be a miracle?"

"I don't know which is more bizarre. You being married, or you not opening your legs. . . ."

"Riley, hush, why don't you go pour me another glass of punch? I want to talk to Dani in private. Go on, go."

I shake my head as Riley scurries toward the kitchen.

"I want some of what Riley was drinking," I say quietly.

"Are you talking to yourself?" Dani asks.

"No, I was talking to you. Now have a seat," I tell her, and I actually feel much more relaxed than I thought I'd be feeling. What is that peace due to? Is it because Dani can't be as big a fool as she's perceived to be? After all, her soon-to-be-husband is in the same room with us. Dani isn't crazy. Flirty? Yes. Whorish? Sometimes. So I will give the girl the benefit of the doubt.

"What do you want to talk to me about? I hope you're enjoying your party. I've had a ball playing roulette and that slot machine is off the chain."

Dani's referring to a poker slot machine we've rented for the weekend. Most people who start playing the machine stay on for hours. Maybe I can lure Dani back to the machine in a few minutes.

"I'm good, Dani. Thanks for asking but enough about me. If you want to get to where I am, you're going to have to put in a lot of work. I feel kind of weird talking to you about these things." Why should I give this hussy tips on how to make her relationship last? Maybe it's because I feel if she's truly happy with Scottie, she won't ever want Neil again.

"Since my mama went back to Cali, I feel a void. And I enjoy listening to other women who've been there and done that. Maybe I'm selfish. And maybe I'm just scared that what I did to you may one day happen to me."

"That's probably the most honest thing you've ever said to me, Dani. I don't know if I should do a cartwheel."

"Hold off on the cartwheels. I–I dunno. I may act big and bad, like I have it all together. But I do get . . . I get scared sometimes. Am I ready to be a wife? I guess I'll have to get over my fear, because we've already reserved the reception hall. We've hired a caterer and a photographer. I have to look at dresses in a week or so. It's so overwhelming. Maybe we should have a summer wedding."

"Well, why are you rushing it?"

"You think we're rushing it?"

"Doesn't matter what I think, Dani. I've heard of couples getting married within weeks of meeting. And they're still together."

"What? A whole month later?"

"Yeah, impressive, huh?"

"I just don't want to do a Britney Spears. If I'm only going to be deliriously happy for forty-eight hours and then have a change of heart, I may as well do something different."

"Tell you what. I have a book that talks about what to consider before you get married. I'll lend it to you if you'd like."

"Why, I'd like that a lot," she says with a curious gaze. "Thank you, Anya. You're a gem."

"It's no biggie." I excuse myself from the den and go search the bookshelves in the library until I locate the manual.

"Here you go. You and Scottie should start answering all these questions. Don't let him get away with not telling you his take on every issue. It's better to know beforehand what you're getting yourself into."

"Hmm, for the record, Scottie and I have already discussed some of these in length. We've agreed to split the chores. If he makes a mess, he'll clean it up. I'll handle the kitchen, the laundry, and things like sweeping and mopping. He'll be my Mr. Fix-It and oversee all electronic things, small repairs, and hanging pictures and televisions."

"Where do you plan on living?"

"My lease is up at the end of January; we'll rent a bigger place in the same complex. He and I want to buy a house, but we won't be ready for that until we've saved for a couple of years."

"And how will you handle finances? God knows that could easily become an issue if one of you loses your job. It's not pleasant to think about it, but you gotta do it."

"Maybe I'm naïve, but even now, it's not like Scottie is wealthy, but we manage to do the things we both want to do. He knows as long as I get my pedicures and manicures and can buy a couple of new outfits and matching shoes every few months, I'm straight. Thank God for child . . ."

I laugh and pretend like I don't know she's thankful for child support. Knowing that a chunk of my hubby's salary goes to Dani every month is something that hurts every time I think about it. Our house could use a few repairs. And I'd love to be able to pay off Neil's ride in half the time, but that's not going to happen.

"Moving right along," Dani says. "Um, may I ask you a question? Something off-topic?"

"Shoot."

"I know we've had our ups and downs and I can honestly kind of figure out why, but one thing I don't understand is why you seem to welcome me in your home lately. Remember, at one time, actually a few years ago, you specifically told me, and I quote, 'You don't belong here,'" she says in this masculine-sounding voice. I do *not* talk like a man. "'And this is the last time you're setting foot in this house.' Unquote."

"People change. So do feelings and circumstances. I had to do what needed to be done based upon what was happening back then. And if it took putting tons of space between us, and making you understand about the boundaries of Neil's and my relationship, that's how it had to happen. Call me the 'B' word, and tell everyone I'm a nut." I shrug my shoulders. "Besides you've never worn a miniskirt and boots to my house again. So I've lowered my guard a bit."

"I see. I was just wondering. The whole thing made me feel so bad back then."

"Oh, right. It's all about your feelings, huh, Dani." I slowly shake my head and continue.

"Personally, I feel whether you or I experience a good day or a bad day, we will never repeat the same day twice. I don't stress out wondering if certain awful moments are destined to repeat themselves."

"Aw, so you just know, I'm not about to walk up in here scantily dressed specifically for someone else's man?"

"*You* better know it. It's just not gonna happen." My voice is calm, sure. I hope she hears what I'm saying and has the brains enough to read between the lines.

"And another way to put it is like this: When I cook a great meal, one that I've done many times before, I will season the food, but no matter how hard I try, I can never exactly season the meal like the last time. The flavor is going to always be slightly different."

"I'm getting hungry again."

"Hush, I'm not done with my speech yet. Anyway, all I'm saying is that even if it looks like a certain awful day *is* trying to repeat itself, well, we already know how it's going to end, right?" I leave Dani alone so I can enjoy my party for the rest of the night.

Turning forty feels pretty good right about now—way more exciting, validating, and lively than I ever imagined.

18

LaNecia

You Got It Bad

Do you really think that just because you're supposed to be getting married to my man on Valentine's Day that it means anything? That y'all guaranteed to stay together? Forever? You are stupid if you think that February fourteenth means something. You'll see."

Karetha gapes at her friend like she's crazy. She knows that although LaNecia is rehearsing the words she wants to say to Dani, that type of confrontation is not likely to happen.

"Necia, c'mon. You really think that lady is going to let you talk to her like that? Admit it. You've lost. Get over it. If I were you, I'd forget about Scottie, and go out again with Reginald Walden. He's your age, he has the hots for you, and main point: *He's not your damn cousin!*"

LaNecia and Karetha are shopping in Frederick's of Hollywood at Memorial City Mall.

"Why is he marrying her? Why they gotta take such a drastic measure? Does she look pregnant to you? That's the only reason two people rush to get married." Large tears form in LaNecia's eyes, making her pupils look glassy and oversize.

"Oh, I get it. She's having his baby but you . . ." Karetha whispers, "I'm sorry, Necia."

"You're insensitive. That's what you are. You're supposed to brainstorm with me. This wedding cannot happen."

"Necia, I'm your girl, but I don't want to be involved in messing up someone's dream."

"You're already involved. You're the perfect distraction. Scottie won't expect you to do anything out of the ordinary."

"I wouldn't count on that. We're thick as thieves. I wouldn't be surprised if he's suspicious of me by now. I hate that, too, because Scottie and I were actually cool before you started flipping out like a gymnast. I wish he'd move back to Michigan. I hate to say it, but I really do."

"How can you say something so cruel?"

"Baby girl, face it. You need a true sit-down with a professional who's capable of helping you sort through this obsession. It's getting painful to watch. And I'd think by now, you'd be tired of what you're doing."

"It's hard to describe or justify, but I feel what I feel."

"Go see a therapist. Like today, for real, Necia."

"I already know what they'd say. Get away from Scottie. Why should I pay good money to hear what I already know. . . . ?"

"Oh, you actually do know you should leave him alone?"

"Look, I'm not saying that. Don't try and twist up my words."

"You got it bad, Necia. I swear to God."

Karetha reaches out to hug her friend, but LaNecia is too busy rummaging through the racks peering at camisoles, teddies, and negligees. She picks an outfit, scans the price tag, returns it immediately, and pretends like she doesn't know it's now falling off the hanger.

"Men are weak. All a woman has to do is throw the pussy at him and he's all hers. They cheat mostly because the opportunity presented itself. I just gotta set up the perfect opportunity." A light sharply gleams in her eyes. "Hot damn. I've just thought of something I can do that's so juicy Scottie can't help but notice. Yep, that's the plan I've gotta carry out. Thanks, Ka. You've been very inspirational today."

LaNecia continues searching for the most sensual and eye-popping lingerie she can find. She's about to give up when she lays eyes on a fire engine red camisole halter with a plunging neckline and matching lace boy shorts.

"How does this look?" She holds the outfit against her body. "You think this outfit is seductive enough to make a man lose his mind?"

"Trust, if Scottie sees you in this, he may forget all about walking down that aisle with Ms. Frazier."

"That's the type of encouragement I need to hear from you. Let's buy this home-wrecking outfit and get the hell outta here."

December twenty-fifth comes and goes, and LaNecia manages to stay away from Scottie all that day and resists the urge to call and tell him about the present she bought.

I'll give him that time. Let me get comfy and then, bam, I'mma put something on his ass.

A couple of days after Christmas, LaNecia goes to work at her second job; four days a week she puts in time at Sista Girl Nail Salon. Her booth is located at the far end of the shop, and she's just finishing up giving a ten-year-old her first pedicure.

LaNecia gets interrupted by the receptionist.

"Hi, LaNecia, I seated your next customer up front."

"Okay. I gotta use the ladies room back here first, so tell her to have a seat and I'll be there in a minute."

LaNecia asks the little girl to go sit with her feet underneath the drying machine; then she rushes to the restroom. When she returns to her booth and slides in her chair, she does a double take.

"Dani?"

"LaNecia? I didn't know you worked here."

Dani stands up, but LaNecia waves at her. "Don't leave." She smiles. "You need a refill or a new set?"

"New set."

"Okay, I'll hook you up."

Dani eyes her warily. "This is a trip. Usually I go to the salon at the mall. It's cheap and fast. But last time I went there, I walked out pissed. I got sick of the nail technicians looking at my toes and talking in a foreign language. I don't know Vietnamese, but I can tell they're gossiping about me. So I thought I'd go give 'us' a try, if you know what I mean."

Is Ugmo too good to let a black professional do her nails? She has some nerve.

"Oh, girl, I know how you feel. You let black folks handle things and sometimes they just fuck it all up." LaNecia laughs. "Like letting Kwame Kilpatrick be the mayor of Detroit. But like I said before, don't worry. I'm going to take care of you real good."

LaNecia grabs one of Dani's hands. "Ew, you got one helluva broken nail. How'd that happen?"

"Well, it probably . . ."

"Are you excited about getting married?"

"Do you really care or are you just making conversation?"

"I do care . . . about *my* cousin."

"Hmm, well, I would tell you, but I honestly don't know what to say. I, um . . ."

"Fine, you don't have to answer. But I would like to ask you something."

LaNecia bares her teeth and engages Dani in small talk as she grabs a nail clipper to remove her acrylic nails.

"So you're supposedly in love with Meadows?"

"I wouldn't marry him if I wasn't."

"And he's the only man for you?"

"Yes! Why?"

"Just checking. I don't want my cousin to get hurt. That's all."

LaNecia takes her time doing Dani's nails and digs for more personal information. By the time she's finished, she knows she's done a great job giving Dani a full set of white pearl French nail tips.

"Hmm, not bad," Dani replies as she stands at the cash register so LaNecia can swipe her credit card. "I actually like how they look. I wasn't sure if I was going to give you a tip. But I've changed my mind." Dani reaches inside her purse and smiles as LaNecia holds out her hand.

"Keep doing what you're doing to stay emotionally stable; life may just end up turning out good for you one day."

And Dani leaves the salon without a backward glance.

A few days after New Year's, when LaNecia knows for sure that Scottie isn't at home, she pays a visit to the Meadows household. When LaNecia rings the doorbell, she's greeted by Reese, who flings open the door and runs upstairs once LaNecia steps inside the foyer. The house sounds quiet, and it seems as if no one is around on this Sunday after-noon.

LaNecia's instincts tell her to go look in the den. When it's apparent that an NFL game is on, yet Neil is snoring on the sofa, she can't believe her luck.

She kicks off her shoes as her eyes dart back and forth around every square inch of the den. It doesn't take her long to find Neil's cell phone lying on top of a Persian rug as if he carelessly dropped it. She slips it inside her pocket and hurries to the first-floor bathroom. She closes and locks the door, then flips open Neil's cell phone.

LaNecia punches a few keys until she locates Ugmo's cell number, then creates a text.

"Hey u. I want 2 talk 2 u. Do u like Frederick's of Holly-wood?"

LaNecia pushes "Send" and hopes Dani responds to Neil's text right away.

Neil's phone buzzes within seconds.

"I want to talk 2 u 2. What about Frederick's?"

"I got u a present," LaNecia types. "And I want 2 c u . . . in it. Meet me in 1 hr at Houston Marriott Westchase."

"R u kidding?"

"No. I miss u and want 2 talk 2 u b4 u marry my brother."

LaNecia's heart feels like it's about to explode. She's never been this excited in her life. She sends another text indicating that a room has been reserved in Dani's name and she can call and check if she wants. She asks again if they can meet and waits for Dani to reply with a yes. When Dani soon replies with "K," LaNecia excitedly slips the cell phone in her jacket pocket again, rushes to put on her shoes, and then stands over Neil, who's still spread out on the couch with his eyes shut. *He looks like he's in a damn coma.*

"Hey, wake up, Neil. I gotta tell you something."

"What do you want?" Neil moans as he rubs his eyes.

"Your baby mama came by the nail salon not too long ago. And guess what she kept yapping about?"

"The wedding?"

"No, fool. *You!* She claims she's still in love with you. But Scottie isn't her first choice; she's getting the next best thing by marrying him."

"She said that?"

"Yes. She was telling me things I never thought I'd hear. It seemed like your girl had been sipping on something real strong," LaNecia sputters, making up things as she goes along.

"Damn, that sounds just like her. When she drinks too much, all her true feelings come out. What else did she say?"

"You know how men have that last fling before they get married? Yep, mmm hmmm. That's exactly what she's hoping to have with you, Neil."

Neil scratches his head and stares into space.

"You don't have time to think about this, Neil. I know you still care about this woman. Anyway, the main point is she knows I was coming over here today. She wanted me to tell you that she's waiting for you at the Westchase Marriott. Right now!"

"S–she did?"

"Yes, the least you could do is drive on over and meet her."

"Where's Anya?"

"She's gone. Reese is upstairs playing with Brax. And Vette is taking a nap," LaNecia claims without knowing if it's all true. "So go see what she wants."

"But why meet at a hotel? That doesn't sound right."

"I already told you. She can't let you meet her at her crib for obvious reasons. That's why she picked a fancy hotel. And she said she'll be wearing this red see-through lingerie from Frederick's of Hollywood."

"She actually told you that?" Neil asks sounding skeptical.

"Hurry, you're running out of time. Now here are your keys. Go on!"

The minute Neil leaves his house, LaNecia places a call to the reservations desk at the Marriott to confirm that they're still holding a room under the name of Danielle Frazier. Once she knows the room is ready, and the rest of her plans seem to be in motion, she heads out the front door and unlocks the door to her car. She feels in her pocket for Neil's cell phone and, satisfied, she speeds away.

She sends another text to Dani. "R u there yet?"

"Almost. Where r u?"

"We'll be together soon."

LaNecia breaks the speed limit to get to the Marriott. Before she gets out of the car she slips her digital camera in her purse and turns it on. LaNecia opens the door and tries to walk at a normal pace inside the hotel so as to not draw attention. The spacious, well-lit lobby is crammed with guests loitering and talking. She continues walking slowly until she spots Dani, who's headed toward the reservations desk. LaNecia tries to remain hidden so she can watch what's going on.

Several minutes pass before Dani is helped at the front desk. LaNecia moves in closer and presses the camera's record button the moment she witnesses the reservationist present Dani with a large, gift-wrapped box. She knows that once Ugmo opens the gift and sees the Frederick's of Hollywood nightie, that she'll be convinced Neil indeed still wants her. And LaNecia prays Dani still wants Neil. And she'll capture the whole thing on camera. *Sure, Scottie will get hurt, but then he'll get it. A hurt man always runs into the arms of another woman. I have to make sure and be there for him when he needs me.*

"This plan better work," LaNecia says to herself. "I spent all my extra salary trying to pull this off."

Dani accepts the package from the reservationist, moves away from the front desk, and rips open the box right in the lobby. She holds the garment in her hand. Then Neil walks up to her. LaNecia's glad they're so occupied with each other that they don't notice her listening in while she tries to stay undetected.

"I'm not sure I'm feeling this at all, Neil. What do you think you're doing?"

"What are you talking about? I'm here because you wanted me to meet you!"

Dani gives Neil a perplexed look.

"I told you, if you ever have second thoughts to let me know. I thought this was your way of asking me to rescue you, before you make a mistake."

"Neil, don't lie to me. Did you set this up to confuse me? You just can't stand to see me happy, can you?"

"I could ask you the same thing. Why'd you tell LaNecia all this garbage about how you still loved me? . . ."

"LaNecia. Oh, okay. Fuck! I know the girl isn't wrapped too tight, but . . . hold on a sec." Dani retrieves her cell phone and shows Neil all the texts.

The color drains from his face. "No," he says somberly. "I didn't send those. I don't even know where my cell phone is. I'm sorry, Dani. I feel like such a fool."

"Don't feel that way. It's not that I don't care. But I am about to marry another man."

"Yet you showed up here, Dani. That says something. What, I don't know. But right now, I gotta find my phone. And LaNecia. 'Bye, Dani," he croaks and he leaves the Marriott appearing more distressed than when he first arrived.

19

DANI

The Pain of Marrying Scottie

It's a few days after LaNecia attempted to destroy the future I'm trying to build with Scottie. One of his projects is behind schedule, and he's put in a lot of extra hours today at the construction site trying to finish the building. Earlier he said he couldn't wait to get off so he can swing by and spend time with me. I prepare a quick meal for him so that we can have a bite to eat before we play with Brax and get him situated for the night.

Once my family digs into a nice helping of baked salmon fillet, rice, and broccoli, I feel so pleased about how everything tastes that I am eager to settle into Scottie's arms.

We're all hanging out in the main bathroom. Scottie is pushing a button that squirts out hundreds of bath bubbles into the tub. Brax keeps screaming and making loud noises as he splashes water and tries to pop the bubbles.

"He's having a ball, isn't he?"

"This boy is gonna pass out tonight, Mariah."

"I'll bet. The more he screams, the more knocked out he'll be." I turn around and open the door to the towel cabinet and locate a sky blue body towel monogrammed with the initials *BF.*

"Scottie, I hope the baby doesn't get confused by all this."

"I think he's too young to even notice," Scottie says.

"No way. Kids pick up on things." I pause and peer at my son. White bubbles cover his entire head. Scottie shapes them so that he looks like Batman.

"Ohhh, that's so wrong."

"Hurry up and get a camera. Go on. You gotta capture moments like this," Scottie says.

"You go get it. I want to stay right here and watch my son have a ball."

"Our son."

"Scottie. Please. We can't do this to him."

"Since you said he's so intelligent, he'll be able to understand that he has two fathers."

"But that's not what I want him to know. Not right now. Maybe not ever."

"I want him to know about me."

"This isn't about your ego, Scottie. It's about the innocence of my precious child. You can play that important role. But he has a father."

"I don't wanna hear that."

"It's the truth." I ignore Scottie's funky mood and try to tickle Brax under the arms. He looks up at me with his mouth wide open, grinning like he's having the time of his life.

"That's how I always want him to look. Sweetly happy like he oughta be, Scottie."

"Sco-tee, Sco-tee."

"Who told him to call you that?"

"I didn't."

I sigh heavily and wonder if I can endure some of the pain that marrying Scottie may bring. Some of life's issues are so complicated, confusingly twisted. Every day I hear of some tragic story involving family issues. Forced marriages. Spousal rapes. Inexplicable physical abuse from a tormented stepparent. Who's to say that, as much as I care about Scottie, one day he won't turn into some sicko who thinks it's okay to harm my child? I don't think it'll happen, but you never know. How can I stop potential harm from taking place if I'm too blind with love to see it coming?

And I can't shake the uneasiness I felt when I got engaged and first heard from my mama once she got back to Long Beach. She told me she was happy for me, but I need to "be careful." Of course, I couldn't sleep well all that night. I called her the next day and said, "If you can't offer me your sincere support, then don't play or pretend. Be honest."

"*You* be honest."

That's all mama said, and now we're here.

"Whatever you want him to call me," Scottie advises, "you better decide soon. Get it in his head while he's young and doesn't know how to question."

"Jeez, I dunno," I mumble. "This is difficult for me. I need your help with these kinds of things."

"Why? You having doubts?"

"I *do* want to be with you. It's just that I get scared. Are the things I'm gaining worth everything I could lose?"

"Oh, I see," he remarks in a clipped tone.

Scottie stands up and heads toward the door.

"Scottie, please don't ever walk away from me. I don't even want to get that kind of thing started. In this relationship, we've gotta be honest. We don't have to yell, curse, threaten, or get physical, but let's have space enough to say how we feel, even if it hurts."

Scottie pauses, then slowly turns around to face me. His

eyes are filled with wounded tenderness. I hear his soul crying. The hands of his soul are beating against his chest. I
can relate. This life-changing decision isn't like going to the
drive-through window of Jack in the Box, where you gotta
make a quick choice out of dozens of menu items. The kinds
of decisions I'm making these days are unlike anything I've
faced before.

"I guess I can't argue with honesty. I don't like how it
sounds when you tell me stuff like that. But if you thinking
about changing your mind about being my wife, you better
be truthful enough to tell me before one o'clock on February fourteenth."

"That's fair," I tell him. He lowers himself to his knees
and splashes water against Brax's little bird chest. Brax
screeches and throws back his head, erupting in laughter.

"Aw, man," I say, "don't let him get you like that, Brax.
Splash him back."

Scottie covers his eyes, looking like an oversize punk.

"Hey, Brax, man, who am I?"

"You my uncle Daddy."

Scottie and I sit on both sides of Brax in his bed and take
turns reading a few poems that celebrate African American fathers from the book *In Daddy's Arms I Am Tall*. The
vivid illustrations portray positive interactions between a
father and child. Brax needs this. He's gonna get double the
love, and I want him to see and understand that's it's a good
thing.

"Love you," he says to me and kisses me on the mouth.
"Love youuu more," he screams at Scottie and hugs him
tight about his neck.

I dab at the corner of my eye and sniff. *It's gonna be okay. We'll feed him what he needs to know one day at a time.*

It amazes me how it feels when I stare deeply into the eyes of a man who's making love to me. It's like we've become one, soul connected to soul, intricately woven together. When Scottie places the full weight of his body on top of mine, it feels like we're human puzzles that naturally connect. My fingers hold tight to the hardness of Scottie's thick neck; he rises and falls above me, stroking inside and stabbing me fiercely as if he needs to touch the deepest part of my soul. I know he's putting his stamp on me, a sexual engraving that marks me as his. Forever. For some reason, these are the thoughts that permeate my mind as we're having sex.

It's mostly dark, but my night-light, which is plugged into the wall next to the bed, causes me to see shadows.

Scottie thrusts his hips, putting all his strength into his stroke. I gasp. Whimper. Then I close my eyes.

Neil is on top of me. As I grip his shoulders, his curvy muscles fill my entire hands. I stroke his smooth arms with the tips of my fingers. I like this. I miss this. He grunts and plunges deeper into me.

Stop. It hurts.

It's not hurt. It's love. And you're mine. Don't you ever forget it.

I quickly open my eyes. Scottie is stroking me. He moves his sweaty face next to mine. My cheeks get wet and moist, and I feel like pushing him off me. But I lie in bed, waiting for Scottie to finish up, my eyes aimed at the ceiling, my mind crammed with odd thoughts.

* * *

Summer comes and picks me up the next weekend.

"Four weeks, baby. Are you ready?"

"Getting there. Hard sometimes. Tons of fun other times."

We're traveling to the River Oaks area of town so I can check on the wedding gown and bridesmaids' dresses.

"Like today, for instance, getting to put on that stunning dress and making sure that the other attire is set, all of that makes me feel happy."

"You oughta be. Not that you'll feel elation every second until the wedding actually happens, but it's damn sure expected that you'll feel some joy during some parts of this entire experience."

"That's what I try to think about. If I concentrate on the parts that worry me, I'd probably end up running away from home."

"Girl, it's just like when I had to move from one place to another. Packing was a bitch, but once I hired someone to assist me and knew that Andre was helping me with the moving expenses, I felt relaxed. A good man will do that for you."

I nod in agreement. "I actually cannot complain. Scottie has come through for me in so many ways. I mean, gosh, the fact that his uncle James is paying for half the costs plus flying my family here a week in advance is amazing. I can't ask for anything more."

"You're lucky, girlfriend. Enjoy all this good stuff because I can count on both hands the number of females who want to be in your shoes."

"Well, that's the problem, Summer. I still feel guilty about what happened with, um, you know."

"Ha! *That*. Well, don't totally blame yourself. That crazy LaNecia didn't help matters. It's not like the idea to meet Neil came solely from you."

"Right, and you better not ever mention this, you promise?"

"Okay, okay. Who am I going to tell?"

"It could slip out. Things happen."

"I doubt I'll ever mention it again. That's your personal business. And I know you just needed to vent. Try not to feel guilty."

"It makes me wonder, though. What would have happened if we hadn't picked up on the fact that LaNecia was involved?"

"Girl, please don't tell me you'll throw all this away over some age-old fling."

"I didn't, which is great, but I'll admit I thought about it. Does that make me a bad person?"

"It makes you a normal person. You thought about doing some bad, but you didn't go through with it. If everyone who ever thought about killing someone went to jail, there'd be nobody on the streets."

The rest of January is filled with a rush of things to do. Scottie and I pick up the matching ring set from I W Marks.

Sola helps me review final details for the food and beverages. We went with Jimmy Dillard's Famous Fifth Quarter Seafood & Catering and voted to place fried turkey at the top of the menu. For people with dietary restrictions, we added grilled chicken breast as an entrée alternative.

Summer agrees to oversee details regarding my floral

arrangements; she also volunteers to check the guest list and note those who haven't responded to the invitation.

"Who is Shay Fleming?" she asks me one day while sitting with me at my dining room table.

"Hell if I know."

"Maybe one of Scottie's family members?"

"I dunno. I think I've met just about everyone in his family unless she's someone coming from out of town. Maybe I'll give him a buzz and ask."

"Hold up before you make that call. How do you like that necklace?"

This afternoon I've been collecting my something old, new, borrowed, and blue that I plan to wear during the wedding. Summer lent me a dazzling string crystal and pearl necklace that her mother gave to her before she passed away.

"Summer, I'm honored you're even letting the jewelry out of your sight. It's beautiful, *beautiful.* Makes me feel like a woman posing on the red carpet."

"That's a good thing, sweetie. Now go ahead and call your fiancé."

I laugh and dial Scottie's cell. He answers with a hearty, "How's my favorite girl in the world?"

"Assuming you're talking about me, I'm good."

"Funny. What other woman would I be talking about?"

"You never know these days, babe. Anyway, I'm calling about the guest list. One person in particular hasn't responded at all."

"Like who?"

"Like Shay. Shay Fleming."

He pauses. "Oh, all right. Don't worry about it."

"I'm not worried. One less mouth to feed. But before I scratch her off the list, who is she?"

"Nobody."

"Nobody somebody, or nobody *nobody*?"

"I–um."

"Scottie, I don't like how you won't just answer the question. Remember our talk a while ago?"

"How can I forget?"

"You must've forgotten because you're choosing not to answer me. That's not honest."

"I feel if the person didn't respond to the invite, then they must not care. If they not respectful enough to let us know they wanna come, then fuck 'em."

"Oh, I get it. Must be one of your exes."

He doesn't say a word. And his silence says more than what his words would have revealed.

"No problem. 'Bye, Scottie." I slam down the phone and instantly regret it. I wait a few seconds and redial his number. The call quickly goes to voice mail.

"Dammit. Now he's pissed at me. This isn't even right. I don't believe him."

"What's wrong?"

I explain Scottie's odd reaction when I mention Shay Fleming and how he refuses to tell me who she is.

"That's easy. Google her and see if there're any photos on MySpace or Facebook. We already know her home address and telephone number. One quick phone call should resolve this mystery."

"But I don't like acting insecure, calling up strange women. I've always wanted to pretend like I don't care and like I trust him."

"But you don't."

"It's important for me to know the basics about what's going on. The rest I can deal with later."

"Well, you know me. I'm game. Hand me your house phone. I'll call. Or log me on to your Internet, and I'll let my fingers do the checking."

"It's not your job, Summer. If my man can't tell me the truth, what am I doing with him? That's why I don't want to google anybody. I'm waiting for him to come to me. That's the last little test he needs to pass."

Later that evening, Scottie shows up at my place. I stand outside my front door with my arms folded.

"You gotta know and believe that you're the woman I'm marrying. Shay Fleming is someone who I used to know a few years ago. I guess it was stupid to invite her. She was the one woman who was gifted at making me feel like an ass. And now that I've lucked out . . ."

"You want to show out? Show me off? Make her regret treating you bad?"

"But I don't have to do that, do I?"

I insert my key in the front door to let him in. "All you have to do is be honest with me even if you think your feelings will harm mine. Thanks for telling me who she is. If you see her at the wedding, will you point her out to me?"

"That's not happening. I decided to call and uninvite her. She cursed me out and hung up on me."

"Good for you. I'm glad she's not coming. Two cars just can't drive in the same lane, I don't care how 'hot' they are," I tell him and silently thank God that Neil and I had enough sense not to go into that hotel room.

20

LaNecia

Wedding Day Blues

Saturday, *February* *fourteenth.*
The wedding ceremony begins twenty minutes late. But when the doors of the tiny rented chapel squeak open, the sounds of sighs and complaining skid to a gentle stop as all the guests crane their necks.

Dani steps into the sanctuary wearing a white beaded floor-length dress with a strapless bodice embellished with rhinestone crystals. Her taffeta skirt is bunched in at her waist. The front of her hair is pushed back from her face; and the back of her hair is curled in long, flowing ringlets that bounce with every step. She slowly walks down the wide aisle clutching the arm of Albert Frazier, her thirty-five-year-old brother, who's prepared to give her away.

All the ushers were warned, "If you see another woman walk through the front doors of the church wearing a wedding gown, first call security, then 911, just in case."

Guests grin, point, whisper, and take photos with flashing digital cameras. Everyone is standing to watch the procession from both sections of the sanctuary.

Someone remarks, "She's radiant."

"That's tanning spray," snaps LaNecia, who's waiting

unnoticed at the back of the church. She's wearing a gray cotton cleaning uniform, and her face has been scrubbed of all makeup. Even her own cousins haven't recognized her. LaNecia moves in closer so she can see.

"Isn't that beautiful? Dani's eyes are wet with tears."

"That's Visine. She's trying to get the red out. Pothead."

"She looks as beautiful as Princess Diana."

"Princess Diana is dead. Dead ain't beautiful."

"Dani looks perfect."

"A perfect man-snatcher. She knows Scottie is mine. He'll always be mine."

A woman standing in the row in front of LaNecia turns around so she can get a good look at the girl who's making disparaging remarks, but within seconds LaNecia ducks from the aisle and heads out of the church, shaking with anger that the day that never should have happened is now a reality.

21

SCOTTIE

Another Man's Wife

It's Sunday afternoon and the new-lyweds are enjoying themselves at home in their living room.

"Yeah, that's what I'm talking about." Scottie groans in satisfaction, then props his feet on top of an oak coffee table. He's admiring the revolving photos from his wedding that are now playing on the digital photo frame with an eight-inch LCD display. Although he and Dani got married only two weeks ago, the twinkle in his eyes has yet to dim. He's holding a cold can of beer in one hand; his other hand rests against Dani's hip while she's snugly perched on his lap.

ABC TV just started airing a doubleheader: Detroit Pistons at Boston; later on they'll broadcast the Lakers at Phoenix. In his mind, life can't get any better.

"What are you talking about, Mister Meadows?" Dani asks.

"I'm talking about how sweet it is to live the good life. If all the haters could see me now . . ."

"Haters? Like who?"

"Like some of my boys who warned me, 'Don't do it, partner.'"

"They said that?" She scowls. "Thank God you don't listen to them."

"I mean, we're tight and everything, but sometimes you gotta watch your buddies. They the main ones trying to break you up."

"And the ones who are full of relationship advice, yet they don't have anyone in their own life."

Sunlight streaks through the living area's bay window of their three-story town house. The lower level consists of a two-car garage and a laundry room complete with a full-size washer and dryer. The second level features a living room boasting nine-foot ceilings, a breakfast bar in the kitchen, a dining room, and a guest bedroom with full bath. The top level houses Scottie and Dani's bedroom and master bathroom, plus a room down the hall for Brax.

"Well, they didn't know what they were talking about, did they?" Scottie beams at his bride and wants to kiss her on the lips, but he thinks twice. He's already kissed her a dozen times since they woke up this morning.

"Mommy, I gotta go wee-wee." Brax runs up to his mother. He's wearing a blue outfit with suspenders.

The doorbell rings.

"Hey, I'll help my man get out of his clothes; why don't you get the door?"

"Thanks, babe."

Dani runs downstairs and opens the door without first checking through the peephole.

Neil stands in front of her, looking dazed. He's dressed in a pair of Dockers shorts and a black T-shirt that emphasizes his muscles.

"Oh, you're here already. Where's Anya?"

"We drove in separate cars."

"I see. Anything the matter?"

"Yeah, can you step outside for a second?" Dani raises an eyebrow but steps onto the tiny porch.

"Apparently, one of the folks at Solomon's Temple saw me at the uh, the hotel," he whispers.

"Oh, shit."

"That's what I said when she told me."

"Did you deny it?"

"I tried to explain to her what happened, but she wasn't hearing it."

"When did this happen? Just now?"

"Yeah. The timing is bad since *you* just invited us to come over to your new place today. Scottie should've asked us."

"Neil, no one's thinking about that old stuff. I just thought it would be nice for all of us to watch the game, eat hot wings, drink beer. Fuck!"

"No, no fucking."

"Shut up, Neil."

Dani abruptly turns and runs upstairs to the second-floor living room. Scottie hasn't returned from helping Brax use the bathroom. And the NBA analysts dominate the television screen with their predictions that Boston will put a hurting on the Pistons.

As Dani moves to stand in the center of the room, she feels Neil close behind her. He places his hand on her shoulder. She slowly turns around and looks up at him.

"Please," is the only word he utters. He looks at the ceiling and takes in the decor and layout of the living area.

"So, this is where the newlyweds hang out. . . ." he says, his voice drifting off.

"Um, make yourself at home. Scottie will be out in a sec. He's with Brax."

"Well, are you going to fix me something?"

"You can make your own plate." She blushes.

"You mean to tell me after all we've been through I'm not good enough to be served?"

"I'll serve you all right." She pouts. "Um, more on that later."

She proceeds to arrange a plate for Neil. "Which kind of wings did you want? We have Cajun, lemon pepper, suicide, barbecue. . . ."

"You don't remember my favorites?"

"Sure, I do. But . . ." She uses the tongs to pick out ten lemon pepper wings and carefully sets them on a plate.

"How are things going with you two? Is he treating you right? If he gets out of order, don't hesitate to call."

"You mean that? I—I can't imagine that ever happening. So far, everything's been . . . um, thanks for the offer."

"How're things going in . . . ?"

Dani is silent.

"Is y'alls room right above us?"

"Not quite, but yeah, we sleep upstairs. All of us."

"Is he better than . . . ?"

"Neil, stop. I don't feel comfy talking about that kind of thing here. I just don't. . . ."

"Hey, don't mean to make you feel awkward. I can't help but wondering, you know."

"I know."

"Hey, big brother, what you doing in here talking to my wife?"

"Daddyyyyyyy!"

Neil ignores Scottie, puts his food on the counter, then scoops Brax in his arms and swings him around, his little legs flailing in the air.

"Neil, you know I hate when you do that."

"Do you let Scottie do it?"

Neil continues swinging Brax up and down in a circular motion; like he's on a ride at an amusement park. Brax laughs and screams, "Weeeee, yeah."

"Nothing wrong with doing this. Plus, he's having fun. I haven't seen my son in a few days. We gotta get to know each other again."

"Don't even try it. You act like I've been keeping him from you. You didn't want to come over here to pick him up on Friday."

"Y'all shouldn't be arguing like this," Scottie says. "Not in front of me. It makes a man wonder where another man's wife is."

"Oh, my wife is on the way." Neil shrugs. "She had some things to do and decided to come on her own."

"Is that what she told you?"

"Yes, Scottie, sweetie, now be nice and get your brother something cold to drink, okay? Thanks, honey."

"When she talks to me like that"—Scottie grins looking at his brother—"she can get anything she wants out of me. Anything."

Neil turns around and carries Brax under his arm. He plops on the recliner and whispers something in Brax's ear. His little legs carry him to the kitchen, where he looks around, spots a plate of food, and picks it up.

"That's my boy, bring that over here and you can have some of my lemon pepper."

Scottie hands him a beer.

"That'll work. Hey, I might get used to coming over here on Sundays."

"I wouldn't count on that. Sometimes me and my wife might be caught up in other things."

"Hey, I'm just asking. I thought y'all wanted to start some couples thing, but . . ."

"No, not really. This is just an invite so you can see how we're living."

"Well, it sure feels good to have that extra room back at my house. But I'm leaving it open and available . . . just in case."

"I guarantee you, my brother, I won't have any need for my former bedroom."

"I wasn't talking about you, brother."

Dani bursts out laughing, then stops. "Oops, sorry. But that was kind of funny. Neil is exposing a side I don't always see. Anyway, we're here to have fun, right? Put down the razors, you two, or I'm going to have to call Sola."

"Aw, man, she used to whip Scottie's ass so bad." Neil chuckles.

"Don't say that word in front of my baby."

"Dani, I don't know why you think you have the right to even tell me something like that, with your potty mouth."

"Mommy has to go potty?" Brax looks up from sucking on a wing.

"Stop listening to our conversation."

"Scottie, don't play with him like that. You can't talk to a kid that way."

"Hey, man, I was just . . ."

"Just don't do it," Neil warns him.

Scottie decides to leave his mouth shut, but he can't help but feel frustrated. Now that Dani is his, he feels he still has to prove his worth as a man. He figures Neil could still harbor resentment but thought at one point he'd have to get over his issues, let him live his life.

I gotta figure out how to handle my brother. Now I kinda know how Anya feels.

Neil changes the subject. "You know Anya goes into the hospital this Tuesday."

"Well, it's about time," Dani pipes up. She's juggling a cup of diet ice tea and a plate.

"Don't get it confused. Come sit right over here."

"I know that, Scottie." She smiles. "How long will she be in the hospital, Neil?"

"Tuesday through Friday."

"You need anything?"

"Not really. Vette's going to fill in and help out with Reese's schooling. We'll be okay. It's only a few days."

"No, but it's the aftercare that's going to be hard, I imagine," Dani responds. "I've never had surgery, but Mama has, and she talked about how hard it is to recover. Your body has to adjust and you're so weak at first. That can be challenging for someone who likes to be active and run around like Anya does."

Right then the doorbell rings.

Scottie says, "I'll get it this time. You just keep sitting on that couch doing what you do best. Looking pretty for me."

The second Scottie runs downstairs, Neil asks, "Is he like this all the time? How can you stand it?"

"Don't hate, Neil. That's how a man is supposed to treat his woman. Of course, you wouldn't know anything about *that*."

"Dani, if my son weren't here I'd . . ."

"You'd what? Huh, Neil? You'd put your hands on me, wouldn't you?"

"I'll bet you'd like to know, wouldn't you?"

They hush up when Anya and Scottie enter the living room.

Anya wears a stony look on her face.

"Um, hello, Anya. We were just talking about you. I do hope your operation turns out okay."

"Scottie, can you get me something to drink? I'm so thirsty I'm about to pass out."

"Anya, did you hear Dani talking to you?"

"Neil, please. Don't think I'm finished with our conversation. I'm not thinking about listening to Dani right now."

"Okay, fine. But why'd you come over here if you're gonna have a bad attitude?"

"Hey, hey, what's going on," Scottie interjects as he hands Anya a beer. "You two are our role models in a way."

"Scottie, if you only knew, you wouldn't make stupid remarks like that," Anya barks.

"Don't call my hubby stupid."

"I didn't say he was stupid, *Stupid.* I said his remarks were."

"Now listen, Anya, I know you're nervous and stressed these days, but if you're going to come into our home and insult us, I think it's best you leave," Dani says in a very serious tone.

"I'm not leaving until we openly discuss what happened between you and Neil."

"Okay, that's fine, but do you have to raise your voice?" Dani stands up, then sits back down. She plays with her hands and strokes her wedding band, sliding one finger across the surface to note its weight and strength.

"We're adults here and I–I think it's okay to talk about things . . . especially since I haven't done anything wrong."

Anya reaches inside her purse and pulls out a red lace cami and boy shorts. "So trying to seduce my husband with your nasty lingerie doesn't qualify as doing something wrong?" she shouts at Dani and throws the clothes on the coffee table. Her hands are trembling. She goes and picks up Brax whose mouth is wide open with a bone stuck in it. "Neil, go ahead and take Braxton to his room. He shouldn't be hearing this."

Scottie waits till Neil leaves the room with Brax. "I–I'm not understanding." His stomach feels like it's dropped to the bottom of his feet. "Someone, please. Tell me what this is about. Dani?"

She stands up. "Scottie, I swear to God. Those clothes aren't mine. It was a setup. LaNecia tried to get me and Neil to hook up at a Marriott."

"When did this happen?"

"Scottie, please don't look at me like that," she shrieks. "You're going to have to trust me. I met Neil but nothing happened. I swear on my father's grave."

"Why didn't you tell me? I thought you wanted us to be honest." He looks like someone socked him in the jaw without warning.

"Well, baby, nothing happened, so I didn't think it was worth mentioning. Plus it was a setup, Scottie."

"That's the main reason you should've told me. You can't be hiding shit like this from me. This is major."

When Neil returns to the room, Scottie leaps to his feet and bashes his head against Neil's stomach. Neil stumbles back a few steps but maintains his balance. They stand in the center of the living room giving each other heated stares.

"Scottie, stop it! Neil didn't do anything," Dani sputters.

"Why are you defending him, huh? That's messed up."

"I'm not defending him. You're overreacting."

"How else should I react?"

"Scottie, calm down. I don't like to be yelled at."

"You're yelling at me!"

"No, I'm not, I'm trying to get your attention. I don't want anyone hitting anybody because it's not even about that. I didn't cheat."

"But why would you even meet him at a hotel?"

" 'Cause she's a ho, can't you tell?"

"Anya, shut up. You sound stupid. And you're wrong! So wrong! I hate being lied on." Dani slumps in the recliner and rocks back and forth holding her stomach. "LaNecia is the one who should be called out. She started this entire thing. Don't blame me for being curious."

"Curious? Is that what they call it these days? You sneaking around behind my back and have the nerve to say you're just curious? That's not gonna cut it, baby. If I'm not good enough to be your husband, tell me now."

"Scottie, you're crazy. Don't do this, please. You don't know what you're talking about."

"Then why, Dani. Why'd you do it?"

"I told you. I got these texts. And I went just to see . . . we didn't do anything. I never went into the hotel room. Don't blame me for something I never did."

"I just hate hearing that you'd even consider going there . . . to meet him. I'm out."

Scottie starts running downstairs. Dani follows him. "Baby, where you going? Let me go with you. I love you and I want to be with you."

"No, I gotta think about things."

He opens the door to the garage and gets in the Escalade. When he ends up at LaNecia's, he sits in the car for several minutes. *Why does she do shit like this? Why did I ever get involved with her? How can she say she loves me and cause me so much heartache?*

Scottie loudly taps his knuckles against the door.

"Hey, how are you doing? Come on in."

"You here alone?" he asks before making a move.

"Yep."

He follows LaNecia into her living room, then swiftly turns her around and forces her to look in his eyes. "What do you think you're doing, huh, cousin? You trying to fuck up what I got just because you haven't had a piece of this in a while?"

"Scottie, get your hands off me," she sputters as he grabs her.

"But all you want is some of my dick, right? Will that make you stop acting so crazy?"

"Hell yeah!"

He angrily pushes her onto the couch and unbuckles his black leather belt.

"You want to fuck me, LaNecia?"

"Y–you called me LaNecia!"

"Answer the question."

"You're scaring me. It don't take all that."

"But this is what you've been working hard for, right? You work harder for me than you do for Pappadeaux and that nail salon put together."

Scottie can feel himself getting aroused. He can tell she's confused. Her hair is uncombed and she looks a mess. But the sexiness he used to know still lies underneath. He tries to ignore his physical reaction to her and moves back one step.

"Can you answer me? You're raising all kinds of hell because you still want Scottie Meadows in your life, in your face, and in your bed so he can fuck the daylights out of you, so come on with it then. We gonna do this or what? Don't just stand there."

He slides his legs out of his slacks and pulls his shirt over his head. He's wearing a pair of purple boxers and some gym socks. His penis is poking from behind his drawers.

"You want me to fuck you, then you're going to have to slip off your panties at the minimum."

"No, Scottie. I don't want it to be like this."

He angrily gets dressed and places his hands on his hips. "If you don't want it to be like this, then do something to make it different. Stop fucking with my wife."

He turns around and grabs the doorknob with one hand.

"Oh, by the way, if you ever get another bright idea about buying my wife a present, pick Victoria's Secret next time. That's *my* favorite."

ANYA

Surgery

Vette, I *swear, this* stuff is so freaking nasty, it's unreal. I'm having second thoughts."

"Just drink it, Anya."

"Yeah, you don't want anything to go wrong, so do everything your doctor asked you to do, young lady." That's Riley Dobson. She, Vette, and I are sitting in my screened patio on Sunday evening. Dusk allows only a small glimmer of light to shine as day gives way to evening.

"Why don't you two know-it-alls drink this, then?"

"I'm too young to drink magnesium citrate," Vette says. I tilt the container of clear liquid and press the opening against my mouth. Grimacing, I try to think pleasant, positive thoughts while swallowing what has to be some of the most awful liquid drugs I've ever stomached. It tastes like lime. Little bubbles form inside my mouth and around my teeth.

"I've been lifting you up to the Lord every morning for two weeks straight," Riley assures me. "Don't worry about a single thing, you hear me, Ms. Anya."

"I appreciate that, Riley. And to know you'll be there with me at the hospital is . . . unbelievable." I am being sarcastic because I think it's a shame that Neil's job won't let him get time off Tuesday morning, the day I'll be checking into Park Plaza Hospital. But when he told me that he'd be there as soon as he can in the evening and that he'd already asked Riley and Vette to take his place, I instantly felt a little better.

"Hey, I gotta be there, hon," she snickers. "I need to see what's happening in case I ever have to experience something of this magnitude. Now, of course, I believe that God will never allow me to be seriously ill a day of my life, and so far I can't complain."

"I hate needles too much to seriously go to a hospital. So this will be a first for me," Vette admits.

"Oh, Riley, you should have seen the look on Vette's face when her brother asked her to be with me during surgery. She was like, 'Who's gonna watch Reese?' He told her that Reese can stay with his mom for a few hours that morning, but he expects her to be in that hospital with me, no ifs, ands, or buts."

"And I was like, 'I didn't make a vow to be with my sister-in-law through sickness and health.' And you know what my big-head brother had the nerve to say?" she asks, looking at Riley.

"What did that man say?"

"He said, 'And I never vowed to let you live with me off and on, and pay your bills, and buy you food, plus let you watch cable for free.' Can you believe he went there?"

Riley and I look at each other and exclaim, "Yes!" and we high-five each other.

"Girl, your husband is something else, yes, he is. I see him outside in the front sometimes mowing the lawn. That's when Scottie lived here. And Scottie would pull up in that beautiful car of his, and it would be shining like he just brought it from the car wash. And hon," Riley chuckles, "he eyeballed Scottie from the time he pulled up till the time he rushed into the house carrying his McDonald's bag, or Taco Bell bag, or whatever junk food he was eating at the time. He'd either be listening to music and snapping his neck like he was in a serious groove, or he'd be on that cell phone talking away, probably to Dani."

The mention of that woman's name causes a sour frown to develop on my face.

"Yeah, speaking of the devil," I respond. "Please keep a watch on my house while I'm in the hospital and let me know if she shows up."

"Anya, you're being silly. What if she needs to pick up Brax?"

"Don't care. People use seemingly innocent excuses to get away with committing all kinds of dirt, but I'm not having it. I can't be worrying about what she's doing while I'm at the Texas Medical Center praying I don't die from too much anesthesia."

"I'm sure you have good reason to be concerned about Dani, given her history," says Riley.

"These days you gotta do what you gotta do. Men are getting slicker, but a lot of times they will never be as crafty as a female. That's why I don't trust Dani. I've tried to be nice, let my guard down, but it's a mistake."

"But, Anya, what if Dani's telling the truth about what happened at that hotel?" Vette asks. "LaNecia can be real over the top when Scottie doesn't pay her attention."

"Who you telling? A marriage license to another chick will hardly slow LaNecia down. If she would've listened to me, to anybody, her life would be going in a much better direction than where she's headed." I shake my head in discouragement. Unfortunately, I have more important things to worry about. Only prayer can help LaNecia. But as I think about it, only prayer can help any one of us. Some problems can't be fixed by human beings.

We walk through the doors of the hospital right at seven A.M. I fill out tons of paperwork involving insurance and payments. That's cool. I can handle those questions. But when the nurse hands me documents that require me to name my power of attorney, I don't feel so confident.

"What's wrong, Anya?" Riley asks, with great concern in her voice. I wave the papers at her. "Here, you sign them."

"I can't do that."

"I don't want to think about who's in charge in case . . ." I swallow deeply.

"Hon, we're going to the ladies room, and by the time we come back, I hope you have filled out those papers. Trust in God. You'll be all right, Anya, I promise."

"How can you be so sure?"

"Because I know in whom I believe. I feel peace. You need to tap in to those things all while you're in the hospital and after you get out. And you should seek peace and faith even to fill out the paperwork. Be right back. Come on, Vette."

Immediately I feel ashamed. Riley is such a strong person. She sees light that seems like darkness to me. And when I declare Neil the power of attorney, I feel like her courage has been transferred to me.

* * *

"It's that time," the nurse informs me. I'm sitting in a wheel-chair in a hospital gown with tan and white socks covering my feet and keeping them from feeling like ice cubes.

Vette bends over and hugs me. "See you, Anya." She never likes saying good-bye.

Riley waits for Vette to move. "Don't forget. We love you, and we'll be here when you are in the recovery room. When they inject you with anesthesia, keep your mind on Jesus. He'll be right in that room holding your hand, you hear me?"

"Yes," I whisper. "Thanks so much. And . . . see you later."

As I lie in bed in the recovery room, I'm so groggy that I can hear voices but can't make out who's saying what. I just know that this couldn't be heaven because I'm lying down on a bed, my body feels like I've been thrown against a wall a few times, and the sounds of characters from *Diff'rent Strokes* are playing on TV.

"What choo talkin' 'bout, Willis?"

"Yes," I say to myself. "Gary Coleman isn't in heaven and if he's in hell, I doubt we'd be allowed to watch a comedy." I succumb to the delicious feeling of extreme sleepiness, and exhaustion, but I'm still here.

Thank God, I am alive.

DANI

A Great Sex Life Keeps a Man at Home

It's a gorgeous Friday evening in April, and I'm going on a date with Scottie. Brax and I are playing with his LEGOs while we wait for Neil to come pick up his son.

Although I apologized to Scottie countless times and told him I'd never meet Neil at a hotel again, I doubt he believes me. He barely speaks to me in the mornings when he leaves for work. But I don't care how angry he is, nothing is going to stop me from going to see *The Last House on the Left*, which premieres tonight at the Alamo Drafthouse.

I hear the sounds of a vehicle pulling up, and I nervously tell Brax, "Come on. Daddy's here."

Minutes later, I'm downstairs in front of our town house strapping Brax into his car seat.

"Thanks," Neil says, grabbing Brax's everyday bag. "We'll see you on Sunday afternoon."

"Wait, don't go yet." I slam Brax's door and look down the street and around me before continuing to speak. "How are things with you?"

"Oh well." He laughs. "It's going to be different around the house. I think Anya gets a kick out of me waiting on her hand and foot. She actually likes being on bed rest."

"I see. How long will she be treated like a queen, so to speak?"

"At least five weeks."

"Aw, shit. You won't have any nookie for more than a month. First of all, she's sore from the surgery, and second of all, you know how weird she acts anyway. Let's double that and say your little dick will be hard as a rock for two months."

"Little?"

"Ooops, sorry, your big-ass Godzilla penis."

"Hey, it's big enough to get the job done."

"I know. I remember."

I turn around to leave, but Neil says, "Hey, Dani."

"What?"

"How much *do* you remember?"

"Ha! Remember we're both in the doghouse from having the nerve to be in the same Marriott lobby. What a joke. It's not like anything would've happened."

"Are you sure about that?"

"Of course I am. Scottie and I have a fantastic love life. But your woman can't compete with me in the bedroom department. Now in the kitchen she has me beat, but it's a great sex life that keeps a man at home."

"That's not always the case, Dani, and you know it."

"I know that you are not a temptation for me." I smirk and turn around to walk back up several steps that lead to the second-level stairwell. "Yep, I can actually be alone with you inside a hotel and we'd never have sex. Ever."

"I'll make you a hundred-dollar bet."

"You must enjoy losing money, huh, Neil?"

"C'mon, here it is." He removes his wallet from his back pocket and reaches in. "Two fifties. You can hold 'em for me.

We'll meet up. See what happens. If nothing happens, the money's all yours. But if you give in like I know you will, you owe me."

"I don't have a hundred dollars."

"You've got two grown people working in a household. You *do* have it. You just don't have a hundred to lose."

"That's it. You are such a fucking dope. I hope you don't always carry around this much money on ya."

"I hope so, too." He turns around and gets in the car, starts the engine, and drives off.

Neil calls me from his cell a few seconds later. "Meet me back at the same spot. Sunday night."

"Sunday?"

"How about Monday? Seven o'clock. It's time for another manicure. I can tell by the way your nails were looking just now. That'll be your alibi when you come and meet me that night."

"Fuck you, Neil."

"That's what I'm counting on. See you on Monday."

I swear if it weren't for Neil, I really could have been fully engaged by the action in *The Last House on the Left*. But when I watch characters get brutally murdered and I don't react, Scottie finally speaks up.

"Hey," he whispers and sips from a glass of beer. "You haven't jumped one time."

"It's not that scary."

"Why are you smiling so much?"

"You can see me?"

"I can feel you smile, Dani."

"I guess I'm deliriously happy right now. I'm sorry I'm

not clutching onto your arm and screaming for dear life. But I am enjoying myself."

"Just checking."

The next morning when I wake up, my head feels heavier than the rest of my body, and watery liquid constantly slides down my nose and my throat throbs with pain. On Monday morning, I call in sick and the nurse schedules me for a four-thirty slot. I lie in bed and don't wake up for another five hours.

When four o'clock rolls around and I see Scottie coming up the stairs of the town house, I signal at him and show him a piece of paper that I typed on our computer:

"Can you drive me to the doctor? I feel awful. Gotta be there at 4:30."

He says sure, and I'm so grateful that all I can do is struggle and smile.

After I sign in and Scottie handles my copayment, the nurse takes my temperature. "A little high, young lady. A hundred and one. Sounds like you're fighting a flu bug, but the doctor can tell you for sure."

The doctor confirms the nurse's assessment, and we leave a half hour later loaded down with several prescriptions.

"Dani, you're scaring me. You have no energy, huh?"

I shake my head.

"Well, babe, I want to apologize for how I've been acting. I ain't mad at you no more. I'm ready to fulfill these wedding vows, seriously."

I nod again and turn around in my seat so that my head is leaning against the coldness of the window.

He's so good to me. I feel like a piece of shit playing this stupid game behind his back.

Scottie drops me off at home and continues on to Walgreens to fill and wait for my prescriptions.

I take the opportunity to call Summer and let her know what's going on. "Hey, there," I groan and wince with pain. "How're you and Andre?"

"Things are still the same. He's planning to take us on a cruise this summer. You sound awful. What's up?"

I tell her that I'll probably be out sick this week due to the flu.

"Swine?"

"Funny, no, just the regular one."

"I hope you feel better."

"Thanks, but that isn't the only thing that's making me feel bad." I explain to her about the encounter Neil and I had the other day and how I'm supposed to meet him tonight at the Marriott.

"You've clearly lost your mind. That's something you shouldn't even joke about. You don't need money that bad, do you, Dani?"

"This isn't about money."

"Then you could have fucked him for free a long time ago."

"I know that. But I won't." I cough and clear my throat.

"Yet you've been thinking about it, which means the damage has already been done."

"No, because I'm calling and letting him know that I'm sick."

"Dani, you're kidding, right? Does that mean if you felt healthy, you'd go through with it?"

"It's just a silly, stupid bet. Nothing like that has happened and never could. Besides, I'm so in love with my husband. He brought me home from the doctor, carried me up the stairs, and tucked me in bed. He boiled some delicious hot tea, and turned the TV to my favorite channel."

"I know you care about Scottie, and I respect him as your spouse, but I've been thinking."

"About?"

"I really wish you had waited before marrying him."

"Why?"

"The fact that he had consensual sex with his relative, any angle you view it, it's gonna be twisted."

"I'm about to go now."

"Don't be this way, Dani. I'm just telling you how I honestly feel. Isn't that the guideline you try to use with your husband?"

"You're not my husband."

"I've said too much. Forgive me for prying. If you're happy, I'm happy."

"I don't know what I am, Summer. I think it has to do with this terrible flu. I'll think clearer once I'm one hundred percent better. I'll call you some other time."

I decide to call Neil instead of texting.

"Hello?"

Dammit. I disconnect the call not caring that I've hung up on Anya. Why'd she answer his cell? I can always say it had something to do with Brax. I hate that she answered.

By the next weekend, I'm feeling stronger. And on Saturday morning, Scottie asks if I want to go with him to Super Walmart.

I'm wearing a pink halter and some white shorts. I slide on my sandals and head for the car.

Once we arrive at the store, Scottie asks me to steer the

shopping cart to the seafood section so he can buy some fresh shrimp.

"I want you to make me a shrimp appetizer where you use lime and tequila and cilantro and parsley. My mom used to make it all the time when we'd have company."

"Eww, it sounds so complicated."

"If you're my wife, you are going to have to learn how to make all my favorite dishes."

"Hey." I laugh. "I know I'm your wife and I can't make all your favorites—just some of them."

"Well, that's gonna have to change."

"In your dreams," I say sweetly and pick up a package of raw shrimp and set it inside our basket. "Scottie, I want us to get some pecans and walnuts; and how about a bag of apples and oranges?"

"Anything for you, darling."

I roll the basket into the fruit and veggies section.

I look over my shoulder and notice a black guy in his early twenties lingering and sucking on a lollipop like he's a little boy.

"Hi." I smile and concentrate on picking out some oranges.

"Hey there, sexy lady. You are just too fine in your outfit. Your legs look beautiful enough to touch."

Within seconds, Scottie is by my side. "You son of a bitch; what you doing talking to my gal?"

"Scottie Meadows! Don't start," I say, flustered. Although I don't exactly like what the guy said to me, it's just harmless flirting.

"Naw, this punk should keep his comments to himself."

"Fuck you, man. You're a punk."

Scottie draws back his hand and pops the guy in the forehead.

"Now who's a punk?"

"Scottie," I scream. "Stop it. Let's go."

I grip the cart and push it until we're near the front of the store. Scottie stops in his tracks and complains, "We haven't even bought our groceries."

"Who cares? I hate when you embarrass me over silly things. I'm leaving!"

I lift Brax out of the shopping cart and hold him on my hip.

Scottie grunts but follows me out of the store and to the parking lot.

Right then I realize that no matter how your heart swells with love for someone, nobody can be everything you wish he'd be.

When we reach the Escalade, I find it ironic that the man who pissed off Scottie is parked right next to us.

When Scottie notices him unlock his car door but continuing to stare at us, he shouts at him, "What the fuck you looking at, man? Get your black ass away from us."

The young man gives Scottie a hurt look and openly gapes even as we drive off.

SCOTTIE

Why Am I Going to Jail?

Two weeks after the grocery store incident, Scottie's behind the wheel of his car on his way home from an event thrown by Bayou Town Construction. The company just signed off on three contracts worth a combined $900 million and organized a fancy party to celebrate on this balmy Monday evening.

Scottie's car speakers pulsate as he jams and spits the rhymes from "Wetter," the latest song by Twista. He's feeling a bit amped, a little bit horny, and he can't wait to get home and rock Dani's world. It's ten-thirty in the evening. He's traveling south on I-59 driving past downtown. He's looking up at the Houston skyline, mesmerized by the lit buildings that shine their light over the bayou city.

"There's Minute Maid Park, the JPMorgan Chase Tower, the Shell Building, the former Enron Building," he says out loud, admiring the architecture of various Houston skyscrapers, and feeling good that with his current job, he's helping to erect outstanding structures that add to the city's landscape. "And that unforgettable Bank of America Center; now that building is the *shizzle*."

Scottie's singing, scoping out skyscrapers, and doesn't

see the car with the flashing lights. He drives for two full miles before he can hear the wail of the siren.

He looks in his rearview.

"Fuck."

Scottie decides to exit the freeway then pulls into an empty parking lot located on the edge of downtown. A white vehicle drives up with the words Houston Police in blue lettering.

Scottie waits for the uniformed policeman to walk up to his Escalade. He quickly rolls down his window and hands over his license and registration papers.

After running a check, the officer returns and stands next to the Escalade.

"I'm going to need you to step out of the car. You have two unpaid speeding tickets. . . ."

"I thought I paid those."

The officer ignores Scottie's protest. "Plus you've got a warrant for your arrest. I'm going to have to take you in." The officer securely places a cuff on Scottie.

"That hurts."

"It's supposed to."

The cuffs feel tight. There's no space for Scottie to move his hands in any direction.

Why do I have a warrant?

Scottie looks around and notices a couple of people walking past and staring at him. His cheeks feel heated. He wants to push the officer down to the ground and run away. He looks around to his left and his right. *Is he really about to arrest me in front of these people like that? I could probably outrun him, but if he catches me he's gonna taser me. Or worse, he may shoot at me and kill me.*

Scottie sighs and thinks about his wife. *Dani's going to*

be worried. She'll wonder where I am. I'm going to call her as soon as I can.

An elderly man walks past the very moment the officer tells Scottie he's being arrested for a simple assault case filed by the young man whom Scottie hit at Walmart.

"What? He said something inappropriate to my . . ."

"Did you throw a punch?"

"Man, I barely . . ." Scottie clenches his teeth and decides to shut his mouth.

After his rights are read to him, Scottie nods his head then ducks down and slides into the back of the police car.

I want to run. Where can I hide? Why is this happening to me? Sure, I shouldn't lose my temper, but still, dude had no business flirting with my wife. That's my wife. And these funky speeding tickets? They arresting me for that? I was gonna pay them! I hadn't gotten around to it.

Scottie knows that law enforcement was getting stricter in Houston lately and had warned citizens they'd be arrested for nonpayment of outstanding tickets. Still, he didn't think he'd be someone who got caught.

I shouldn't even be going to any jail.

"Hey, man, are you a Christian? You believe in God?"

"Of course," the officer replies.

"Um, you got a wife?"

"Yeah, happily married for sixteen years."

Okay, he responded. He's human. But will he let me go if I try and talk him out of taking me down?

"I've only been married since Valentine's Day."

"Not long at all."

"I love my wife," Scottie says with conviction. "And our son. His name is Brax."

The officer doesn't respond. Scottie keeps his thoughts to himself for the duration of the trip.

By the time the car comes to a stop and Scottie is let out, he feels frustrated and worried. He shuffles along, walking with his hands behind his back. His stomach feels like it's about to explode, and he has a strong urge to pee.

The ride to the jail was brief, but because they drove through a tunnel, he still doesn't know exactly where he is. He walks into a room filled with hundreds of mostly African American men, Hispanics, and a few Caucasians. Soon he's led inside a cage surrounded by a metal fence. Rumbles of voices bounce off the walls filling the room with nervous energy. He notices men, so many men, their ages ranging from late teens to the mid-sixties. He's so agitated he can't clearly focus on any one individual.

His cell phone, wallet, and keys are removed from his slacks and set on top of a wide counter. One guy eases Scottie's watch from his wrist. Fellow inmates chitchat with one another, sizing up the seasoned prisoners from the neophytes; some are full of excitement and quiz the men they're chained to and learn if any of their neighbors, old friends, or family members are in jail.

What's Dani doing right now? How long will it be before I can get something to eat?

Scottie waits so long he can't predict what time it is. When he finally hears his name being called, he stands up and walks in a single file behind other men who've been arrested.

An inmate standing behind him whispers, "If a female officer walks by, stop right where you are, turn around and face the wall until she's out of sight."

What kind of mess is that?

"A lot of horny motherfuckas in the pen," the guy continues. "Dick hard as ten bricks, but if they catch you rubbing your meat, that's your ass."

Scottie is led to a room that is noticeably empty except for a single phone with people standing in long lines in front of it so they can call someone collect. Scottie wants to hear from people in the "free world," but he can't. Hundreds of other men are waiting.

He gets frisked again, men feeling on his balls. "You got any tats?" asks a tall, black man in processing.

Scottie nods. But his arms are bound, so he can't show the man.

"What's your height? Weight? Eye color?"

Scottie answers each question in a monotone voice.

"Do you have diabetes or any medical condition we need to know about?"

"No, my w—wife does," he says, his voice breaking.

"Do you hear any voices and are they telling you to harm yourself?"

Scottie glares at the man then whispers, "Nope."

He's instructed to stand in front of a digital camera and doesn't realize his mug shot is being taken. A white man with puffy eyelids takes Scottie's hand and fingerprints each finger once, both his thumbs, the sides of his hand, and entire hand.

Processing takes twenty minutes. Then he and a dozen other inmates stream down the hall single file inside another cage.

"We'll be here till court jail calls us," one guy mutters like it doesn't matter to him one way or the other.

"I miss my gal," another says.

"Amen to that," Scottie responds.

Hours later, Scottie and the others are corralled into a holding tank where hundreds of men lean against the wall; sit on the hard, cold floor; and lie on their backs, trying to get some sleep.

Wonder how long I'll be here? If I ever get out of here, I'm never going to break the speed limit again. I promise to not lose my temper. Or not even look like I'm about to hit somebody. I'm going to start going to church every Sunday, and I will never shout at Dani again. I just want to hear her voice and tell her I love her and not to worry.

DANI

Waiting on You to Come Home

I am so pissed at Scottie I want to scream. He told me he was going to some work function, but it's almost three in the morning. Every time I dial his cell, it goes straight into voice mail. When I call one of his coworkers, he said he saw my husband leave the party around ten. So where is Scottie? I am so tempted to call LaNecia and listen for background noises to see if that's where Scottie is hiding. He'd better not be. I'd kill him, and her, too.

The house phone rings with such a piercing sound I jump out of bed and run to catch my landline.

A recording says it's a collect call from an inmate in Harris County Jail.

Oh, Jesus!

After a few minutes of listening to a recorded message, I finally hear his voice. "Baby, I'm sorry. I got picked up, but I'm okay. Damn, I hate this. You all right?"

He tells me that the young man he hit copied down his plate number and filed a police report. Even though no bones were broken and there was no bloodshed, he had the right to press charges. The police determined the registered owner of the car and pulled up Scottie's driver's license picture. The young man identified Scottie out of a photo lineup. I guess the warrants are so backed up that the only way HPD can catch someone is to pull them over for a routine traffic violation.

"Scottie, where exactly are you?"

"Downtown. We're just sitting around waiting to go to the court jail. I haven't been able to sleep and I'm hungry. What time is it?"

"It's three-thirty. Are you okay? Is anyone messing with you, babe?"

He assures me that he's fine. He's ready to go to sleep and couldn't do it until he talked to me.

"Well, babe, there's someone waiting to use the phone. But if I go get back in line, you probably won't hear from me for another hour. Just try and get some sleep. I'll call you tomorrow. I mean later. Fuck!"

"I love you."

"Love you, too. Kiss Brax for me."

What we thought would be an overnight jail adventure has turned into something more devastating. Scottie told me the San Jacinto Jail houses over one thousand inmates. The overcrowding results in a backup that won't allow him to go to court jail until God knows when.

"I've been talking to other dudes who're on their second and third go-round. They said it may take a week, babe."

After I gasped and felt my knees go weak, I had to switch to independent, responsible, clear-thinking mode. First line of business? Contacting my husband's job and explaining the situation without telling too much. To feel my heart sag with worry over this is something I don't want anyone to see, especially Brax. Every day he asks, "Where's Uncle Daddy?"

"He's on a trip."

"What's a trip?"

"It's like an adventure where you go to a place you've never been before." I meditate on what I tell Brax and think to myself, *I'm on an adventure, too, except you can still see me every day.* Then I dash over to Brax's bookcase and pray I'll find a story that deals with vacations, road trips, anything that can help my child to understand why people sometimes disappear.

The days are long, but I stay busy at work; my mind's split between concentrating and doing a good job so I won't get fired, and wondering how I'll manage to pay all our bills on my salary alone. The nights seem like double the length of daytime. I miss talking to Scottie, running behind him all throughout the town house, begging him to rub my back, and asking him to run my bathwater. And sex? I lie in bed wrestling to fall asleep. Before long, my fingers begin stroking my twat, rubbing it up and down, and pretending like Scottie's the one making me feel good.

And now it's Saturday. Scottie's first weekend in the jail. Last night when he called, he told me, "I thought I'd be outta here by now, but since it looks like I don't know when I'll get released, come visit me."

"Babe, I'm still mad at you for not letting me come downtown before now."

"I–I just don't want you to see me like this, Dani."

"I know. But now that it is, let's deal with it."

Summer agrees to go with me to the 701 Jail, a redbrick ten-story building located downtown.

We enter the overcrowded lobby and fill out a small

white sheet of paper that notes Scottie's SPN (his jail number), our name, and other info. Then we wait in line to go through security.

When I walk through the metal detector, it starts beeping. "Oh, so even this thing knows Dani Meadows has arrived, huh? Like it's announcing me."

"Remove your jewelry and you'll be fine," says an officer leaning against the wall.

Summer and I ride an elevator to the second floor. Even though fluorescent fixtures fill the room with light, the splashes of ugly green paint make the room feel depressing. Security cameras watch our every move.

We enter a narrow hallway and sit down on a large slab of gray stone. It's so dirty it looks like a million nasty people have sat on it. Each side of the room has glass windows that appear to be six inches thick. On the other side of the window are seats where the inmates sit after they're notified that they have a visitor. A roll of paper towel is sitting on the seat. I assume it's for the visitors and I tear off a sheet and vigorously clean the window closest to me.

Soon about fifteen men dressed in orange jumpsuits and orange socks pile out of their secured area, to the little space where they can visit with a loved one. Scottie sees me and lowers his eyes, then sits down. I offer him a smile, but I want to cry. The window between me and Scottie feels so thick. His hair looks wild, and he needs a shave. He looks sad, frustrated. Other people who are visiting are talking loud, conversing with their loved one. Although I feel self-conscious and don't want people to hear my business, I have no other choice. This place is nothing like the jails usually depicted in the movies.

I lean in toward the glass and contort my body so that my mouth practically touches a tiny screen.

"You trying to do a *Shawshank Redemption* thing yet?" I yell.

"What?" He presses his ear against his side of the glass wall.

"You better not drop the soap, buddy."

He laughs, which makes me laugh. We only have twenty minutes to talk, so he first tells me he loves me, then gives me a list of things to do.

"I should be out soon . . . but in case I'm not . . ."

I'm listening to what he needs me to do, handle business, be strong.

"If I'm here a long time, who will you call on to take care of what I normally handle?"

"I dunno."

"You know," he says and gives me the saddest look I've ever seen.

The next week, I beg Neil to come by my place. I open the door before he can ring my doorbell.

"How are you making out?" he asks as he walks past me into the foyer.

"I'm good," I say in a high, chirpy voice.

"You look like hell, Dani."

"Whatever!" I climb a couple flights of stairs until we reach the living area. I know Neil's staring at my ass. *Is it wrong to want attention from the opposite sex?*

"Have a seat. I barely cooked anything."

"I didn't come over here to eat food."

He sits and throws his hand lazily across the back of the sofa and his legs spread wide apart.

I go stand between his thighs.

"What you come over here for?"

"Well, Dani. Have you talked to Scottie at all today?"

"No, I haven't. What's up?"

"He called this morning and asked me to come see him tonight. We spoke a few minutes. He wasn't talking about anything. You know how it is."

"Ha." I smirk. "I know, all right."

For the longest time, Neil just stares at me so intently I feel he's trying to read my mind. Earlier I was stressed and went for a swim in the complex's pool. Right now I have on a white bikini and a knee-length halter top that functions as a swimwear cover-up. It ties up in the back and is the same color as hay. Neil's eyes follow me from my face down to my knees and exposed legs.

"What else did he say?"

"Scottie told me his release date is May fifteenth."

"Three more fucking weeks? Oh, hell no!"

"You know what else he said?"

"What?"

"He's scared you're going to cheat!"

Scottie knows me. He and I are accustomed to having sex at least four times a week. For me, making love is like breathing air. I have needs. Scottie has to understand that.

"What did you say to that?"

"What could I say, Dani? I haven't forgotten how much of a tigress you were."

"Were?" I smirk.

"Well, um, I wouldn't know that these days."

"Mmm hmmm." I see. He may not have physically made love to me for the past few years, but Neil has definitely fornicated with me mentally. I know when he's putting his penis inside Anya, he wishes it was me.

"But check this out," Neil continues. "I decide I should pay the man a visit in person. Just to see how he's holding up. And I go down to 701 Jail. I pay money to park. I stand in a couple lines. Wait a good half hour because there are a lot of people there. It's a busy night, right?"

"Right."

"Finally, they let a new group up to the second floor. I put my little piece of paper under the window and go take a seat. After five minutes of waiting, they call my name over the loudspeaker. Guess what they tell me?"

"What, Neil, just tell me."

"They tell me Scottie can't have any visitors."

"Why?"

"Because inmates are allowed one visitor per day."

"Of course," I say, alarmed. "So who came and visited him?"

"LaNecia!"

I've gone to see Scottie a few times, but what about the days when I couldn't make it? Has she been down there, in his face, still trying to convince him that there's nothing wrong with them being a cousin couple and I don't deserve him?

I think about the hell LaNecia's put me through since the day we met.

"Neil, I gotta have some dick."

He bolts to his feet; one hand grips his dick, the other hand folds me against his warm, strong chest. I close my eyes and press my breasts against him. Hot tears splatter against my cheeks.

"Oh, Dani," he mumbles and kisses the top of my hair.

He releases his penis and places his fingers on my back. They are so warm, gentle, yet electrifying. He rubs my shoulders, caressing them like I'm a precious little baby. His lips move from my hair, to my cheeks, to my neck.

"I want you, baby, I do. Oh, God." I wrap my arms around his waist. His dick pokes my clothing. Double-layered fabric doesn't feel too thick when the lust of a man makes itself known.

He rotates his hips, humping against me.

"My pussy is so wet . . . because it's crying."

"Why is it crying?"

"Because it's so happy."

Neil moans and lifts me up in his arms. He carries me and looks like he's about to go upstairs where my room is located.

"No," I say, "guest room."

With my head leaning against his neck, he carries me through the guest room doorway, drops me on the bed, and closes the door.

Oh nooo! What am I about to get myself into?

My va jay jay is throbbing like a time bomb is ticking inside of it.

Neil wrinkles his nose as he pulls open his shirt and slides in bed next to me.

Instantly I'm transported to our wicked past. The wrong things we do sometimes feel sooo good.

What if Scottie finds out? Or Anya? But Anya said a day never repeats itself.

I swallow hard and look at Neil lying partially naked in my guest bed.

She wasn't lying.

I try to make my body act faster than my mind.

Neil whispers, "What are you doing?"

"Getting ready."

I lie on my back and stare at Neil. He kisses me above my breast where lots of skin is exposed due to this little skimpy bathing suit cover-up outfit.

"I love your outfit."

"Me, too. I feel naked in this. And since I feel naked, I may as well get naked. Help me?"

He unties the string and pulls off my cover-up. Now I'm only in my bikini. But it doesn't take long for him to unstrap the bikini top. I don't wait for him to remove the bottom. Soon we're totally naked. I've never wanted a man so much in my life.

Neil presses his warm lips against mine. They're so soft I want to chew 'em and suck 'em. And I do.

You stupid ass. Why can't you wait three more weeks for Scottie? What kind of wife are you? You better hope he never finds out.

I shiver, then push Neil away from my face. I grab his hand and lead it to my vagina. He caresses me; his hand's so wet it's like he has lotion on the fingertips. He inserts his fingers and strokes me while I arch my back and moan. I pant and cry and grab the sheets with the back of my hands, pulling on them like they can stop my orgasm. But they can't. I explode and scream so loud Neil covers my mouth with his hand.

And when my panting subsides, we lock eyes. He stares at me for the longest, like he knows what we did must remain a secret. He rolls out of bed, gets dressed, and all he says is "Technically, the hundred dollars is yours. You've won." Then he leaves my home without even saying goodbye.

As I lie there in bed, thinking about what just happened, in more ways than one, I feel so utterly relieved.

ANYA

I Hear Love

Neil and I are in bed. He's turned away from me, his eyes glued on the small LCD television that's mounted on the wall above a chest of drawers. The tension in our bedroom is so thick it's like a tall barrier separates us and the only way I can get through to Neil is by jumping over the wall.

"Neil, I'm sorry," I apologize to his back.

"Anya, it's okay, really."

"Hmm, since when are you fine with us not having sex, unless you're doing it with someone else?"

"Woman, please. Just because you're struggling emotionally with postsurgery doesn't mean I'm having an affair."

"Who said anything about having an affair? Fucking some whore isn't the same as being involved long-term."

"Well, I haven't done either. So please shut up so I can finish watching *Family Guy.*"

His tone sounds harsh.

He turns toward me. "Anya, I didn't mean to talk to you like that. I've had a hard day at work. Scottie's bugging the hell outta me about making sure his debts get paid. 'I'll pay you back, I promise.' That's what he tells me. So, out of the goodness of my heart, I'm paying the mortgage."

Anya sits up in bed. "What? Their mortgage is not our problem."

"I'm going to help my brother."

"You're such a fool. Are you fucking Dani again? I don't know why you gotta pay her ass child support plus the mortgage for two straight months. You must be out your mind. Plus you never even discussed this with me."

"Anya, please. You don't bring a single dollar into this household. . . ."

"Shut up before I do something you regret."

He jumps up and storms from our room, slamming the door so loud that the wall clock crashes to the floor.

I get out of the bed and open the door. "If you broke this clock, you're paying for it." I slam the door as hard as I can and jump back in bed. Here we go again. Every time Dani has a problem, we have problems. We've been snapping at each other for days.

Neil barely kisses me anymore and I guess it's because of how he feels about me now that I've had a hysterectomy. Supposedly, he thought he'd be getting a brand-new woman, but the only thing brand-new about me is my attitude.

I hear a light knock on the door. "Is it okay to come in?"

"Come on, Vette."

She sits on the side of the bed. "What's with all the yelling? Neil burnt rubber trying to get out of the garage. Y'all too big to be acting like kids."

"Leave it to you to make jokes at a time like this. I hate to go here, but I feel sometimes his family issues bring us down."

"Like how?"

"Don't get me wrong. I know Neil is responsible and caring, but that leaves us in a bind. We ain't Oprah or P. Diddy. What if Neil loses his job? Who will y'all depend on then?"

"Look, Anya . . ."

"I'm sorry if I hurt your feelings. He's your brother, but he's my husband, and when things aren't going right in our house, I get all riled up."

"I guess I understand. I'm just offended by the way you said things. People get in trouble and need help. Our mother taught us to be compassionate, no matter what."

I decide to change the subject. "Well, we're preparing for Scottie's homecoming in a couple of weeks. Did you hear about how our relative girl went downtown to see Scottie and acted such a fool they escorted her out of the building and banned her from visiting him anymore?"

"No, I hadn't. What happened?"

"LaNecia was talking very inappropriately, nasty talk, and begging him to leave Dani, as if *that's* gonna happen," I say, laughing. "Anyway, Scottie called Neil and made him promise not to allow her within one hundred fifty feet. . . ."

"From the state of Texas, or your house?"

"Both," I say, jokingly. "I'm glad he's coming home, yet I can't shake this bad feeling. Neil is hiding something from me. Have you noticed him acting weird?"

"No more than usual, Anya. Don't worry. He probably has a lot on his mind. He asked Uncle James to chip in and throw down with some money for Scottie. I think Uncle James gave some cash, but not what he'd normally give. Remember the wedding expenses? Anyway, leave my brother alone for a change. He's a good man."

"Only a sister would say that, but if he were your husband, you'd be singing a different tune."

There's nothing worse than when a woman senses her man is hiding something, yet he won't admit he's hiding anything. And since Neil is tight-lipped, I decide to take a different route to find out what I need to know.

A couple of days after me and Neil's screaming match, I call Dani and invite her over to the house.

"Hey, Dani. Neil and I want you to come by. I know you've probably been lonely in that big ole town house with your baby. We're having grilled chicken breasts, pinto beans, cabbage, and long-grain rice, with German chocolate cake for dessert."

"Neil's favorite," she says in a barely audible voice.

"Come on over. We'll be waiting for you."

I answer the door when they arrive.

"Neil will be back in a second. He made a run to the store for a case of beer and a newspaper."

"Oh, okay, no problem. He's not the reason why I'm here." She laughs, then stops.

"My cooking is, right?"

"Exactly."

She follows me into the kitchen holding Brax by the hand. I'm shocked when she presents me with a wicker basket stuffed with bubble bath, soap, scented candles, bath water crystals, and a big chunky soap bar.

"Hmm, milk and honey. That's my favorite."

"I know."

"You know? Who told you? And why?"

"Well, um, Mother's Day is coming up and I've been saving this for you. I may as well give it to you now."

"Why? You've never given me anything like this before."

"You're so good to Brax, and it's just something I want to do." She sounds like she's forcing me to take the damn gift or else.

"Let's eat."

She makes a plate for Brax and gets him situated. Then she sits in the chair right next to me and for the first time I notice how she's dressed. Even though it's ninety degrees outside, she's wearing a long-sleeved blouse, baggy slacks, and some dingy-looking gym shoes with dried-up mud caked on them.

Twenty minutes pass. I throw all kinds of questions at her.

"How've you been holding up since Scottie's been gone?"

"Fine."

"Does it get lonely in the town house?"

"Huh?"

"You ever too afraid to be there by yourself with just you and Brax?"

"Sure."

She gives me short answers and squirms in her seat, looking at the doorway every few minutes.

"Hey, Neil is taking so long. Why don't I pour you a glass of wine we've had around the house forever. Zinfandel."

"That's my favorite. Oops, one of them."

I forcefully smile at Dani, fill up her glass, and hand it to her like a good hostess should. Even though I gave her a present to warm her up, I still feel heated inside. My instincts suggest she's been up to no good. And I'm not very good at camouflaging my true feelings. So it takes everything within me not to splash the wine in her face, but I can't waste it for trivial reasons.

She sips. I talk. She sips more. I talk more about Obama,

the last movie she's seen, and how Brax is faring without Scottie around.

When Dani hiccups and giggles, I lean in. "When's the last time my husband has been at the town house?"

"Oh, a few days ago? Or was it last week? Whoops, excuse me. I dunno really. Not too long."

"What did he do when he was there?"

"He did good. Real good. Mmm hmmm. He's so kind and wonderful. Anya, you're lucky to have Neil, I swear I envy you."

"What did he do good?"

She gives me a blank stare, and I hear "Uh-oh" slip between her teeth.

"What were we talking about?"

"We're talking about why my husband was recently at your place without Scottie around!"

"Brax! Anya, you know he comes and picks up the baby. What, is that a crime these days? You want Neil to go to jail, too? You're insane." She belches.

Ten minutes later Dani gulps the rest of her wine, wipes her mouth with her sleeve, stumbles into the den, and passes out on the couch. My strategy to get this woman drunk so the wine will loosen her tongue doesn't go quite the way I hoped.

The girl is too wasted to realize I made up the part about Neil going to the liquor store. He doesn't know this, and he won't know. As long as he keeps info from me, I'll pay him the exact favor.

But because my inner suspicions refuse to leave me alone, I'll have to execute my second plan.

Every Thursday morning I try to listen to 104.1 FM, KRBE, which is mostly a pop radio station. The Roula & Ryan show is hosted by Roula, a Greek woman born and raised in H-town. Ryan is her sidekick and seems to be one of the rare males who can provide truthful and sensitive commentary on male-female relationships. But what really lures me to this show each week is when they air "Roula & Ryan's Roses." I sent them an e-mail because I wanted to be on the show just so I can take a chance and find out if Neil will send a dozen roses to me or to another woman.

So when I get the call from Roula, I am shocked that I get selected. Then when I realize I'm talking to her, I feel nervously excited and try my best to act normal. Roula explains that she and Ryan will be calling Neil, pretending they are representing a national florist company that's doing a promotion involving free roses.

"If it's free, he'll be game," I tell her. "I need to know if he's being unfaithful."

"Who is the woman?"

"I hate to say it, but she's someone he's cheated with before." I start to admit they had a child together, but I already look like a fool as it is, so I keep my mouth shut.

I stand by in nervous anticipation, and when I hear Neil's voice as he's talking to Roula, I know the moment of truth is here.

"Hi, I'm with National Flower World and we're doing a little promotion where we'll send a dozen free roses anywhere you want just to introduce our company. You're under no obligation. No credit card is needed or anything."

"You say it's free?"

"Absolutely free, sir."

"And you won't need a credit card?"

"Not at all. We're hoping you'll use our services in the future if you take a chance on us today."

"Good. My credit card is really charged up." Neil chuckles.

My hands are sweating like crazy as I grip the phone and hold my breath.

"Okay, Neil," Roula says. "Who do we make the card out to and what should it say?"

"To my wife, Anya. Love you."

"Ah, okay, well, Neil, we need you to know you're actually on the radio right now. The reason we're calling is because your wife, Anya, wasn't sure if you'd send the flowers to her."

"What? Anya, why are you doing this on the radio?"

"Neil," I cut in. "I'm sorry, but it seemed you were becoming distant. I had a bad feeling, and I needed to know if anything was going on."

"Anya, you should have come to me."

"I did, but you blew me off."

"I answered your questions, but I guess if it's not what you want to hear, you think I'm hiding something. I haven't done anything with anybody. I am done with this conversation. Just know I love you, no matter how you feel inside."

Neil disconnects the call. I want to get in bed and pull the covers over my head.

Is he telling the truth? Can Neil truly care about me when I feel so much of who I used to be is no longer there?

Days later, I take a seat in the waiting room of my physician's office. I am facing a plain white wall that is adorned with photos of Tiger Woods swinging a golf club.

A few outdated magazines lie on a small table next to me. I pick up one and begin thumbing through its pages.

Moments later I hear a man and a woman's voice; they're holding a conversation as they enter the waiting room. Their feet slowly shuffle across the floor. They ring a bell to let the receptionist know they've arrived. The chair right behind me makes a whishing sound, and I know they've taken a seat.

"Dodie, don't worry. You will be okay once you see the doctor," I hear a man say who's seated behind me. He sounds like he's eighty years old. His voice is soft and soothing.

"I know, Paul. I can't wait to get out of here, though. I have a taste for a cup of cocoa."

"I'll make you some as soon as we get home, okay, Do-si-do?"

"Thank you, Paul." She starts laughing, and he joins in. Their laugh sounds like a full orchestra.

While listening to them, I want to turn around and look at them. But all I can do is listen and smile.

I don't hear old. I don't hear age. I hear love.

SCOTTIE

I'm Going to Make You Love Me

The day of Scottie's homecoming, Dani waits three hours for his paperwork to be processed. When Scottie wanders into the lobby, walking with a bounce, Dani yelps and jumps into his arms. He swings her around in a circle until she starts screaming with joy.

"Okay, put me down. Let me take a good look at you."

Scottie's wearing the same clothes he wore the day he got arrested. He smiles and flexes his muscles.

"Ooo, baby, you're looking good. I love that you worked out while you were here," she says, and squeezes his plump arms. "You already had a tight body. . . ."

"Well, I kept it tight for you. You were all I thought about every second I was here." He takes one final glance. "Hey, let's bounce. I've had enough of this place."

She grabs his arm tightly, and they walk out the door into the brilliant sunlight. Downtown Houston looks awesome today.

"Man, the fucking sun is blazing down on me, and I love it. And I love you, Dani."

She grins at him, and they plod down the street, settle in Dani's truck, and drive toward home.

"Okay," Dani says. "Your boss has been kind enough to grant you that leave of absence. But now that you're back, you should report to work on Monday."

"No problem. I've never been so eager to go to a job in my life."

"And, of course, Anya's throwing a party for you, so we'll head straight there. You can take a shower. I got you a brand-new outfit. Everything will be different."

"Will it?" Scottie says calmly.

"Well, yeah," she says, pouting. "You're going to definitely become a better, more conscientious driver. And I insist that you attend anger management classes. You can't threaten or try to fight anybody just because you don't like what they say to me or anyone else."

"Those are the changes you want me to make. But what about *your* changes?"

"M—mine? What do I need to change?"

"Word gets out, Dani. Even when you think no one knows your business, they do."

"Um, what on Earth are you talking about?"

"Don't play the innocent role. Someone from the outside came to visit me. . . ."

"Is LaNecia really anyone who can be trusted? Please don't insult me, Scottie."

"She may make up shit from time to time, but when she knows the truth, she's gonna tell me that, too."

"You believe that sicko over your own wife?"

"Yes, if I know for a fact that you sneak around behind my back."

"Y—you don't know that."

Scottie glares at his wife as she presses her foot on the accelerator.

"Going faster ain't gonna change anything, Dani. If you need to tell me something, now's the time to do it."

"Look, Scottie, if you're asking if I had sex with another man, the answer is hell no. Are you kidding me? LaNecia needs to check herself. She's so desperate she'll do anything to get you away from me. And, since we're on this subject, why do you allow her to do the things she does? Is it because you told the girl you still care about her? You love her? You're as guilty as I am. . . ."

"What did you say? Keep talking, Dani. I want to know how *guilty* you are."

"Don't try to put words in my mouth. Scottie, if I didn't love you, I wouldn't be here. I wouldn't have accepted your collect calls, put my manicure and pedicure money in your inmate fund so you can eat a bag of chips or whatever they served y'all down there."

"You never even wrote me a letter. I saw other guys getting mail all the time, but not me."

"That's crazy," she says seductively. "We talked on the phone, honey bun, and I have the bills to prove it."

"Don't try to sound sweet now. I'm mad at you."

She laughs. "I'm so glad you're out, baby. It wasn't any fun without you there. And Brax . . . oh my goodness, he's practically reading now. You'll see."

Scottie begins to relax as he considers her reasoning.

"I guess I need to chill. The main thing is I did my little time. This is just a funky Class C misdemeanor. It's gonna be on my record, but at least I'm not on probation. I'm straight."

"I hope you mean that literally," Dani teases.

"Seriously, baby. I appreciate the little things you did for me. Every inmate's fear is that his woman is gonna leave him, or sleep with another man. I guess I'll take your word for it, but if I ever find out you lied, ten anger management classes won't help."

"You need to quit," she says, laughing hysterically.

It's almost five o'clock on a Friday. They get stuck in rush-hour traffic but take the time to catch up on the details of everything Scottie's missed out on.

They arrive at Neil's and notice lots of cars parked in the driveway and in front of the house.

"People have been waiting to see you all day, honey."

"That's a trip. I never thought folks would care this much about a brother."

"Lots of people love you. You'll see," she says as they exit the truck.

Colorful purple and orange streamers are mounted on all the doorways. A huge Welcome Home Scottie banner spans across the arches that lead into the den.

"Hey, cousin," says one male cousin.

"What up, what up. I see the cards over there. I'm dying to whip you in spades. Set up the table."

Scottie goes around hugging Vette, Reesy, Riley, and Karetha.

"Where's your girl?" he says folding Karetha into his arms for a warm hug.

Karetha averts her eyes. "I don't know, but wherever she is, I know her mind is only on you. You know Necia."

"I know, Ka. Be good. I'm glad you're here."

Scottie breezes into the kitchen and opens the refrigerator. "Real food," he screams at the top of his lungs.

"Don't you dare walk in my house looking for something to eat without first saying hello to us." Anya is standing near the breakfast bar with her hands on her hips. Sola waits beside her, clinging to a large photo album.

"Scott-Scott!"

"Mommy!" He leaves the refrigerator door open and races into his mother's arms. She hugs him and softly cries. "Thank you, Jesus. I was so scared for you. And sorry I didn't visit. I just couldn't bring myself to come down there. I don't want to see my son behind bars."

"Except the kind of bar that serves Crown Royal, right, Mama?"

Neil steps into the kitchen, his presence almost filling the room. He locks eyes with his brother, then walks up to him and pats him on the back.

"Yo, man, thanks for looking out for me. I appreciate everything you've done. Took care of the attorney, paying my bills. I owe you, man."

"You don't owe me anything," Neil says and walks out of the room.

"He's so weird," Dani says nervously. She's been standing in the shadows, observing all the action.

"Anyway, it's time for you to take a nice, long shower, hubby. You smell worse than a pig."

"You know what? You right. I can smell myself. So, y'all give me twenty minutes. I'm going upstairs to shower and I'll be back down to get the party started. Now, make sure my favorite music is playing. Oh, guess what. When you're in jail . . ."

"Oh no, here he goes trying to liven things up with his prison stories," Anya says, laughing.

"Listen up. Everyone gets a nickname. Know what they called me? 'Radio.' 'Cause I was singing all the time. Scottie was making hits up in the joint."

Everyone beams at Scottie as he leaves the kitchen.

He runs up the stairs, enters his former bedroom, sees

clothes lying on the chair, and scoops them into his hand. Just as he's about to turn around and leave the room, he hears a click; the door locks.

He quickly turns around. LaNecia is staring at Scottie as if she's looking right through him. Her long, unbraided hair is a tangled mess.

"What are you doing here, cousin?"

"I came here to see you. I heard you were getting out."

"But why aren't you downstairs with the rest?"

"You don't want to see me alone, Scottie? What can I do to make you see I'm special because I'm all out of answers? How can I make you love me?"

"You gotta stop stalking me, cousin. I feel like you're following me on Twitter."

"Do you have a Twitter account?"

"See, you're scaring me, baby girl."

She steps closer to Scottie and tries to grab his penis. He slaps her hand away and steps back.

"That is enough. You need help, cousin, for real. Leave right now or else I'm going to call the cops."

"You wouldn't do that."

"Yes, I would."

"Do you know what *I'm* going to do?"

Scottie watches her pull a 9-millimeter gun from behind her back. Her hands shake as she points it directly at his face.

He screams, *"Please,* LaNecia, *don't shoot!"*

DANI

Marriage Isn't Always What It Seems

I casually walk upstairs to find out what's taking Scottie so long. As I approach the bedroom, his door is closed shut. I hear voices.

"What's wrong, Scottie? You scared? Are you now ready to take me serious?"

"LaNecia . . ." He raises his voice in a weird sounding way. "Please."

"You son of a bitch. You said you love me, but you lied. You act like you want to fuck me, yet you end up teasing me. All you gotta do to release me is tell me the truth."

"I *have* told the truth."

"No, you haven't," she wails.

Feeling tense, I lean in closer, not yet ready to knock.

"LaNecia, nooo!"

"You scared of this gun, huh?" She laughs. Then I hear an animal-like howl.

"If I can't have you, *nobody* can."

The air fills with yelling, a loud gunshot, then complete silence.

I rattle the doorknob and bang my fist against the door, pounding on it till my skin begins to sting. "Scottie! Scottie! Are you all right? Talk to me, Scottie!"

The door squeaks opens. LaNecia stumbles back away from the door. She lowers herself to a sitting position on the edge of the bed. She dumps her face in her hands, rocks back and forth, and wails at the top of her lungs, "I can't make this man love me. I can't make *any* man love me. I have to learn how to love myself. That's the only love I know I can get."

"Where's my husband?"

She points. Scottie's standing in the doorway of the walk-in closet. His eyes are bloodshot. His face is ashen. He begins removing bullets from the gun and drops them in his pocket. I smell gunpowder and look up. A bullet hole punctures the ceiling. I take one look at Scottie and collapse in my husband's arms. I thank God he spared Scottie's (and LaNecia's) lives.

They tried to warn me. "Marriage isn't always what it seems. Every married woman I know is miserable and wishes she were single." Blah, blah, blah. I wish they'd have told me this before I said "I do." But wait. They *did* tell me. When did I ever listen? Well, I'm all ears now. It's funny how young folks reject good advice until they have no other choice but to listen because all the sharp warnings finally come true. Your life brings you to a cold, lonely cell. Door shut. Locked. In jail. Believe me when I tell you. Scottie wasn't the only person behind bars. Don't get me started.

Thankfully, Neil and Anya heard the gunshot that day and escorted LaNecia out of the room. Once Scottie and I were alone, I saw him differently than ever before. When I realized how close I came to losing the one man who proved his love to me in every imaginable way, I had to make a drastic change. I had to do things that made life better for Brax, Scottie, Anya, Neil, and especially myself.

And two weeks after our ordeal I adopted what I refer to as the Neil Braxton Meadows rules.

I'm a happily married woman. And because of this, I told myself, and my baby daddy, no more being alone in a room or house with Neil. No more wearing skimpy clothes around him. No more reminiscing about a past that should have been long buried.

Because Mrs. Danielle Meadows promises to be an excellent wife who's always on her best behavior. After what Neil and I went through, and seeing how LaNecia almost lost her mind over a man, I can never put myself in those tempting situations again. Thank God LaNecia finally agreed to go to a therapist. Maybe a professional will prescribe a permanent cure for her unhealthy fixation.

And now that the drama has subsided, thank God Scottie doesn't pester me anymore about Neil, or any other guy these days.

Besides, what Scottie doesn't know can never hurt him. Or can it?

Special thanks to my editor, Heather Lazare, for her editing expertise, and to Claudia Menza for being a wonderful literary agent. Thanks to Emily Lavelle for everything you do to promote my books, and to both the copy editor and the copy department for your superb work!

Shout-outs to Electa Rome Parks, Shelia Lindsay, Cheryl Robinson, Marissa Monteilh, Lexi Davis, Claudia O'Hare, Margaret Johnson-Hodge, Kole Black, Wilt Tillman, Cynthia Gibbs, Albricka Gordon, RAWSISTAZ Reviewers, Patrik Henry Bass of *Essence* magazine, Carol Hill-Mackey, The Pink Reviewers, Trice Hickman, Philana Marie Boles, Ta-Nisha Webb, Sylvia Hubbard, Niobia Bryant, Chelsia McCoy, Tia Ross, Shani Greene Dowdell, the one and only Karen Hunter, Sam Redd of MaverickMedia, Heather Covington, Vanessa Davis Griggs, reviewer Cheryl Hayes, Antoinette Hosley, and every book club, reviewer, library, and bookstore for your support.

Blessings to Lt. Derrick McClinton for his input, and to Duane Gordon for the "inside" info.

Can't forget Facebook and MySpace friends, and the University of Houston crew.

Acknowledgments

To all the aspiring authors who ask for advice: keep hanging in there and never give up.

Thanks to the Lord for blessing me to live my dream.

Last, thanks to my mother for the support, and to everyone in my family (What's up, Detroit).

E-mail me at booksbycyd@aol.com.

Also by Cydney Rax

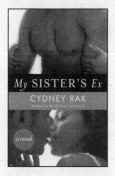

My Husband's Girlfriend
$13.95 paper ($18.95 Canada)
978-1-4000-8219-3

My Sister's Ex
$14.00 paper ($17.99 Canada)
978-0-307-45440-9

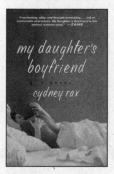

My Daughter's Boyfriend
$12.95 paper ($17.95 Canada)
978-1-4000-8313-8

My Best Friend and My Man
$13.95 paper ($15.95 Canada)
978-0-307-39377-7